Among the Colours

by

James Gregory Randall

AOS Publishing, 2024
Copyright © 2024

James Gregory Randall

ISBN: 978-1-990496-79-0

Cover Design: Jessica James

Visit AOS Publishing's website:
www.aospublishing.com

Painting is something that takes place among the colours

-- Rainer Maria Rilke

Among the Colours is a work of fiction. The author's use of historical names, places, and events does not change its imaginative nature. With the faith that story tellers share with writers, James Gregory Randall has imposed a narrative structure of hope on what otherwise could be interpreted as a series of random occurrences. The hero grows into adulthood, suffers devastating loss, and somehow recovers victorious to bring life to a broken world.

Any resemblance to persons living or dead is coincidental. In this regard, *Among the Colours* is a true story that gives shape to the past but compels readers to draw their own conclusions in the present.

James Gregory Randall is not a historian, scholar, or academic, His research is dependent upon Google, published secondary sources, and Wikipedia. Michael Bliss and Sherrill Grace are giants in his work. They provide him with the framework of credibility for his imagining.

His writing echoes the scholarship of the works listed in the Bibliography.

Among the Colours is a story fit for telling, not for citing. It is a catalyst for further discussion, not the final word.

For Ric Johnson

(16 July 1955 - 21 April 2023)

A friend who was closer than a brother

Part One

1
1924
With His Song

Frederick Grant Banting (1891-1941) rolled off his new bride, Marion Wilson Robertson (1896-1944). Covered in sweat, he tossed aside the sheet from their wedding bed. It was hot, hot, hot.

God, what an inferno! He didn't know how he was going to survive the next six weeks, cruising the Caribbean. With her all heated up and dressed to the nines and formal dinners every bloody evening. What had he gotten himself into? Banting needed a drink, but first a smoke.

He opened the doors to the balcony, stepped to the railing, and looked to the choppy water below. Good thing their suite was midship. He had his share of ocean crossings in fore and aft cabins. Just below the upper decks was his first choice, and not too far from the dining room. Marion wanted to be close to the dancefloor, but Banting couldn't abide that. He wasn't a dancer, and while he could shake off the strictures of most of his Baptist upbringing, this was one he couldn't. His were two left feet and woe to the woman who was his partner.

He lit a cigarette. Maybe he should have married Edith, he thought. But she refused him — said everyone would think she accepted his proposal because he was the most famous man in Canada. Now, he was stuck with this prima donna.

Banting heard Marion sobbing. He returned to the cabin and sat on the far edge of the bed; his back turned away from her. "It'll get better," he told her. "Sex is never great the first time," he admitted. In spite of his misgivings, he did want the marriage to work. He tried to be tender.

He had wistful dreams of a dutiful wife and a house full of rambunctious children. He offered her his cigarette. She refused. Wordlessly, she rose from the bed and padded barefoot to the bathroom. The faintest scent of Chanel No. 5 trailed after her. She bought it for their honeymoon. It lingered in the air as she walked away from the man she had been so desperate to marry. Now, she could hardly stand being in the same room as he.

Banting watched her as she left the room. Her hair was tousled by their lovemaking, her figure tall and stately. Without thinking, he blurted out that she was more beautiful than any of the French women he had ever met on leave. He made the situation even worse when he assured her that he had taken precautions.

Her spine stiffened and her face coloured. She needed a shower and stepped into the bathroom, clicking the latch shut behind her. Marion leaned back against the door, making sure it was locked. She couldn't believe what she had heard. The words her new husband spoke drove away any vain hopes and illusions she had been harbouring in her heart.

Some weeks after photos of them together began appearing in newspapers, she received an anonymous letter from *The Girl about The Man.* Marion tossed it out as rubbish. The writer wrote that she was one of many young women Banting had ruined. Marion refused to believe the malice that was spilled in scarlet on the white sheet of paper. Now, she rued her naïveté. Newlyweds are supposed to be inexperienced lovers, faltering their way toward a lifetime of ecstasy. Or so she foolishly dreamed.

But Fred knows his way around a woman's body far better than he should. He's done this before, she could tell immediately, and it broke her heart.

New husbands aren't supposed to be any good in bed. She'd been warned not to expect too much. It'll be over in a flash; her married friends told her. But it wasn't. He was languid and leisurely. He waited for her, and they came together. She experienced first-hand the long extent of his sexual history. It felt good. It couldn't have been better. But she was a virgin, and he wasn't. That made her blush. The only men she'd seen naked were her patients. There was that one boy who fumbled with the buttons on her blouse a few summers ago. What was his name? Dick? Peter? Rod? No, it was Harry. He was as charming as a prince.

She smiled at the memory, disappointed now that they hadn't gone all the way. He did not press her beyond the point of no return. She could still wear white on her wedding day. It was a moral victory over deep human desire, she thought at the time and believed with all her heart. Now, she wasn't so sure.

Fred, however, was well-schooled and experienced. The bastard. But how could he not have been? She knew the answer before she spoke it. She couldn't expect a farm boy and a war hero to remain innocent after all he had gone through.

He had the opportunity when he was overseas. He faced death night and day. He needed to enjoy all the good that life had to offer before a bullet, or a piece of shrapnel snatched it from him. Honestly? She couldn't blame Fred. If she had been in his place, she'd have done the same thing.

And now that he's won the Nobel Prize? Hordes of grateful women are ready to give their all to the Discoverer of Insulin.

He didn't have a chance. She had hoped against her better judgement that she would be his first, like he was hers. To think that she pushed their wedding date forward before someone else could lay claim to him. She could not believe what the other woman had written. Marion had wanted him to be all hers and now laughed bitterly. She was a woman aggrieved. Her sham of a marriage to Fred Banting will never be what it could have been, had he been honest and true.

His double standard galled her. He expected her to be unsullied. The two-faced prig! Well, the sheet on their wedding bed was his incontrovertible proof, and she had hers. His ill-thought words and her foolish heart! She had been entrapped by the very man she set out to capture for herself. She was the fool, forcing him to bend his knee, and then giving him her heartfelt yes.

No wonder Edith called the whole thing off. She had waited for so long, only to have Marion swoop in and mesmerize her fiancé. Fred forgot his promise, and Edith escaped in the nick of time.

At least, they came to terms. Good old Fred, confessing his selective pre-marital sins. Not the whores, of course but innocent girls, maybe even a housewife or two.

Edith demanded the engagement ring, $2,000 in cash, and a promise that he would not foul her reputation. There'd be no kissing and telling, on her part or his.

Edith proved to be a woman true to her word, but Marion had doubts about him. Frederick Grant Banting may have been smart enough to be in the right place at the right time when insulin was discovered, but he never learned to treat women with respect.

Marion showered, toweled off, and returned to their bedroom. Doing her best to prepare herself for the long day that lay before her, she told Fred that it would take a while for her hair to dry. She suggested that he go ahead, and she'd meet him in the lounge when she was dressed.

Eager to show her off to his new drinking pals, he urged her not to take too long. The United Fruit Growers was footing the bill, and the young couple needed to fulfill their duty. UFG paid a fortune to have a Nobel Laureate on board. With Marion at his side, Banting was bringing far more to the table than the company executives ever dreamed.

Marion gave Fred a glorious smile. "As long as we are dancing afterwards," she said.

He winced at the thought. For years he told his mates that he preferred his dancing to be done by proxy. His half-drunk male friends always guffawed at the joke but not Marion. She wanted to dance with her husband, not his surrogate.

She watched Fred leave their honeymoon suite to spend the afternoon drinking himself stupid with men who were more than happy to put their gin and tonics on the UFG tab.

It's not often you get the company to pay for your drink, the business managers and sales reps thought as they ordered another round and laughed at Banting's jokes.

When Fred began singing, she'd join them, but not a moment before. He had a glorious voice. That's how he first seduced her — with his song.

2
1920
A Terrible Beauty

Edith Roach (b. ca. 1895) was a long-necked and graceful woman with thick, dark brown shoulder length hair that she wore swept to the side. She bore with grace the hard luck of being childhood sweethearts with Fred Banting. Edith had a small, kind mouth and intelligent, hopeful eyes.

Banting was bull-headed and tough to love. When he returned from overseas in 1919, he was not the same rough-and-tumble country boy she agreed to marry when he enlisted. He drank, he smoked, and he swore. These new habits pushed her Methodist upbringing to the limit. She believed in holiness and the sanctity of the body. Smoking, drinking, and whoring weren't part of her vocabulary.

But she couldn't toss her darling aside, not yet anyhow. He still held her heart in his hands.

Before the war, they shared an unshakeable and certain belief in God and the unfolding miracle of the universe. While serving as a battlefield surgeon, Fred began to wonder about the nature of God and faith and wandered further afield than Edith dared imagine. While she queried and doubted but reserved judgement pending further investigation, he strayed beyond the pale of thoughtful questioning to self-justification and absolute certainty. He became his own moral arbiter. He did whatever he thought was right in his own eyes. This grieved Edith's spirit. It caused her to question the wisdom of loving him the way she did.

Working day and night, Banting treated the maimed and torn apart. They arrived on stretchers from the front. In his moments of reprieve over whiskey and smokes, he remembered his Sunday School lessons and found them wanting. This broke Edith's heart.

She knew that she could never settle for an agnostic as a husband. However, she was willing to give him the benefit of the doubt.

Let's see how things play out, she thought. His story isn't over yet. He still might redeem himself. Then she waited, and waited, to no avail.

Banting was brusque and hot-tempered; he cut people off and turned the conversation back to his experience, his concerns, his trials, and his tribulations. Edith was kind and patient. She listened with compassion to the stories students, friends, and strangers told her. She gave them her full attention without waiting to jump in and tell them a story of her own. They had something valuable to say. She put them at ease. They shared their pain and joy and loved her all the more for listening.

Armed with a Gold Medal in Modern Languages, Edith taught high school at Ingersoll Collegiate, a few miles from London, Ontario. She was a woman who knew what she was about, where she wanted to go, and what she needed to do. She faced the fact that if she were to transform her infatuation for Freddy into a strong and lasting marriage, she'd have her work cut out for her.

He may have once been a darling from the golden cornfields in southern Ontario. Now, he was a blowhard who had been east of Eden and returned with the mark of Cain. He had changed utterly. A terrible beauty was born.

Edith was at his side when he was about to face the hard luck of being granted his deepest yearning and most heartfelt desire. His prayers for fame and fortune would soon be answered in such a way he could not, in his wildest imagining, have ever dreamed possible.

Before becoming Canada's most eligible bachelor, Banting set up a practice in London in 1920. He did not get the position at the Hospital for Sick Children that he assumed, given his war record, was his for the taking.

In his newly established surgery, he had more time on his hands than patients to keep him busy. While he waited for referrals that were slow in coming, he painted to fill his empty days. He had little to no money in his bank account. Banished to this obscure backwater on the edge of the universe, he stewed and fretted. Was this any way to treat a decorated war hero?

Damn those Ivory Tower bastards in Toronto! Didn't they know who he was? At least he had the balls to go overseas and do his duty. Them and their caps and gowns. He had medals on his chest. White feathers festooned theirs.

While on a visit in October, Edith stood back from the easel. She smiled as she gazed upon Fred's latest effort — a landscape, the oil still wet and glistening. His work was getting better. Her voice was full of encouragement. She liked how he mixed his colours. He'd been practising.

Unused to receiving compliments, Banting didn't know how to respond.

Ever since returning home, he was determined to keep the military bearing he had adopted overseas. He preferred being in command to taking orders.

Edith fiddled with the engagement ring he had given her before he was mobilized. Even after four years, it seemed a new and wonderful delight.

But would he ever marry me? she asked herself. Do I want to risk jeopardizing my happiness by yoking it to his perpetual discontent?

No longer a foregone conclusion, the question niggled in the back of her mind. Fred had turned into an unhappy man, and that gave her pause. She wasn't sure she was ever up to the challenge of him wallowing in despair.

Banting had his shortcomings, that's for sure, but he also had his charms. He was hale and hearty, the centre of attention, and the life of the party. He was also domineering, bellicose, and insecure.

His reasons for delaying their wedding were always practical and full of good sense. While he dithered, she used the time to her advantage. Perhaps she couldn't fault him for his logic, but she could question his fidelity. Edith knew that he had been unfaithful. While she waited, he strayed, but she was no man's fool, especially his.

Banting lit his pipe. Visiting the Art Gallery of Toronto with Edith the February before gave him the idea that he should try his hand at painting landscapes.

Banting waved his arm about his studio. It was full of drawings, water colours, and oils. All these months later, the sketches he had attempted were still that of a rank amateur. Turns out landscapes are a lot harder than they look.

"Tom Thomson (1877-1917) knew what he was doing," Banting said.

Edith remembered the crowd of men at the Memorial Exhibition swarming to the front of the gallery. She couldn't see a thing. What stayed with her was hearing the pert young woman who had the temerity to ask all those questions about Thomson's death. Edith admired her cheek but couldn't remember her name.

Banting couldn't either. He hadn't given the strident grey-haired gal a second glance. What he remembered, though, was the harridan in black, the one with the blue hair. Of all the strays at the gallery that evening, she was the most memorable. Everyone gave her a wide berth. She smelled of the devil.

Edith thought that Thomson painted the north like no other. She admired his work on small boards and large canvases. His *Jack Pine* was a testament to Canada's great loss. We may have won the war, but at what cost? She mused. All those men who survived came home bereft and alone. Their lives were blown apart.

Thomson's trees are lonely sentinels on a craggy shore.

"That may be all well and good," Banting protested. "Thomson fussed around while the rest of us served King and country. Algonquin Park is not a battlefield."

"He died living the life he was given," Edith said.

"Hiding from the Hun, more like," Banting scoffed. "He certainly didn't risk his life in the trenches."

"Thomson enlisted and was rejected," Edith said. "What was he supposed to do? Not everyone is cut out to study medicine. He's an artist."

"Bully for him, the coward," Banting said. "His family got him off. I signed up and did what needed to be done. Now, I paint to take my mind off my troubles. I am not cowering in the backwoods. All painting does is make me realize how incompetent I am."

Edith knew better than to argue with him when he got an idea in his head. "You could always take some lessons," she suggested, careful to keep any hint of criticism out of her voice. She stepped away from the easel, trying to see more promise of his potential. "I bet that there is someone at the A&L who'd be eager to take on a capable student like you."

"The Arts & Letters club?" Banting asked. He looked at her, askance.

"There's nothing like expert advice to shorten a long apprenticeship or an eager student to gladden a teacher's heart," she said. "Remember that quotation from Chaucer? *The lyf so short, the craft so hard to lerne.*"

"Indeed," Banting laughed. "A lesson once a month would give us a reason for visiting our old haunts."

"And rekindle our love," Edith dreamt.

3
On The Verge

Edith knew how sensitive Freddy was, and she did not want to set him off again. Not today of all days, she thought as she looked at his brush strokes. Perhaps he'll say that their wait is over. After the cups, the marmalade, and the years of delaying, perhaps he will give her the nod and she'll buy her wedding gown, or perhaps she will call the whole thing off.

Is today the day she lets her guard down? As meagre as her teacher's salary is, she is more than able to help with the expenses, at least until Freddy gets his practice established. He has no real excuse to delay their wedding any longer.

Edith, on the other hand, has many concerns. She needs him to come to her on her own terms. To be a loving, faithful, and dutiful husband. She could not allow him to take the upper hand. She was her own woman and was accustomed to making her own decisions. She did not want him to force her hand.

Fred relit his pipe. Painting helped him forget how slow his practice was.

Edith told him to be level-headed and persevering. She reminded him that he was a resourceful surgeon who knew better than most how to treat traumatic injuries. Any hospital would be lucky to have him on staff. London and the surrounding areas were in desperate need for the skills that he had to offer.

She reassured him not to worry about the future. Hard work and good luck go hand in hand. When a man lays a proper foundation, his ability and determination will bring him success. Given enough time, he will flourish.

But Banting was tired of waiting. His expenses kept mounting. He needed more money coming in. When Edith suggested that after their wedding, she could continue teaching until his practice was flourishing, he nearly snapped the paintbrush in his hand.

"Don't be absurd!" he shouted. "No self-respecting man would ever marry when he couldn't support his wife and children."

Edith blushed and turned her face away. She looked out the open window and kept her mouth shut.

In addition to his surgery, Banting was working as a part-time demonstrator at the university. It brought in a few extra dollars a month. He assisted Professor F. R. Miller (1881-1967) with his neurological experiments on cats. It was quite the stretch for Banting. He was used to amputating limbs, treating head wounds, and removing shrapnel. Delicate surgery on small animals was new to him. However, he loved the adrenalin rush that came from being pushed to the very limit. He was used to life on the edge. It was addictive.

During the war, wounded soldiers overwhelmed Banting's surgery. He didn't have to molly coddle them or worry about his next paycheque. The aches and pains and skin rashes he had to deal with now drove him mad. Get over it, he wanted to say to his patients. Get back to work, you malingerers. It made him furious, their whining about this ache and that pain. Give him real medical problems to solve. He'd much rather leave delivering babies and such like to others. He wanted to do serious medicine that made a difference in people's lives.

"But obstetrics is no small matter, Freddy," Edith said. "The future of humanity depends on each safe labour and delivery. Women need good doctors."

"I'm not an idiot," Banting said. "It's just I can't be bothered with all the emotion and drama. I'd rather treat a catastrophic wound and move on."

He shuddered. People weren't all that interesting to him. He couldn't care less about how they felt. He struggled to relight his pipe. He wasn't ready to hear the good words that Edith was saying.

"You don't have to be on the front lines to do your duty. Sometimes God calls us to live extraordinary lives in alleys and by-ways, away from the madding crowd. A good life can be lived out in the everyday. Small things that do not garner attention are grand."

Her and her sermonizing, Banting thought. He took a long draw on his pipe. The nicotine made him meditative. The only thing better would be a small dram, he thought. But Edith wouldn't like it.

"You're probably right," he said. "It's just that I'm not quite ready for the straight and narrow."

"Probably right?" she asked. "We grew up in Alliston, reading *Pilgrim's Progress* and attending Sunday School. Since going to Europe, you've forgotten Bunyan's Vanity Fair. In the end, its allure is always disappointing."

Not liking the direction this conversation was heading, Banting walked over to his desk and picked up a note he had scribbled on a scrap of paper. On Halloween, he came across an article by Moses Barron that got him thinking about the islet cells of the pancreas in relation to diabetes. An idea came to him that might lead to a cure for that terrible disease.

"For diabetes, Freddy?" Edith asked "Really? All those people who keep their blood sugar low by starving themselves. They eat vegetables that have been boiled three times. The latest treatment doctors prescribe restricts patients to foods that won't raise the sugar in their blood or urine. That's no life."

Banting was astounded that she could speak intelligently about something he had just discovered. He shouldn't have been surprised. Edith may have been a language major, but she read scientific and medical journals. They helped her get on with students who attended her class only for the credit. She wanted to know what interested them and what she could do to make her teaching more relevant to their studies.

"There's nothing more practical than a solid grounding in a second language, no matter your field," she often said to her half-bored students. Some perked up their ears, while others refused to listen. Edith focussed her attention on students who were struggling to learn. She left the recalcitrant ones to their own devices.

"If you find a cure for diabetes," she said, "you'll become the most famous man in the world."

"This is my first original idea," Banting replied. "It's come out of nowhere. I know I don't have the background. For God's sake, I use hammers and saws and drills in my work, not beakers and flasks."

He poured himself a whiskey. Edith gave him a stern look, but he didn't care.

While prepping for Professor Miller's lectures, Banting learned that researchers had known about the relationship between the pancreas and diabetes since the 1890s. Minkowski (1858-1931) and von Mering (1849-1908) discovered that the islets of Langerhans played a role in preventing diabetes. No one knew yet what, why, or how, but Banting had an idea.

There must be a way of isolating the yet undiscovered enzyme the islets may or may not be producing. He has to prove the existence of this active principle.

"How do you think you'd do that?" Edith asked, taking the whiskey from him.

"Capture some of it for analysis," Banting said. "Find a way to purify it for human testing."

"Is that all?" Edith replied, having a sip, shuddering, and handing the glass back. "I imagine more experienced researchers than you have thought of this before."

"You're not kidding," Banting admitted, growing suddenly irritated at her. It galled him that she could speak to him as his equal. "But they haven't figured out the how." He finished the last of the whiskey and poured another.

"Given your determination, I have no doubt that you will find a way," Edith attempted to mollify him, but he refused to listen.

"The pancreas secretes enzymes that are involved in digesting what we eat and drink," Banting said. "They may also be producing an internal secretion that controls blood sugar levels. That's what I want to discover — if there are two stages in the process. I suspect the enzyme that aids digestion destroys the blood sugar enzyme before scientists can examine it. My idea is to isolate the one from the other. If we can separate the external from the internal, we'll be on our way."

"Are you sure that you want to do this, Freddy?" Edith asked. "Can you handle the unrelenting scrutiny of an adoring public? If you think that the pressure you are under now is unbearable, you have no idea of what could be coming."

"As a surgeon, I know that blockages of the pancreatic duct will lead most of the pancreas to atrophy, while leaving the islets of Langerhans intact. To keep the external secretion from digesting the internal, I'll need to tie the ducts. This will destroy the cells that produce the external enzyme, but not the cells that produce the internal. After we tie the ducts closed, we'll need to keep the dogs alive long enough to allow the pancreas to waste away. The surviving tissue should only contain the internal secretion. That is my assumption. Isolating the internal secretion and proving its ability to reduce sugar in the urine is the secret, I'm sure. All I need is some lab space, a few dogs, and maybe an assistant. We need to experiment on dogs because the canine pancreas is similar to the human."

"What about here at Western with Professor Miller?" Edith asked.

"He stores the lab animals in his office," Banting replied. "The university has no space for his experiments. I volunteer my time to assist him. There's no money to spare. Besides, he doesn't have the expertise. I already asked him. He suggested Toronto."

"The University?" Edith asked. "But what about your practice here, Freddy? Will you be able to do both?"

He ignored her.

"Professor Miller thinks I should talk to a Dr. MacLeod. His speciality is the behaviour of sugar in the blood. A couple years ago, he wrote a monograph on diabetes. He's the world's leading expert. He's the man I need to talk to. He'll know if my idea is viable or not."

"Does that mean you'd move back to the city? Are you sure about that? You'd be leaving everything here behind. Is that what you really want?"

She saw into the future and realized that his dream of a happy life was not hers at all. She needed to make her own plans before it was too late.

4
Diabetus

Banting bristled at Professor James John Rickert MacLeod (1876-1935), who was leafing through some correspondence on his desk and thinking about his next appointment. You know it's spelled D-I-A-B-E-T-E-S, don't you? MacLeod sighed when he looked at Banting's scribbled note, titled "Diabetus."

"I was in a rush."

"And you didn't think to prepare a formal presentation?"

"I didn't know if my idea had merit. I wanted to meet with you first before wasting any of my time."

"And you thought you could waste mine? The truth is, Dr. Banting, you know nothing about diabetes research. Generations of fully trained highly competent scholars have been studying it for decades. I know. I've read everything that's ever been written and attended every conference on the subject worth attending. How do you expect me to believe that a notion for a cure has fallen from the heavens into your lap when it has eluded so many others for so long? Miraculous discoveries may sometimes be divinely inspired, I know that. Most of the time, however, they are the result of hard lessons learned from disappointing failures. You may have been a competent surgeon in the battlefield, but you don't have the skills to carry this project to its completion. You do not have the background or the experience to transform this nebulous idea of yours into something tangible."

"But no one else has connected the dots," Banting interrupted. "Only me! Dr. MacLeod, I have never failed at anything I set my mind to. I do not lose. I know a thing or two about facing insurmountable odds. I know what it is to be pushed to the horizon of my competence. That's how I learn."

MacLeod sat back in his chair, puffed on his pipe, and looked at the brash young man across his desk. For some reason, he let him go on.

"I know I'm out of my depth. But I have served in a battalion. I value teamwork."

"As long as you are the one giving the orders?" MacLeod asked.

"I know what I can accomplish if I have the right people at my back."

MacLeod nodded, and Banting continued, stumbling with his words, and wringing his hands. "If you agree to supervise me, I'll do it without asking for compensation."

MacLeod perked up. "You're willing to do this on your own without asking the university for money?" He was incredulous at the thought.

"I need a lab, dogs, and an assistant who can run the experiments. I can do the actual surgery. I need to ligate the ducts so the pancreas atrophies. It shouldn't be a problem once I get the hang of it."

MacLeod puffed on his pipe. "It's a lot harder than it looks."

"Please, sir."

"They are easy to miss. They are so small, believe you me."

"I'm a quick study," Banting replied. "I can learn if you show me."

MacLeod shook his head, marvelling at the tenacity of this man who would not take no for an answer. "I can see that you're bound and determined."

McLeod had never before met anyone who was so committed to an idea that he was willing to gamble his life for it. Sell his car, certainly. But give up his growing surgical practice to test a hypothesis that, in all likelihood, would fail? That was unthinkable. He relit his pipe and considered Banting's proposal more closely. "It does have promise," MacLeod admitted. "First, you atrophy the pancreas by ligating the ducts. Then, you collect the internal secretion from the islets of Langerhans. Perhaps this hypothesis merits further consideration.

The pancreas produces both an external digestive enzyme, and an internal enzyme that regulates blood and urine sugar levels. Once the pancreas atrophies, it stops producing the external digestive enzyme. The islets of Langerhans continue to produce the enzyme that controls blood sugar. If such an enzyme exists, you should be able to extract it from the islets of Langerhans in the depancreatized dog.

Your job over the summer, if I get approval, will be to prove that this supposed enzyme exists. If you can do that, you might be on the way to finding a cure for diabetes."

Banting was incredulous. He sat there stunned.

"I'll need time to get the department on board," MacLeod mused. "I have a state-of-the-art animal operating room that hasn't been used in years. You'll have to clean it up. Will you consider starting in the spring term? Can you wait that long?"

Banting jumped to his feet. "Wait?" He shouted. "Of course, I can."

He paced around MacLeod's office, his mind racing. "I'll shut down my practice in London. I'll serve notice as soon as I get home. Then, I'll need to talk to Edith." That made him pause and he caught his breath.

"Wait a minute, young man. You need to settle down. I have some inquiries to make before you charge full speed out of here. I have to confer with my colleagues. We'll have a meeting and decide whether or not to allow you to sink or swim. I'm not the only one you need to consider. As far as you are concerned, I may be the University of Toronto, but let me assure you, I am answerable to the president, the provost, not to forget the various deans and trustees. There is a chain of command here.

I am also responsible to my colleagues in the field. They hold me accountable for the decisions that I make in this office. I need to make a few judicious inquiries before you do a thing. Most everyone will be away for the summer, so space won't be a problem. I also have a few extra dogs. If you need more than the ten that we keep on hand, you'll have to find your own."

"That's easily done," Banting said. "I learnt at Western that people are always trying to get rid of unwanted pets. All I have to do is knock on a few doors in the neighbourhood. If I avoid answering any direct questions, I'll soon have more than I need."

"As far as a lab assistant goes, let me see," MacLeod began to shuffle through some papers on his desk. "There's that young fellow graduating this spring. His aunt died from diabetes. He'd be keen. Charles Best (1899-1978). He'd need a stipend, though. The department has some money for him. But not for you."

"That's okay," Banting said. "I'll sell my car and sleep in the lab."

"I'll be in Scotland the entire time you're here mucking about," MacLeod replied. "When I return in September, I'll examine your results and see if your idea still has merit. If it does, I'll find some money for you to keep up your research over the fall and winter. If it doesn't, you and I are finished. You will not be compensated for your effort. Is that clear?"

"You won't be disappointed, Professor MacLeod," Banting said. That Best fellow and I will work night and day to bring a positive result to you."

"Even a negative has scientific value," MacLeod said. "You won't go wrong if you follow proper lab procedures and take meticulous notes. Your idea is worth exploring."

"Thank you, sir," Banting said, pumping Professor MacLeod's hand.

Against his better instincts, MacLeod had relented. He couldn't control the man, but he couldn't afford to lose him either.

"The two of you will be alone, which I suspect is how you like to work. On your own, in charge, and following your nose. Without me interfering or holding you back. I'll allow you that much freedom, at least until September. When I return, however, things will be different. I'll hold you to a strict accounting. Under my supervision, you will do things properly and to the highest possible standard. Can you accept that?"

"In the army, I learned to obey orders without question," Banting said.

"It's not easy, getting along with lesser lights," MacLeod cautioned. "It takes tact and diplomacy. What can be accomplished in one day on your own takes a week with others. You'll have to be patient, Banting. It's infuriating but the process works.

If your experiments find anything positive, I'll assemble a team of first-rate scientists to refine the extract for human trials in the New Year. But the initial idea is yours, Banting; I'll never forget that. You'll be the one who shares the results, first to the University's Journal Club, then to the annual meeting of the American Association of Physicians, and finally to the world.

Your name will be forever associated with diabetes research. You will be its public face. The rest of us, hopefully, will toil on in anonymity — full professors with tenure, able to walk down the streets without the press hounding our every move. That's what this will cost you. Your face will be known across Canada and the world. Your life will no longer be your own."

5
Golden Summer

Professor MacLeod put the last of his books into a steamer trunk and wondered what he had gotten himself into. He had taken time away from packing to meet Banting at the animal operating theatre. It gave MacLeod a small measure of comfort to know that Banting had been operating on cats under Dr. Miller's close supervision. One might think that performing pancreatomies on dogs should be easier, but it's still microsurgery.

Banting may be an oaf, but he's onto something. His idea could change the course of human history. But the man himself, what at a piece of work! He'll be more trouble than he's worth.

At least the lab is empty over the summer, MacLeod consoled himself as he walked to the campus. There'll be no witnesses if it turns out to be a debacle. But if Banting succeeds, the department be getting something for nothing. The benefit outweighs the risk. That pleased his frugal, Scottish heart.

I'm willing to gamble because the suffering diabetics endure is so terrible. Besides, no one in the field has had any luck so far. Maybe I'll make medical history without it costing a penny.

However, after spending an irritating afternoon with Banting and his insecurities, MacLeod was ready to call the whole thing off. Instead, he kept his mouth shut and went on his summer idyll.

Ligating the dog's pancreatic ducts to the duodenum is a long and tiresome chore. MacLeod had done it several times and it had never been easy. The ducts are so small that they are easy to miss. He hoped Banting would soon catch on. It made him smile, though, the sight of Banting dry-heaving from the smell of dog shit and piss.

Just wait until the hot, humid days of summer, when the sweat is pouring down your face, MacLeod chuckled to himself.

This place will be rank, and I will be breathing in fresh air on the bonnie banks of the Clyde.

Banting put his fist to his mouth. "You're right, Professor MacLeod. This surgery is far trickier than I could have ever imagined. I will get the hang of it if I ever get over the stench."

With that, MacLeod tossed his gloves and bloodied surgical gown into the laundry tub. He scrubbed his hands.

"You'll do fine Dr. Banting," he said. "Best is a capable lab assistant. There's also Dr. Clark Noble (1900-1978). The one could work with you for the first half of the summer; the other, for the second half. Best needs to attend military training for a couple weeks. That'd be a good time to do the changeover. See you in September."

MacLeod smiled to himself as he strode down the hall. If Charlie Best can survive the summer with that modern Major-General, he'll someday make a good scientist. For once, I'd love to see him apply himself to his work. He's had a pretty easy time of it so far, I'd have to say.

I'll assay their results when I return. If there's any gold in the pan, we'll be on our way. If not, we'll have eliminated one more futile endeavour. Not to brag, but I've made sure that the scope of this summer's work is well within their limited ability. Banting's a good enough surgeon and Best is competent enough in the lab. Neither are experienced researchers.

The question that remains foremost in my mind is whether or not they will follow strict enough protocols so that their results can be replicated. Best needs to be diligent in his work and Banting needs to be meticulous both in the surgery and with his record keeping. He needs to write everything down. There can be no dismissing things because they are dissatisfied with the results.

In the worst case, I'll have them repeat their experiments in September. Once their results are confirmed, I'll call in Bert

Collip[1] (1892-1965) on leave from the University of Alberta. It sure is a feather in their cap that Edmonton got him. Our loss that we didn't. He'll take this project to the next level.

I have no problem with Banting and Best using their extract to experiment on a few lab dogs. But I'll leave it to Dr. Collip to refine the solution for human trials. Within a year, we should have a cure for diabetes, beating Nicolae Paulescu (1869-1930) and the Romanians to the prize. In the meantime, I'll let these two muddle their way through this golden summer. It'll be a crucible that may transform Banting's theory into something worth considering. If it turns Charlie Best into a research scientist, all the better.

With that, Dr. McLeod hurried home. He and Mrs. McLeod had a train to catch. They were shipping out from Montreal and didn't have a moment to lose.

---

1. James Bertram

6
On Their Own

Charlie Best returned from a two-week training stint with the Canadian militia that interrupted his summer's work with Banting. Rather than let Dr. Clark have his chance, Banting kept Best on. He was turning into a decent surgical assistant and the two got on well enough. Sometimes, the devil you know is better than the one you don't, Banting mused. Unfortunately, he spent most of the first week, cleaning up the mess Best left behind.

Best opened the doors to the laboratory. If there's another war, he'll be ready to serve. Once a soldier, always a soldier.

Worn and haggard, Banting looked up from his work as his tanned and handsome protégé entered the lab. He noticed the time and shook his head.

"Dr. Banting, how are you?" Best asked. He was bursting with energy, hale, and eager to get back to work.

"Tell me Best," Banting demanded. "Are you happy you won the coin toss with Dr. Noble?"

"Yes, of course," Best replied. "It got me here, working with you. This is a once-in-a-lifetime opportunity."

"Then why the hell is your work so sloppy? I've had to redo all your tests. Dirty glassware and inconsistent solutions have invalidated our results. If you want to continue working with me, you'll have to change your attitude.

In case you haven't noticed, this isn't varsity. People's lives and well-being are at stake. We have the opportunity to alleviate their suffering. Diabetics are starving to death, waiting for a cure. But you're too busy playing baseball, courting, and riding horseback to pay attention. Your duty to me comes first.

For God's sake, you better wash everything in this lab. Throw out all those irregular solutions and make new ones that are completely normal. If you have to, reread your Ringer.[2] Get the formula right for once, will you? We have a job to do."

Best flushed red with anger and embarrassment.

"This is far too important for you to be so slipshod," Banting continued. "It's a privilege. You have a care and a duty."

Banting grabbed his jacket. "I have had more than enough for today. This place better be shipshape when I return tomorrow."

He stormed out of the lab.

Charlie Best was not accustomed to this kind of criticism. Tall, blonde, and handsome, he was used to floating through. Good grades came easily to him. He'd learned to put in enough effort to get what he wanted. He never really had to apply himself. With Banting furious, however, Best knew he had to shape up or lose everything. He put on his lab coat, went to the sink, and spent all night washing every bit of glassware in the lab. He dried and polished every surface until it was gleaming.

Before going home to collapse on his bed, he made a new batch of solution, checking and rechecking the formula and following the outlined procedures exactly.

There you go, Dr. Banting, sir! He said to himself, saluting. The finest Ringer's Solution you'll find on the planet — sodium chloride, potassium chloride, calcium chloride and sodium bicarbonate balancing the ph. Just as Ringer himself prescribed. It's as normal as plasma flowing through veins.

He turned out the lights and stumbled home for a few hours' sleep.

When he returned the next morning, Banting nodded his approval.

"Good work, lad. We better get going before the heat of the day makes this lab unbearable."

With that, Best loosened his tie. "What's next, sir?"

___

2. Ringer's solution is a mixture of salts administered to human and veterinary patients for intravenous or subcutaneous hydration. Its precise proportions vary from species to species.

"We have to ligate ducts so that we can begin the two-stage operation of depancreatizing lab dogs. You are about to become a fine surgical assistant.

First, we ligate the ducts and situate the pancreas under the skin. Second, when the pancreas has atrophied, we remove it entirely. The depancreatized dog should live for up to four days without treatment.

While the ligated pancreas atrophies under the skin, it stops producing the digestive enzyme. The islets of Langerhans, however, keep producing the enzyme that reduces blood sugar.

Once the pancreas has atrophied, we remove it. Then pulverize it. Filter the thick brown muck and inject it back into the dog. If the animal survives beyond four days, we've found our miracle cure."

"Seems unnecessarily complicated, don't you think?" Best asked, prepping for the surgery. "There's got to be an easier way to do this."

"There may be, but we'll follow MacLeod's directions exactly," Banting replied. "We don't want to give him any reason for getting rid of us, so that he can take all the credit for our work."

7
Convenient Grace

"Not one that's atrophied?" Banting cried out four days later. In frustration and despair, he opened up the two surviving dogs whose ducts he had ligated. He wiped the sweat off his face. The lab was sweltering. He could barely breathe; the stench was so high.

"Yes, sir, this one is healthy too," Best said. "So's this one. Their pancreases are still in good working order."

"MacLeod gave us 10 dogs," Banting said. "Only two are left? He'll be livid."

"What do you think went wrong?" Best asked.

"Shit, Charlie. I don't know. I must have missed some of the ducts. Damn it all. He looked around the lab, his eyes frantic. Oh God, I could use a drink."

"MacLeod warned you that the surgery was trickier than it looked."

"It sure as hell is," Banting replied. "With all the battlefield operations I conducted in France? I was certain that this would be a simple task. How hard can it be, operating on a dog? I'm a surgeon after all, not a lousy veterinarian."

Banting instinctively felt for his flask, but it was Prohibition. There wasn't a drink to be had anywhere he knew of in the city. He hadn't time to make any connections. If only he were back in London — there, he knew a guy.

"Dr. Banting, please," Best said. "In France, you were dealing with blunt trauma in appalling conditions. It was battlefield triage, not fine surgery like this."

"We had to keep soldiers from bleeding out," Banting said.

He stood at attention.

"Stabilize him as quickly as possible and ship him out. Make room for the 1000 other lives in the line outside."

He saluted.

"Yes, sir!" Banting barked, before slumping. His face fell. "I'm not used to losing lives on the table. My patients live."

"Our casualties are indeed heavy," Best continued, trying to calm his superior down. "There's no denying it, but you have to keep working, sir. Redo the operations and wait for the pancreases to atrophy. Then, we'll be back in business."

"Yeah, yeah, yeah, Charlie. I know the spiel," Banting clenched his jaw. "I kill dogs for the greater good. That's why we numbered them. Could you imagine, Charlie? Giving them names and treating them like pets? Do you love animals, Charlie? I grew up on a farm. We raised animals for a living. Their lives had purpose. God, I could use a drink."

"What we have to do is an unspeakable sacrifice," Best admitted.

"Slurry the pulverised pancreases in Ringer's solution, Banting said. "Inject the filtered extract back into the dog and see if it lives. All this to create an extract that may or may not contain an unproven enzyme from the islets of Langerhans that may or may not be there. But we don't know, Charlie."

"We're like two idiots, flying pell-mell into the darkness," Best admitted.

"We wreak havoc wherever we go. All the good, all the ill we are doing? It's based on an idea that came to me on Halloween night. Can you imagine?

While children were out trick-or-treating, I was cowering in my study. I didn't have enough money to give out candy and apples. Then, there's Edith judging my every move. What kind of nightmare have I gotten myself into?"

"What's her opinion of you holed up here with me?" Best asked.

"She thinks I'm bound and determined to ruin my life. I'm heading straight to hell. She says I'm too good a man for the misfortune I'm chasing. There's a better way, she insists. To live humbly. To live peacefully. To doctor in the byways of some backwater in southern Ontario. And marry her, of course.

But abandon my idea? Leave it to MacLeod and his bigwig cronies to scoop up and steal? It's not as if they don't have enough already is it, Charlie? That you and I have to settle for crumbs when we could have gold? They have tenure and status. The best tables in restaurants. We cook our suppers over Bunsen burners here in the lab."

"This idea of yours is the motherlode for us," Best said. "With it, the world is ours for the taking. All I know, Dr. Banting, is that you must be brave. If you want to see your idea through, you have to keep working. You can't stop now."

"We have to prove the extract exists," Banting agreed. "Prove MacLeod wrong. Then, this summer and all these dogs we've sacrificed, won't be for nothing."

Banting and Best spent the rest of the day and long into the night redoing the ligations. After Banting finished each surgery, Best closed the dogs up. This time, they made doubly sure every duct was ligated.

While Best checked in on the dogs, Banting searched the storeroom for a bottle of spirits. He poured a couple ounces into a tall glass and filled it with water. It turned cloudy. He took a sip and grimaced. "It's no martini." He took another sip. "That's better." Then another. The alcohol hit his system and he relaxed.

Best stepped into the doorway. "Oh, I was about to turn off the light."

Banting raised his glass to him. "Do we have any olives?"

"Only in your dreams, sir," Best replied. "Surely, we can now move on to the next stage in our experiment."

Banting took another sip of his drink. "As long as I don't go blind, Charlie, or die. If I do, tell Edith that she can have my second-best bed."

Banting roared with laughter, pleased with his Shakespearean wit.

Charlie was sombre and subdued. "When you've sobered up tomorrow, we can chop and mash the pancreas; create a slurry with Ringer's Solution; filter the extract; and inject it back into one of the dogs. Then, we'll record how long it lives. The untreated dog will be the control. If it dies and the other lives, we'll make history."

Banting struggled to light his pipe.

"It grieves my spirit that we have to kill animals to prove our hypothesis. Will my conscience ever be clear, Charlie? Because I have minimized the loss of life? Remember, I trained as a surgeon and have vowed to do no harm. Every life is significant. Even these blasted dogs."

He finished his drink.

"Yes sir, your conscience will be very clear indeed."

Banting looked at the young priestly acolyte and took his absolution at face value. "You must believe in Prevenient Grace."

"Pardon?" Best asked. "I'm not much of a theologian."

"God's forgiveness for sin before we commit it," Banting replied. "I'm no longer a churchman, but I was hoping for something more down to earth."

"Which is?" Best asked, immediately wishing he hadn't asked the question.

"Convenient Grace, Charlie. Forgiveness for the sins we intend to commit, come hell or high water. Sins of wilful commission. Acts that we have justified in our own minds yet know beyond a doubt are plain wrong. That's the kind of grace that I need — grace that allows me to do whatever the hell I want."

8

A Baptism in Dog

"How about we take a break?" Best suggested. "We need to get our strength back. Maybe grab a bite to eat?"

Banting nodded.

"There's a deli around the corner. Do you have any cash, Charlie? I, uh, left my wallet at home."

"Again?" Best smiled, knowing Banting slept in the lab.

"Again," Banting replied. "I'll make it up to you one day."

They hung up their lab coats, washed their hands, and took their leave. The lab smelled of dog shit and death. A brisk cool wind would do them a world of good. Instead, they breathed in heavy humid air.

The sun was unrelenting, but they found an empty park bench in the shade.

"You stay put, Dr. Banting, while I get those sandwiches. Want anything in particular?"

"Whatever's the daily special, Charlie. Thanks for this."

Best hurried off down the street.

Banting pulled a little sketch book out of his pocket. It's good to relax a bit, he thought to himself. He put his fingers together to form a square and held his hands up to frame the scene. He began to sketch the horizontal and vertical lines in front of him. I'll learn perspective yet, Banting smiled.

When Best returned, Banting put down his pencil.

"What did you bring us today, Charlie? Beef with mustard and lots of pepper. And a pickle, Charlie?"

"And a pickle, Dr. Banting. I'm starving."

"Me too."

As they ate their lunch, a group of well-dressed young women strolled by. "Don't they pique your interest the slightest bit, Charlie?"

"Not really, sir. Margaret and I are planning to get married as soon as I land a full-time position."

Banting shook his head and laughed. "I've been engaged to Edith for six years now. Hasn't kept me from enjoying the smorgasbord laid out before me."

"Does Edith know?" Best asked.

"Probably," Banting answered, "not that I have ever asked her. As a Christ follower, she has a bounden duty to forgive and forget. Mine is to get as much out of life as possible. Because after death, Charlie, there is nothing. Do all the living you can now, while you still have the chance."

Best noticed Banting's pencil sketch of the scene in front of them. "I didn't know you were an artist, sir.

"More of a dilettante," Banting replied. "I could while away my life here. Sitting in the sun with an easel in front of me and a brush in hand. Have you ever had the joy of painting en plein air, Charlie?"

"No sir, can't say that I have," Best replied. "I'm not even sure that I know what that is."

"Painting out of doors," Banting said. "To lose yourself in a landscape, creating a piece of art on canvas, pine board, or scrap of paper. At the very least, crafting something that is entirely for your own peace of mind, not for anything else. It's therapeutic."

"An indulgence that keeps one from committing suicide?" Best asked.

"I suppose," Banting replied. "No one will ever kill himself when he is doing what he loves, especially an artist with an unfinished painting on his easel."

"What about those rumours about Tom Thomson on Canoe Lake?" Best asked.

"Smoke and mirrors," Banting said. "Someone trying to make something out of nothing. The creative force that compels one to paint is too powerful for anyone to ignore. Not that it is ever easy."

"Are you talking about those Group of Seven boys," Best asked. "They're always in the paper raising a fuss."

"They work outside at their painting regardless of the frigid winter, bone-numbing spring, or God-awful summer. The best light for painting is in the autumn. When the sun is on the horizon, with the colours at their most brilliant.

The leaves falling from the trees, so you can see the trunks and the branches. Unobstructed and uncluttered. Those men do their greatest work outside, capturing the light, mixing paint, and getting colours right. It's alchemy. Transforming a smear on a palette into a luminous image."

"Could you imagine spending an entire day out in the fresh, clean air?" Best asked. "Doing something that doesn't kill or harm? That is somehow transformative?"

"That's exactly what an artist does," Banting said. "I sketch a scene, but my work has no real power. It doesn't arrest a viewer's eyes or change a life. It is an ornament that distracts from the main event. Something that probably doesn't match the furniture. I paint for the pure pleasure of the act. The mechanics, that's what I'm good at. I'd love to retire someday and go on expeditions to Canada's north. Or out west."

"I've never been to the Rockies," Best admitted. "Just Algonquin Park. That's as far north as I'd ever want to go."

"The best part is the potential on a blank piece of canvas," Banting said. "The hope that I could capture the essence of a brief moment in time. As far from this hell hole as you can imagine."

Banting tore the sketch out of his book.

"Do you want this? Keep it as a reminder, for years down the road, of our friendship. It was born in excrement and christened in urine. A baptism in dog."

9
July 30, 1921

Best took a healthy dog out of its kennel. She was bounding with energy and ready for a walk. When he led her to the animal operating room, she cowered in fear and pulled back, stiff-legged and frantic. Best tried to comfort her.

"If you survive, old girl, every diabetic will thank you. We are sacrificing your life for the greater good."

She pissed all over the floor.

At the end of the week, Charlie Best checked Dog 408's blood sugar. "It's down again, sir."

"That's what? Four times in four days we've injected her?" Banting asked. "And each time, the extract drove down her numbers?"

"That's right," Best said. "They do not lie."

Banting looked at Best's report. They both laughed and shook hands.

"I think I'd better sit down and write Professor MacLeod a letter," Banting said.

In it, Banting named the extract "Isleton," but MacLeod later deferred to Sir Edward Albert Sharpey-Shafer's 1910 idea that there was a chemical missing from the pancreas in people with diabetes. He called it "Insulin."

"Don't forget to ask about new gloves and gowns," Best said. "Maybe someone to help keep the place clean? How about a complete refitting of the animal operating room?"

"And while I'm at it, a contract for the coming year," Banting said. "I've run out of funds and could use some back pay for this summer's work. I could even start buying your lunch."

"That'd be a treat," Best said, wiping his brow. "Now I know why everyone abandons this place at this time of year."

"What are you talking about," Banting asked. "100° Fahrenheit and 100% humidity in an airless lab. This is a cake walk compared to the minefields in France."

"I hope we're not asking MacLeod for too much," Best said.

"I hope we're not asking for too little," Banting insisted.

Best checked the dog's temperature. "She's burning up, sir. She may have a fever."

"Or maybe an infection?" Banting asked. "You watch over her while I mail the report to MacLeod. I'll ask to keep you on this project with me. We work well together."

While Banting went to his office and sat at his desk, Best nestled Dog 408 in the recovery kennel. He spent the rest of the day scrubbing the lab clean.

When Banting returned later in the afternoon, they checked in on the dog together. She had died in her sleep.

"Well, this is a screw up," Banting said. "I just put the report in the mail."

"Shall we do an autopsy to see what happened?" Best asked.

Banting cut the dog's body open. The wound from the surgery was full of pus. "Good God, Charlie! Whoever discovers an effective medication against bacterial infection will deserve the Nobel Prize, not to mention a knighthood."

"Must be my turn to carry the body to the funeral pyre," Best said.

"I believe you're right," Banting replied. "I'll prepare the next two dogs for depancreatizing. We'll treat one with the extract and leave the other as the control."

"Then, we'll compare and see if the extract really works," Best said.

With that, he carried Dog 408 out to the incinerator and Banting prepared Dog 92 for surgery.

Without treatment, 408 lasted four days before dying. However, 92 responded beautifully to the injections. She was frisky, friendly, and cooperative. Until they ran out of extract.

"We need more, Charlie, and we need it now," Banting said. "We can't wait two weeks to scavenge extract from atrophied pancreases."

"What'll we do?" Best asked.

"I don't know."

"Figure out a short cut? We need an inexhaustible source," Best said. "The demand will be too great. Diabetics and their families the world over are desperate for a cure."

"We need to develop a means for mass production."

"How about we use the fresh pancreas we've just removed? Best asked. "Process it the way we would an atrophied one?"

"We have nothing to lose, Charlie. It'd certainly speed up the process. Let's see what happens."

Best chopped up the fresh pancreas and minced it into Ringer's solution. He created a slurry that he filtered into a brown muddy coloured extract.

Banting injected his beloved 92 and had a smoke. He then tested her blood sugar. "It's reduced, Charlie, but nothing significant. The result is so miniscule, it's not worth considering. The extract is too weak to be efficacious. It needs to be more concentrated. I knew right from the beginning that this would be futile. I'm not writing this up. It's a waste of time."

"Are you sure?" Best asked. "This could be a vitally important step. MacLeod said to record every result. No matter what."

"I've made my decision, Charlie," Banting said. "Let's move on."

10
Peace Offering

In Scotland, MacLeod opened Banting's letter, wondering what he would have to deal with when he returned to Toronto at the end of September. Then he read what Banting had written. Well, I'll be damned, he said to himself.

Without its pancreas, Dog 92 survived for 20 days, receiving daily injections of the extract. They might be onto something.

To avoid wasting department resources, MacLeod ordered Banting and Best to stay within the original parameters of the project. They needed to concentrate on redoing the experiments and collecting the data, building an unassailable fortress for the assault that was sure to come.

There'll be time enough for further exploration when I return and can supervise their work. Their methods need to be sound and their data collection complete. Banting might as well move to Toronto. I better poke around for some funding. Maybe Velyien Henderson (1877-1945) can hire him as a special assistant in Pharmacology with light enough duties, so that he can continue to work for me.

He is an outsider, but he has discovered something that escaped the rest of us. That I'll grant him. But there'll be a storm a-brewing. Lord, help me. I worry about what's to come. Banting will need to gird himself. When his idea becomes public, he'll be stepping onto highly contested ground.

Academics have been fighting for years to find a cure. Careers have been lost and won and more casualties are on the way.

Far more experienced researchers than he will scrutinize his hypothesis, criticize his methodology, and find fault with everything he says and publishes. Is he ready to present his findings to an eager if hostile audience? People will be highly skeptical. He will not be well received. He'll need to develop a thick skin and learn not to take criticism personally.

This is a battle that he is destined to lose. Many people have too vested an interest to allow him to steal the credit they have spent their lives pursuing. They'll exact their pound of flesh; of this I am certain. No one ever emerges unscathed from ground-breaking discoveries. It's all a question of what a person is willing to sacrifice to win the prize. McLeod packed his steamer trunk with books, tobacco, and tea to last the long year ahead of him.

While Fred Banting and Charlie Best waited for Professor MacLeod's return, they fumbled around the lab like a pair of amateurs — the blind leading the blind. They failed to make any more headway on their experiment and lived in fear of MacLeod's arrival. They couldn't replicate their results. His return to work would be their day of reckoning.

11
i' the name of Beelzebub

When MacLeod heard a sudden rapping on his heavy oak office door, he looked up from the tower of papers on his desk. He replaced the cap on his precious Mont Blanc fountain pen and blew the wet ink dry before turning the page over. The rapping continued.

"Knock, knock! Who's there, i' the name of Beelzebub?" he muttered to himself. He rose from his chair and stepped out from behind the desk, strewn high with books to be reviewed. There were files to be sorted; letters to be answered; research proposals to be considered. By yesterday, he had to respond to innumerable memos. Interdepartmental circulars about the building's faulty heating, holiday requests, and leaking roofs. Then, there were the sticky locks, squeaky wheels, staffing changes, teaching schedules, and drafty windows. And the course syllabi consultations with new professors who wanted his advice, job applications, tenders, bids, sales pitches. Last but not least, reference letters for grad students applying for jobs, scholarships, and research grants. Then there were the schemes, bickerings, complaints, charges founded or untrue, wounded egos and the like, that he had to sort out before the department imploded.

"It's all in a day's work," he sighed. "It's what I signed up for when I accepted this thankless position."

He walked across the well-trodden floor to the door, which was more of a barricade to keep people out than an entryway granting them access. He braced himself and tugged it open, the hinges screeching in high dudgeon.

"Ahh, there you are, Dr. Banting. Come in. I was wondering when you'd show up."

Banting strode into the office and stood at attention. "Sir," he said.

MacLeod shut the door after him.

"Give me your coat. I'll hang it on the rack."

MacLeod pointed to a pair of high backed leather chairs in the corner. They were turned away from the never-ending, futile tasks that waited brooding on his desk — glowering and unquiet, the western front of his work at the university.

"Have a seat," he said. He wondered whether or not Banting would ever relax and live in peace, instead of being wound to the breaking point. It must be exhausting, all this tension, he thought.

"Thank you, Dr. MacLeod," Banting said. He settled uncomfortably into the luxurious chair MacLeod offered him. His eyes scanned the vast bank of floor-to-ceiling windows that looked out over the courtyard. He couldn't help but wonder about having an office like this — sitting in a seat of authority, having the power to shape the destinies of brilliant scholars like himself. And cut short the careers of lesser rivals.

"It must be nice," Banting seethed with inner turmoil. "But why should he have all this and I nothing? He had better give me what I deserve, or I'm taking my idea elsewhere."

"I have just the thing for an occasion like this," MacLeod said, hoping his peace offering would mollify the angry young man. He picked up a tin of Mac Baren pipe tobacco.

"Ever tried this?" MacLeod asked.

Banting shook his head.

"I bought it when I was in Scotland over the summer. Care to have a pipe before we begin?"

"Most certainly, sir," Banting said. He fumbled in his pocket, searching for the *Bruyère*[3] he picked up in France. He was more of a cigarette man; they suited his budget, but he kept a pipe in his pocket if someone ever offered him a smoke.

---

3. Pipe made of French briarwood

MacLeod handed him the tin and settled into the chair beside Banting. "This one's for you if you like. I always pick up several when I go back home. They're impossible to find here."

"Thank you, sir," Banting said. He was disarmed by MacLeod's generosity.

With their guards up, the two men spent a few quiet, meditative moments cleaning out their pipe bowls. They tapped the ash and old tobacco into the crystal tray on the small side table between them. Each schemed about the best way to survive this tête-à-tête.

"I know exactly what I want from the little bugger," Banting swore to himself. He steeled himself for the attack he would most assuredly win.

The amiable Professor MacLeod loosened his jacket for the knife blade that would inevitably slip between his third and fourth rib. The Scottish biochemist and physiologist was much loved and well-respected the world over. He was a diligent department head and conscientious graduate-student supervisor. He nurtured his charges and enabled them to find success in their chosen fields. They received all the credit that they were due. In return, he received their accolades, honour, and life-long respect.

He had devoted his career to researching physiology and biochemistry but was chiefly interested in carbohydrate metabolism. This foray into diabetes research was a lark, an adventurous side trip on the glorious Grand Tour that was his professional life. It interested him and he was up for the challenge. Now, he had a dilemma, the likes of which he had never encountered before.

Banting's idea warranted further investigation, there was no denying. However, the man himself was unpredictable, insecure, and unprepared for the task ahead of him. If things didn't go his way, he'd make life hell on earth for everyone else. MacLeod would have to surrender to the self-centred Banting if he were to keep him at the University of Toronto. As a consequence, he needed to prepare himself — to suffer the intended slights, indignities, and slurs of a wounded, powerful, and influential man.

Banting made friends easily. He gathered loyal acolytes and devotees, and strung women along. He kept them close, tied secure by a knot that only he could undo. When he tired of one, he would discard her, and troll for another. Catch and release, he angled for women, and they took his lure.

Could MacLeod accommodate the unreasonable impositions and special allowances that Banting would surely demand? And not go mad? The question was front and centre in his mind as he tamped the fresh tobacco into his pipe. What would be worse? To endure Banting's fractious nature and find a cure for diabetes? Or hand the greatest discovery of the twentieth century to a team of Americans? The University would never absolve him if he were to choose his personal well-being over its own prestige and glorification. Banting would be the death of him, regardless.

"This is the spot where I do my best thinking," MacLeod said. "If you want to succeed in the academy, you need a place of sanctuary — a sacred space where thoughts arrive unbidden.

Opportunities for exploration show up when I'm enjoying my pipe, and they take me off in new directions. I admit, they're often a waste of time; but once in a while, they're eureka discoveries. You never know. This chair is my seat of inspiration. I've had my best ideas come to me while I'm relaxing here."

MacLeod lit his pipe.

"Where do you find your safe haven, Banting? When you're not out there in a frenzy doing absolutely everything that should have been done yesterday?"

Banting took a puff before answering. "I am happiest when I'm outside, with a paint brush in my hand and a canvas on an easel in front of me. When I'm trying to capture the lay of the land or the play of light through the leaves on a tree. I can lose myself and completely forget my troubles. Recreating a scene in oil, water colour, or pencil, I couldn't care less. I want to paint

Canada and its vigour. My best thoughts come to me from out of the blue. Like this diabetes idea. I was working on a scene, a small thing of no real consequence. Then it appeared, the notion of capturing the pancreatic endocrine secretion before it's destroyed by the exocrine."

Banting's candour took MacLeod aback.

"This overbearing farm boy has artistic depth?" he asked himself. "How is it that such an impossible, insensitive, tone-deaf creature could have an artistic impulse? For those who oppose him, he is as brutal an opponent as a Mark IV battlefield tank. Yet, this fury of contradictions is also a perceptive soul."

MacLeod relished the smoke from his pipe and exhaled slowly. He felt the calming effect of the nicotine, as he thought about this hitherto unconsidered aspect of Banting's nature. "Maybe there is a way. He isn't always a beast. He could sometimes be a likeable and convivial fellow."

Virtually everyone who encountered Banting found him full of integrity, honest, and true. Ordinary people loved him. He spoke their language. They understood every word he said to them. He was an easy man to respect.

"It is quite a thought, Banting," MacLeod finally said. "I hope for diabetics of the world that your idea has more going for it than initially meets the eye. While I know that your physiology is flawed, I think your idea is worth exploring. You may be onto something here. The two of us, however, will need to work together, if you want your idea to come to fruition. You don't have to like me, but you do have to accept my authority as your supervisor. Are you prepared for that, Dr. Banting?"

12
October 1921

Banting was gung-ho to get the job done. People were dying and MacLeod was dragging his heels. He'd had enough of MacLeod's tripe. He'd heard it all before. You don't win wars by dithering. But MacLeod was adamant.

"There is much that needs to be done before we can start clinical trials. We cannot risk injecting humans with your extract until we know exactly how it works and what its effect will be."

"In my experience," Banting said, "there are no advances in any human endeavour without peril. Life is always a high-stakes gamble. The only question that should be asked is if the benefit outweighs the risk."

"However," MacLeod interjected. "We are constrained by the university and by our Hippocratic Oath to do no harm."

"But the longer we delay, the longer our patients have to suffer."

"All of us here at the university know the risks of delaying," MacLeod said. "We are honour-bound to cause no pain. This is our vow."

"I'm not implying that we should endanger people's lives," Banting replied. "But life is a risky endeavour. It exacts a toll, whether we press forward or straggle behind."

"The university has processes in place to protect its research subjects from our enthusiasm for winning prizes," MacLeod replied. "Practically speaking, that means you will have to submit to my authority. It is my responsibility to manage the project. I determine the start date and whether or not we have achieved our objective. Having supervised many undertakings like this over the years, I know how to administer multiple research teams. Yours is one of many that I have on the go."

"But surely none are as important as mine," Banting said, his tone of voice sharpening.

"Every scientific advance is vital," MacLeod said. "Yours however has the disadvantage of a frenzied media. The public is clamouring for a cure. Whoever finds it will be canonized. You will be given your due, Dr. Banting, but make no mistake, my department has far more demands on its limited resources than it can afford to fund. You and Best need to develop a new and more efficient way to produce the extract. The two-step pancreatization of dogs is untenable on a large scale. We need a streamlined process that is commercially viable."

"I had initially dismissed Best's suggestion that we use fresh pancreas instead of atrophied ones," Banting admitted. "Now, I'm having second thoughts. As a farm boy, I know that before heifers are slaughtered, they are routinely impregnated to speed up the fattening process. The pancreas in a fetal calf doesn't start producing the digestive extract until after the birth. It produces endocrine secretions only. Abattoirs have an unlimited supply that is free for the taking."

"That may be," MacLeod said. "Nevertheless, the scientist in me wants to see if there is another viable source. I've asked Dr. Noble to conduct a series of experiments on the East Coast with fish pancreases. Monk fish have discrete islet organs, while the islets in mammals are scattered throughout the pancreas. This anatomical separation might facilitate extraction and purification."

"Dr. Noble is a good and capable man," Banting acknowledged. "I would have enjoyed working with him. When it was time for him to have his turn in the summer, I refused him. I had spent an entire month training Charlie as a competent surgical assistant. I didn't want to start over with Clark. It would have set our project too far behind schedule."

"I'm not criticizing you at all for your decision," MacLeod assured him. "Besides, I have other work for Dr. Noble. He will not be forgotten. While he evaluates the inshore fishery[4] as an alternative source for the extract, you and Best will work on ways here to improve its production. I'll put together a team of biochemists who can purify it for human clinical trials."

"Dr. Collip is the ideal man for that job," Banting said. "He sat in on one of our early discussions. I thought him an ally and a valuable resource while you were away. Someone I could talk to when I needed direction."

"I agree," MacLeod said, "but let's hold off a bit for now. I don't want to call upon him until you and Charlie can guarantee a safe and steady supply of the extract. Once that's in place, we can start to think about clinical trials."

"I've always seen myself working directly with patients," Banting said. "I'm a trained and licensed medical doctor. Having spent the summer toiling away in the lab, I now realize I am not a research scientist. I miss interacting with my patients. There is nothing in lab work that compares to the gratitude people have when you guide them through arduous pain and suffering to wellness. It's a journey of healing, a pilgrimage that leads one small step at a time to recovery."

"That may or may not be a decision you or I can make," MacLeod said. "The university has a committee headed up by Duncan Graham (1882-1974) that determines who can treat its patients. Dr. Graham will scrutinize your qualifications and competencies. He will lead the process and you will be thoroughly vetted. The decision is his and his alone. In the meantime, you and Dr. Best should keep working on the extract. I'll pay a visit to Henderson and see if we can scare up some funds to keep you in pretzels and beer."

With that, Professor MacLeod stood. "Let me grab your coat," he said, bringing their meeting to a close. He had other

---

4. Fishing in waters less than 90 feet deep and within sight of the shore

matters hounding him and they were all as pressing as Banting's urgent need for lab space and support.

Banting also rose. "But what about the lab, sir? It's in terrible condition."

He put on his jacket.

"I'll find someone to help with the cleanup," MacLeod said. "But you'll have to make do. The new one's almost complete, and I don't want to waste department funds on a facility that's about to be dismantled. What I'd like you to do, Dr. Banting, is to prepare a presentation for the upcoming departmental Journal Club meeting. The audience will be friendly, made up of colleagues from the department. I'd like you to share the results of your summer project. This is your idea, and you should be the first one to talk about it publicly."

"Thank you, sir," Banting said. "I'll start work immediately on the lecture. I don't mind sharing my idea as long as no one steals it."

13
White Hot

The days since Banting met with MacLeod dragged into months. While their work held promise, it was still inconclusive. The question that remained uppermost in MacLeod's mind was if it was safe enough to treat human diabetics. Dr. Collip had purified the extract, but MacLeod was unconvinced.

By the end of November, Banting was so frustrated, he injected himself with the extract. It seemed harmless and had no side effects. Without telling MacLeod or anyone else on the discovery team, Banting and Best administered the extract to Dr. Joseph Applebe Gilchrist (1893–1951), a diabetic colleague who was declining rapidly. Rather than inject him with the extract, however, they gave it to him orally. It had no effect whatsoever.

Disappointed, Banting could think of nothing more than returning to his room and finishing off that bottle of booze he had opened the night before.

In early January, Dr. Walter Campbell (1890-1981) injected a 65-pound, fourteen-year-old boy named Leonard Thompson (1908-1935) with the extract. His clinical trial was a disaster. Thompson had an allergic reaction that nearly killed him. There was no significant difference to his blood sugar.

"What went wrong?" everyone asked.

"It worked before," Banting reasoned. "It should have worked now. Here are Dr. Collip's instructions."

He pointed to the blackboard. "See?"

- Grind up a whole beef pancreas in an equal volume of slightly acidic alcohol
- Evaporate most of the alcohol in a vacuum still
- Wash the solution with toluene[5]
- Sterilize it with a Berkefeld filter

"What did we miss?" Banting asked. "What didn't we do?"

Banting's extract failed its first clinical trial, and he was desperate for a drink. He loosened his tie and removed his lab coat. He walked through the lab to the small room where he and Charlie kept a dog cage, their equipment, and hung their jackets for the day. He twisted the handle and gave the door a push.

Strangely, it was blocked from the inside. Then it opened, and Charlie Best stuck his head out.

"Ahh, there you are, Dr. Banting. Just in time. Dr. Collip and I have been talking. He has some exciting news for you."

"Is that right?" Banting asked, suddenly suspicious. He stepped into the room, and saw Collip sitting there, slight and on edge. Banting sat in a chair across from him, immediately wary and ready to jump.

"Well, sir? How are you?" Banting asked.

"I've finally figured it out," Collip said. "How to purify the extract."

"Congratulations!" Banting said. He stood. "Oh, that's good news. It couldn't have come at a better time."

He shook Collip's hand.

"How'd it happen? Charlie and I followed the exact procedure you laid out in December. It worked then, but we aren't having any luck now."

"I really can't say," Collip replied.

---

5. a colorless, water-insoluble liquid with the odor associated with paint thinners

"Pardon?" Banting asked. The bile rising to his throat. He became angry and could hardly control himself.

"What do you mean? Can't? Or won't?"

"I can't," Collip admitted. "I was working feverishly, ever since the Thompson debacle, tinkering with the extract to purify it, mixing, filtering, blending, trying to find the perfect ratio to purify the extract. I gradually increased the concentration of the alcohol to the point where the proteins precipitated out. I knew that centrifuging would extract the lipids and the salts could be washed out. At somewhere over 90%, the active principle precipitated out. The problem is how to get rid of the alcohol without destroying the active principle."

"But you took notes?" Banting asked. "I'm sure that Charlie and I can replicate your process. Give us the broad strokes, while they're fresh in your memory."

"That's the crux of the matter, Dr. Banting," Collip said. "I have time to write anything down. It's now all a blur."

Banting scoffed.

"More likely you met with MacLeod before coming here. The two of you cooked up a scheme to get the patent and cut Charlie and me out of any further action."

"Don't be ridiculous, Dr. Banting. This isn't a competition or a battle for credit. I'm here to treat patients, not make a fortune from their misery."

"That I have a hard time believing, the way the two of you confer without Charlie and me. You work in secret and make decisions without us. You and MacLeod are up to something."

"That's because you can't do sophisticated biochemical research. You're a surgeon and Dr. Best is just beginning his career. You are completely out of your depth. To get this extract ready for human clinical trials, you need to step aside and let specialists do their work."

Banting was white hot. He stood, faced the door, and readied himself to leave before he'd say or do something he'd live to regret. All of a sudden, he whirled around and grabbed Collip by the throat, slamming him against the wall.

"It's a good thing you're such a runt, otherwise, I'd finish you off. Where is that MacLeod, Charlie? Call him up and tell him to get his ass over here. We've got business to discuss. There'll be no secret patents. There'll be no changes in policy without a joint conference between us. I will not be pushed aside."

He let Collip go, and the poor man slumped into a chair. Collip loosened his tie and gasped for breath. He feared for his life and wondered why the hell he agreed to work with Banting in the first place. Whatever he hoped to gain from this collaboration was not worth the price.

Let someone else find the cure for diabetes. He needed to get back to his family. They were ill. He prayed it wasn't another outbreak of the Spanish Flu, oh God.

14
An Earthly Grace

Banting's room was a mess. The curtains were drawn, and the windows completely blacked out. No light penetrated the darkness. It smelled of stale smoke and unwashed laundry. Ash trays were filled to the brim and overflowing. Empty bottles cluttered every available surface. An unfinished painting on an easel stood in the corner. It was partially covered with a ragged piece of cloth that was torn in frustration and ripped in despair.

After the episode with Dr. Gilchrist, Banting was *persona non grata* at the lab. Nobody at the university trusted him anymore. He was in a bad way, and he knew it. Something had to give, and it had to be him. He stared at the nearly empty bottle of hard liquor in his hand.

When MacLeod came through with his funding, Banting found this place. What luxury, he thought when he moved in. What freedom. No more sleeping on couches or scrounging meals from Charlie. It felt good to have a room of his own. Where he could exhale the disappointment of the day, lose himself in the canvas in front of him, and breathe in hope for what was to come.

To put it bluntly, holding a palette in one hand and a brush in the other kept him from drinking his woes away. His art would never make him famous, but it would allow his imagination to soar above the thunder clouds. Now, the room seemed tiny, claustrophobic, dank, and blue with tobacco smoke. The walls and ceiling closed in on him. The space that once seemed open and expansive was now shrunk down and unwelcoming. All the life was being squeezed out of him.

When he returned home in the evening, all he could think about were his failures. In the autumn when he and MacLeod first met, everything had been in his favour.

Now, all was lost. Collip purified the extract, Leonard Thompson was on the mend, but Banting was still on the outs. There was nothing for him to do in the lab. He felt that he was being deliberately pushed out.

"Collip and MacLeod will get the credit, and I will be forgotten," Banting fumed.

The squalor in his apartment sat in stern judgement against him.

The near-empty bottle, though, was a completely different matter. It offered him an earthly grace from the stress that was driving him deep down and under. He held it close to his lips. His whole being ached with worry about where he would get his next drink. This one was almost gone. He tipped it back and caught the very last drops. They hit his throat but burned through to his soul.

Sweet Jesus, this feels good, he thought. I can't let something this precious go to waste. Every drop is essential. Especially with MacLeod on the warpath. I'd hate for him to catch me stealing another bottle of 90 proof from under his nose. That'd flip him over the top, the bloody bastard.

Him and Collip certainly share gleeful laughs at my expense. Smart asses. He doesn't mind thieving for himself when it suits his fancy, the little big man. As soon as his juniors rise up, he smacks them down. The hypocrite, all smiles and welcoming to your face, and a complete bastard behind. Collip's just like him. The two are one and the same.

First, he invites me to prepare a paper for the Physiological Journal Club. The audience would be made up of amicable colleagues and students, or so he said. It wouldn't be hostile in any way, a friendly get-together where you share your summer's work. Everyone wants to know how you're progressing. They might make some helpful suggestions. That's what he said, the bastard.

Banting pawed his way through the cabinet, hoping to find another soldier he had forgotten about.

"Ah, there you are," he said when he found one. He twisted out the cork and drank deeply, sitting down to relish the hit of alcohol to his system. Then, MacLeod gives such a detailed introduction to my paper that when I'm finally presenting, I'm merely repeating everything he's already told them. And the bloody free-for-all afterwards? I couldn't get a word in edgewise. The questions came pell-mell, all directed to him because he's the Big Man and I'm his tongue-tied lackey. The delightful MacLeod is always ready to wax eloquent. I hate his guts.

Then to realize, the room is full of his students and colleagues. I was the stranger in their midst. I'd come from nowhere. I didn't have a chance. No wonder they deferred to him. I was the authority, but they hardly noticed me. What a bloody fool I was to think that I could make a mark here in his bailiwick.

Banting took another long drink. I'm the poor old sod who came up with the idea.

Not the world-renowned tenured professor. Just a mere sapper in the trenches, shovelling out the muck, so the big man won't get his polished boots muddy when he deigns to visit the front lines.

I'm a dunderhead without a clue. Now, everyone thinks that he is the lead researcher and that my idea is his. But I am not his dogsbody. I bloody well knew this would happen. Him and that Collip stealing my thunder and getting the glory for my discovery.

And who is Collip, really? He wouldn't give me the process for purifying the extract. Now, he can't produce it on his own. What a sweet irony this is. He needs me more than ever.

Banting raised the bottle in a toast and took another swig.

I'm a simple surgeon without a clue. It's a good thing I didn't strangle him when he refused to tell me. Or I'd be on my way to Kingston. Who in God's name does he think he is?

If it weren't for me, he wouldn't even be on the team. I urged MacLeod to invite him to join us. Otherwise, he'd be back in Edmonton in some bloody old building, freezing his balls off.

That one-trolley town is as far away from civilization as you can get. A town of mud roads and cattle tracks if there ever was one. And a bridge you can jump off when you come to your senses. Collip's worried I'd patent the process myself. And me trust him? Not on your life.

Him and MacLeod want to leave Charlie and me out in the cold, the way MacLeod consigned Clark to the East Coast fishery. What a waste of time that is. Why bother with fish pancreases when the packing plants have more than enough beef pancreas? The only good thing is that cockamamie MacLeod has gone out there too — chasing after red herrings or whatever he's doing on the East Coast. Probably eating lobster like there's no tomorrow.

Knock, knock, knock.

Banting thought he heard something at the door but wasn't sure. *Knock, knock, knock. Whence is that? How is't with me when every noise appals? Maybe it'll stop.* He shrunk into his chair and shushed himself. "No more muttering out loud, Banting," he shushed himself. "You fool."

He grabbed the bottle by the neck and took another hard drink.

Now, Edith's on my case. She wants me to quit. She thinks I don't really want to marry her. Threatens to call off the engagement if I come up with one more reason for delaying the wedding. Can't she tell? I'm on the verge of a breakthrough. I can't get married when I'm this close to victory.

"But you're always this close," she says. "To someone else," she screeches. The banshee accuses me of betraying her.

So what if I've been messing around? At least I haven't committed the unpardonable sin. Besides, adultery isn't really adultery if you're engaged. It's all her fault. If she weren't so straitlaced, I'd be completely satisfied.

But no, not with her. We have to wait until our wedding before I can bed her. Well, screw her shrill, outdated hectoring. No one can blame me for looking afield. I have needs, too.

This isn't all about you, Edith Roach. You're the one responsible for my supposed infidelities. They occurred because you keep refusing my entreaties.

Knock, knock, knock.

"I can hear you, damn it all," he said as he tried to stand. "I'm coming."

He slumped back into his chair, his head swooning from all the booze. That Paulesco's really on my tail, he thought. Good thing Charlie found the article about his research in Rumania. Otherwise, we'd be lollygagging.

In some cases, his results are even better than ours. We don't have time to waste. I can't marry Edith right now. I can't. She'll have to wait. And if she doesn't? It'll be her loss. Can't she understand? I mean, what's one more year?

Banting emptied the bottle and scanned the room, searching for another he was certain he squirreled away somewhere. Who else would risk their all for this undertaking? So what if I missed a few ducts, and my longevity experiment with Dog 92 failed. It isn't the end of the world.

I gave up my practice, moved out of my house, and apparently lost my girl. I've humiliated myself in front of strangers. Even injected myself with the extract before we administered it to anyone else.

Of course, I wasn't going to ask MacLeod for permission. He's hamstrung by those imbeciles at the university. They butter his bread, and he isn't going to cross them.

I'm no hero, but I had to see. It was a matter of honour. That poor Joe Gilchrist. It broke my heart to see him starving to death. Only a fool would think that undernourishment is an effective way to treat diabetes. Treat the patient by denying him bacon and eggs? Idiocy.

Charlie and I couldn't bear to see him suffer any more. We couldn't think of a better Christmas present for him than to lower his blood sugar levels before the holiday. But damn it all, the extract had no effect. And that MacLeod?

Thought he'd have a heart attack when he learned what we did. Coward. He doesn't have a clue about defeating an enemy. You have to take risks. The most foolhardy gambles have had the best results. We didn't defeat the Hun by waiting until the coast was clear. General Currie[6] sure knew how to put human lives on the front line.

"Give 'em hell boys," he said, and he ordered them to their deaths because he knew that there was only one way to win the war. Kill or be killed.

Then the bloody knocking, again louder, and even more insistent. Oh, God, that's all I need. It better not be Charlie.

Knock, knock, knock.

---

6. During the First World War, Sir Arthur William Currie (1875-1933) was the first Canadian commander of the Canadian Corps.

15
Where You Go

"I know you're in there, Dr. Banting. Open up and let me in."

Banting jerked his head around. "Charlie? Is that you? What are you doing here?"

He stood and tripped over his untied shoelaces. "Damn it all."

He swiped the side table to prevent his fall. Bottles and glassware tumbled to the floor. Shards of glass flew everywhere.

The door burst open. Charlie ran in.

"Dr. Banting. Are you okay?"

He hurried over to his fallen comrade.

"Your hand! It's bleeding."

Banting glanced at his wound and laughed bitterly at his misfortune.

"I survived shrapnel in France, only to be felled by a sliver of glass here in Toronto? You're not needed, Charlie. This is a flesh wound. I can look after it myself."

"At least let me clean it up," Best said. He grabbed the rag off the painting to staunch the blood. It was the cleanest thing in reach. He wrapped it around the cut. Charlie sat there for a second collecting his thoughts. He removed the cloth.

"The shard of glass is still there. You have tweezers somewhere, Dr. Banting?"

"Over there. On the shelf. He waved with his hand."

Charlie made his way through the mess, appalled that his friend had fallen so low. He found the tweezers and returned to the great man, half-drunk and ready to pass out.

He removed the sliver and poured some alcohol over the cut. He rewound the cloth around Banting's hand and tied it.

"This'll do quite nicely. I don't think I need to go to the hospital," Banting slurred. He looked around the room. With his friend there, he was suddenly ashamed of how badly he let his life fall apart.

"God, Charlie. My place looks worse than the lab last summer."

Charlie smiled.

"You've fallen off the wagon. Have you any intention of ever getting up?"

Banting's head clearing, but still too drunk to stand, he nodded. "I can't let Edith see me like this. She'll say, 'I told you so.'"

"Edith's right," Best said. "You have to beat this thing before she claims the victory. If you don't pull yourself together, that'll be the end of our collaboration. You need to take back control. Don't let that bastard MacLeod or that idiot Collip take what's rightfully yours.

Gerry Fitzgerald (1882-1940) is in an uproar. He's all alone. As head of the Connaught Laboratories, he's taking control. Nobody's working at the lab and there's not a drop of extract to be had. I can't produce it. We need you back in full fettle, Dr. Banting. I need you to help me. My career's over if you don't get back in shape. You are wanted. You are needed. The world is desperate for what you have to offer.

"Come on, Charlie, you're exaggerating. Nobody's indispensable."

"Your destiny, for good or ill, is to be the one who finds the cure for diabetes," Best decreed. "That is your duty. This is rank dereliction. You need to pull yourself together. There is too much left for you to do. Stop feeling sorry for yourself."

With that Best swept up the broken glass and gathered up the empties into a box. "God, that's a lot of booze," he said.

"I'm no researcher Charlie, and if that Graham won't let me practise medicine at the university, I might as well surrender to Edith and become a country doctor. I don't know where else I'd fit in or how I'd contribute."

"There is a way for you to get around this impasse. The government of Ontario has licensed you as a physician. No one can stop you from setting up your own clinic. You don't need university authorization to care for patients who come to you privately for treatment.

I suggest that you return with me to Connaught and help me rediscover how to produce the extract. I'll give you whatever extract I produce for clinical testing."

"You may be on to something, Charlie. This could be a way for me to get out of this standoff. Tomorrow, I'll sober up."

He grabbed for the bottle. "One last swig, and nothing more until we've reproduced the extract."

Best grabbed the bottle from his hand. "Forget about the booze, sir. I need you up and running today. Fitzgerald's bellowing like a bull. People are writing him from all over the world, asking for progress reports. This is your opportunity to get back in the action."

"And if I don't?" Banting slumped back into his chair. "What if I take my idea to the Mayo or the Rockefeller Institute?"

"Where you go, I go," Best said. "Without you my career in Toronto is over."

"Come on, Charlie, don't be ridiculous. You haven't been tarred and feathered. Those bastards have blackballed me. They can't stand the thought that a country bumpkin beat them to the punch. You, on the other hand, are still in their good books. They have room for you in their world."

"But I'm American. They want a Canadian to be credited for finding the cure. And certainly not a Scot. Whether you like it or not, whether I like it or not, our lives are intertwined. Where you go, I go. I bloody well wish it weren't so. I have the misfortune of trailing in your wake. You are my duty, care, and destiny. I can do no other."

"Well, no more whining then, Charlie. You must do your own work and live your own life in your own way, because you are responsible for both. I, on the other hand, could sure use another drink."

16
Let History Be the Judge

Fitzgerald was furious. He stormed through the empty lab to his office. Pressure was mounting on him to produce the extract, and no one from the diabetes team was on-site. Exactly how was the Connaught Anti-toxins Lab going to fulfill its obligations when the only one around was that floundering Charlie Best?

Fitzgerald couldn't believe it. Not one of those blockheads had the sense to write the process down. Banting was a lout and an inexperienced researcher, at that. He had some excuse, but Collip? The legendary biochemist who mixes and matches solutions with a bit of this and a little of that and makes monumental discoveries on the fly? That genius? He couldn't make a batch the same way twice if he tried.

With MacLeod out east, Collip at home with his family who were struck down by the flu and Banting caught stealing bottles of lab alcohol , Fitzgerald was at a complete loss.

I'm the one about to be made a laughingstock. I wish Charlie would get Banting back. I don't care if he's hungover. If he had the good luck to discover the extract last summer, maybe he'd find some again. God, this is infuriating. The news is out, and people are calling for the extract. Every day, they want updates. They want to know how MacLeod's serum is doing. I don't care whose it is. As long as someone in our lab figures how to produce it before the Americans. We need huge vats of the stuff, not test-tube samples.

As far as I am concerned, I'm willing to pay the devil any price to get this project back on track. If Banting wants the credit, let him have it. If he's willing to be the public face of diabetes research in Canada, so be it. The time for squabbling is over.

Where is that bloody MacLeod when I need him? No wonder he's hied himself off. Everyone in scientific circles knows that the majority of breakthroughs are a collaborative process, not the work of a singular genius. Besides, as soon as Banting opens his mouth, people will see him for the buffoon he really is.

Let history be the judge. The truth will eventually come out. I am beyond caring about these petty, temporal rivalries that are derailing our work. People are dying, and the cure is within our grasp.

Fitzgerald heard a sound and turned to see Charlie Best entering the lab.

"Charlie, there you are. Where in God's name is Banting?"

"Still hungover. I'll get him after lunch."

Fitzgerald shook his head.

"The time for waiting is over. Focus on what you know. You and Banting did it before. You can do it again. I'm counting on you Charlie, to get us out of this mess. Do you think that he's in any shape to come back to work?"

"He lost himself in the booze, but he'll sober up," Best replied. "We had a long talk. I know he wants back in. With MacLeod and Collip out of the way, there's a chance he can contribute something useful instead of spending all his energy fighting them. Just give him what he wants. Is that too much to ask?"

"But follow university protocols, okay? Banting lost everyone's trust over Joe Gilchrist and Leonard Thompson."

"Thank God, Thompson's responding well to Collip's treatment," Best said.

"Hopefully Joe will too if we can start treating him soon. For his sake and ours, we've got to get back on track."

"No one better die. The consequences would be devastating for everyone. There's that little girl on death's door, Dr. Fitzgerald. She's in a coma. We gave her a massive dose. It eliminated the acidosis, but we've no more extract. Now, she's unconscious and we can't revive her. She's not going to make it, and we're powerless to help her."

"I've made my deal with the devil, Charlie. There's not much more that I can do. Duncan Graham has it out for Banting. There's no way he will practice medicine at the university. I'll talk to Dr. Robertson,[7] head of the Toronto Hospital for Sick Children, okay? Him and Banting are friends. I know that he's completely fed up with the infighting. All he wants is for us to find a cure. He'll talk some sense into Graham."

"Diabetics are dying, and we're wrangling over God knows what?" Best asked. "Besides, there's a real chance that Dr. Banting will take his idea to the Americans. All Canada will lose out. Can you imagine the fallout from the government? For letting the cure for diabetes slip out of our hands?"

"There'll be hell to pay for this tit-for-tat bickering," Fitzgerald said. We aren't out playing on a school ground during recess."

"Roy Greenaway (1891-1972) sure is on Banting's side," Best said. "The stuff he's writing in the *Toronto Star?* The people are eating it up. He's turned Banting into a champion. People want to meet the discoverer, not some Johnny-Come-Lately who's out to make a name for himself."

"Whether we like it or not, Banting is the name everyone remembers. Most people see him as the principal discoverer of the extract."

"If the Americans are the first to receive the treatment that was initially invented here in Canada, it'd be a nightmare" Best said. "For the sake of the university, for the sake of Canada, you have to convince Graham to give Banting a permanent appointment. Grant him a sinecure. Surround him with highly competent people. Make him the figurehead. He may be incompetent, but he sure has the public relations savvy to come out on top. He's a well-liked and popular war hero. His military record has won the hearts of nearly everyone.

----

7. David Edward Robertson (1877-1942)

His story is the one people will remember for generations to come. The rest of us will live on in his shadow, forgotten and mentioned only in passing."

"Without Banting there'd be no extract," Fitzgerald admitted. "He's the one who got us looking closely at pancreatic secretions. Without MacLeod, however, there'd be no clear research objectives and parameters. Without Collip, there'd be no purified extract. It's been a team effort, with everyone playing an important role. We are dependent upon each other.

Your job, Charlie, is to get that man back in here. The two of you can continue your work with calf pancreas tissue on the Connaught farm site. We already have calves there that are involved in smallpox vaccine production. I might even be able to scare up some spare cash."

17
The Culprit

Charlie saw Fred Banting march down the hall towards him. "Where have you been, sir? Dr. Fitzgerald has been asking about you. He wants you back in the lab, working with me. He figures that I can't do it without you."

"Don't be ridiculous Charlie. Of course, you can. You're smart, strong, fully qualified, and completely professional."

"Please, Dr. Banting, diabetics across the world need you."

"I signed a lease for a clinic on Bloor Street, Charlie."

Banting stormed ahead and Charlie could hardly keep up. "I'm hanging out my own shingle. Thanks for the suggestion. The landlord knew immediately that I was ex-military. When I told him what I was up against, he said it's about time the little man stood up to the brass. If we don't claim what's rightfully ours, they'll steal it from us.

He gave me a cut on the rent, Charlie. That'll help until I have patients of my own. Let me tell you right now, I won't be charging what those fat-cats get away with. Nobody will ever accuse me of turning away patients who were too poor to pay for my treatments, or of me trying to get rich from their suffering."

"The sooner you and I figure out why the solution we're currently making is completely ineffective, the sooner you can begin seeing patients," Best said.

"Then, we better go back to the beginning."

They continued walking, but at a slower pace.

"We know that the active principle from ground up fresh pancreases is just as effective as that from atrophied ones. That's not the issue. What we need to determine is what is different from last summer."

They reached the door of the lab and opened it.

"For one thing," Best said, "instead of mixing the ground pancreas in Ringer's Solution, we're using alcohol. Do you think the alcohol is neutralizing the active principle?"

"Not sure. It worked with the Ringer's, but now it's not. The variables are mind-boggling. The amount of the alcohol, its strength, maybe how we're getting rid of it? It could be a myriad of things."

They put on their lab coats.

"We're all working in the dark, aren't we?" Banting asked.

"The processes we're trying to analyze are sophisticated," Charlie acknowledged. "Our equipment is make-shift, and our techniques are primitive. We need more accurate measurements."

"Now, what's this I hear about Eli Lilly?" Banting asked.

"They're on board."

"Pardon?"

"Dr. George Clowes (1877–1958) has persuaded the university to collaborate with them. In fact, he's coming to Toronto to hammer out the details.

They're asking for the exclusive rights to the American market for a year."

"I better have a meeting with him," Banting said. "I don't want the university making any side deals without us. We need to be in on it, Charlie.

Our extract will be the most important drug they will ever produce. This is huge. With them onside, diabetics will finally receive the treatment they need. Maybe even be cured. We're making history, Charlie.

I don't want to be swept out of the picture when it hits the news."

"Eli Lilly's having the same trouble we are," Best said. "They can produce the extract in the lab, but they cannot mass-produce it. Something unknown has been inadvertently added to the process. We all have to figure that out. And the sooner, the better."

At least they aren't hobbled the way we are by university protocols and bureaucracy," Banting said. "They can make a decision and act immediately, not wait for it to be sifted through committee after committee until it's too late."

"They're out to make a fortune, I know that but diabetics will be the ultimate beneficiaries."

"But can we trust them not to hold out on us?" Banting asked.

"From everything I know, Eli Lilly has an impeccable record. They are committed to quality and the well-being of the people who depend on their products."

"Have you been taken in by their sales pitch, Charlie? There are a lot of charlatans out there."

"I don't think Eli Lilly is one of them. They aren't making promises they can't keep."

"They may be our salvation, Charlie. Let's hope that the meeting with Clowes in July is profitable for everyone concerned."

"When we produced the extract last summer, we filtered out the sludge and injected the brown liquid into the dogs," Best said. "The active principle was still effective.

The problems began after we filtered the solution. We evaporated off most of the alcohol and sterilized the remaining solution with a Berkefeld filter."[8]

"Heating the extract to evaporate the alcohol might be the culprit" Banting suggested.

"But how can we remove the alcohol without raising the temperature of the solution?" Best asked. "MacLeod has set-up fans and is dispersing the alcohol that way. Collip's using acetone."

"Acetone!" Banting laughed. "It may have a higher evaporation rate than alcohol, but it's also far more volatile. Any fool knows that. A small spark and the entire lab could go up in flames. Imagine the headlines! Greenaway would have a field day."

---

8. a water filter used in microbiological laboratories

UNIVERSITY LAB BLOWN UP!
LARGEST EXPLOSION SINCE HALIFAX!
NO SURVIVORS!

"Please, sir. This is no joking matter. Let's figure this out first," Best said.

"Once we have rediscovered the process, we can talk to MacLeod about patenting it," Banting said. "And who's to get the credit. I don't want either of us to be forgotten when this takes off. We deserve our place in history."

Best looked askance at Banting in his lab coat with the sleeves cut off.

"You know that looks ridiculous. Right?"

"Can't help it. After last summer's heat wave, I got into the habit. Besides, no one ever steals mine. It's always on the hook where I hung it the night before.

18
If Wishes Were Horses

Banting hung his threadbare suit jacket on the hook behind the door to his Bloor Street clinic. He knew it wasn't much, but it was his, and it was a start. He lit his pipe. This feels very good; very, very good, he muttered to himself. I can be my own man and follow my own destiny. I am, after all, responsible for both.

Now, if only those chemists at Connaught would ever get their act together, I might even start treating patients. It's a crying shame that I have to wait for someone else before I can get on doing what I know needs to be done. I hate depending upon other people to do what I'd rather do myself. I won't wait for much longer.

He settled down to the mountain of correspondence on the desk in front of him. I will make my own way, one letter at a time. These people need me, and I will not ignore or forget them.

Banting spent the rest of the day fielding inquiries from diabetics, begging for their lives. At present, we are trying to treat the symptoms, not find a cure. That will come much later, if at all. He opened one letter after another and wrote the same depressing reply to each.

I'm afraid that these are the blunt truths that need to be told. The supply of extract at present is sporadic and its effect inconsistent. Sometimes it works perfectly, other times not at all. Researchers on both sides of the border are working night and day. An effective therapy is in the offing, but it is not yet in hand. As soon as it is, you will be notified. Your name has been added to the list of people to receive the extract. I will not abandon you to your misery. You will not starve to death under my watch. That is my promise.

Banting had to admit that as soon as they solved one problem, another would arise setting them even further behind than before. Discovering a treatment seemed a nightmare from which there was no waking. First, there were no pancreases to be had — no beef, no pork, not even fish from that brilliant MacLeod and his half-baked summer research project on the East Coast.

Then, there was an acetone shortage. To make matters even worse, the American government — in its puritanical, teetotalling judgement — changed the quality of alcohol that could be supplied to research laboratories. The new stuff was vastly inferior to the old, not to mention nearly undrinkable.

If the lab ever produced any extract, it had such painful side-effects that patients refused to take it, or it was so weak that it had no effect whatsoever. The idea that had once seemed within reach was now unfathomable. Banting was out of his depth. MacLeod was right.

I didn't have a clue what I was taking on. The devil was not in the idea, which was a godsend. Rather, it was in the working out — making the treatment reliable. That was the challenge. He shook his head.

Why are good things so hard to accomplish and hurtful things so easy? This keeping death at bay. This enabling people to flourish in their lives, not waste away, starving and skeletal. It's beyond me.

Diabetes is a monster. Banting vowed that he would not rest until it was slain. He had his work cut out for him. That was plain and simple. And it would take its toll, a telling from which he'd never recover.

He looked at the pile of correspondence still remaining in front of him. The letters were all from diabetics who were pleading with him to treat them. They were in dire straits. Each was as special as the other, each as deserving, and each as hopeless as all the others.

His hours of work had made no appreciable difference at all. He had put pen to paper in the early morning. All he had to show for his effort in the late-afternoon was an ink-stained and cramping hand. He needed an administrative assistant.

Banting looked at a gold-embossed letter from Antoinette Hughes (1864-1945), wife of Charles Evans Hughes (1862-1948), the governor of the state of New York and the 1916 Republican presidential nominee. What could he tell her that he hadn't written a thousand times before? The treatment is within sight, but the extract is unreliable.

Once we figure out the means of producing it on a commercial scale, there'll be more than enough for everyone. Do what you can to keep your daughter Elizabeth alive. It's really a matter of months, not years. Surely, she will last that long. She must persevere. As God is my witness, this young woman has to live.

With that, Banting closed the cap on his pen. He put on his jacket, stepped out his office door, and made his way home. He had an empty liquor bottle on the shelf to remind him of his vow to keep away from the booze until a treatment was found.

In the corner, an unfinished painting stood on the easel.

I really should get back to it. I need to take some lessons. Maybe someone at the art gallery will take me on. All I need is some money to pay him. There might even be an exhibition I could take in. Maybe get some inspiration. It'd be a welcome relief from all this stress. Edith was right. I could have been a happy country doctor, living a beautiful life with her and a houseful of children.

If wishes were horses, diabetics would ride.

19
1922
New Suits and Celebrations

It was the middle of July before George Clowes of Eli Lilly came to Toronto to go over the results of Banting's first clinical trials.

"I can't believe how few supplies you have here," he said to Banting. "I'll wire Indianapolis and have them ship you more."

"I'd be grateful," Banting said. "My patients are desperate."

Banting gave Clowes a tour of the facility at Connaught. Clowes shook his head when he looked at MacLeod's wind tunnel system for evaporating alcohol.

"This is untenable on the scale we need. It's impossible to regulate and too unwieldly for a commercial application.

You need to get a vacuum still. That's the most efficient and controllable method for evaporating the alcohol at the lowest temperature possible. Heating the extract is killing off the active principal. There's your problem in a nutshell."

"That's exactly what Dr. Best and I thought. But Fitzgerald and MacLeod have invested too much time and money in this evaporation technique to back out."

"We need a system that is useful for the patients and profitable for the producers," Clowes said.

"The university doesn't give any consideration to the needs of private industry for making a profit," Banting said. "I understand that you are in this to make millions."

"Of course," Clowes interrupted him. "However, Eli Lilly has always put the patient first. We sell only to doctors and hospitals. If we do our work properly, the money will flow in. Yes, we expect to profit, but not through cheating, fraud, or deception."

"I'll talk to the Board of Governors," Banting said. "But first, I need to become better acquainted with what is going on at Eli Lilly."

"Pack your bags then," Clowes said. "I'll give you the grand tour myself."

With that, Banting was on his way to Indianapolis. When he arrived, the people at Eli Lilly fêted him like a hero. It felt good to receive the accolades he was due.

"That Banting really is a fine chap," J. K. Lilly[9] (1861-1948) said. "We must back him to the limit."

Clowes showed off the state-of-the-art equipment Eli Lilly was using. He explained how they were dealing with the challenges of making the extract.

When Banting returned to Toronto, he was convinced that Connaught Labs needed the new vacuum still. All he had to do was try and get the money from the university. Surely, they had a contingency fund for such an expenditure. This would establish Toronto as a preeminent medical research facility. He had faith that the Board wouldn't be so short-sighted as to refuse him.

At first, Banting tried to chase down the university's senior administrators, only to find that most of them were out of town for the summer. Only Sir Edmund Walker (1848-1924), chairman of the Board of Governors, returned his call.

"Sorry, Dr. Banting," Walker replied when they met. "Only the Board can authorize such an expenditure. I can't sign for this on my own. We won't be meeting again until university begins in September."

"That's too late, Sir Edmund," Banting said. "Diabetics are dying and need insulin immediately."

"I can't help you. Even if I could get enough Board members together to form a quorum, it wouldn't be for several weeks. This is the middle of summer. Everyone is away on holidays."

Banting couldn't believe what he was hearing. It made him furious. He roared with contempt. "If I get the money for the vacuum still, will the Board accept it?"

---

9. President and chairman of the Board

The old man stammered. "I can see no objection."

With that, Banting strode out of Walker's office. He hurried home once again to pack his bag. Disgusted, he felt like the disciples shaking the dust off their feet when the people of the village refused to listen to their message.

I've done all I can for the university, he thought as he hurried to the train. He had not forgotten what Dr. H. Rawle Geyelin (1884-1942) volunteered.

Geyelin knew Robert Bacon, the rich parent of a very ill diabetic child. "If you need money for your research, I might be able to help you."

Banting decided to give him a try. After a quick phone call, Geyelin asked Banting how he wanted the cheque made out.

Banting wired the $10,000 donation to R. D. Defries (1889-1975) of Connaught Laboratories who ordered the still. Then Banting contacted Eli Lilly to add Geyelin's name to the list of physicians who would receive the extract when it was ready.

"I will wait for no man," Banting vowed.

He travelled to Morristown, NJ and met with Dr. Fred Allen. (1879-1957) who prescribed starvation diets as low as 400 calories per day to his diabetic patients.

"Would you please introduce me to your patient Elizabeth Hughes (1907-1981)?"

"Let me make a phone call," Dr. Allen replied. "Perhaps you can see her before you board your train. You won't be disappointed. She is a heroic and brave little girl, with an indomitable spirit."

Elizabeth Hughes, daughter of Secretary of State Charles Hughes, weighed 45 pounds when Banting met with her and her family. He agreed to take her as a private patient.

She arrived in Toronto with her mother on August 15, 1922, and began receiving insulin from Dr. Banting. Placed on a 2200-2400 calorie diet, she recovered quickly. When she returned home to Washington, D. C. on Thanksgiving Day, she was the perfect picture of a healthy 15-year-old girl. The family and the world canonized Banting. He could do no wrong.

He took the train to Boston and met Clowes at his lab in Woods Hole, MA to discuss how they could protect his priority in the discovery.

"It was my idea, after all. I got everyone looking at the relationship between the pancreas and diabetes. I do not want to take anything away from Minkowski, or all the others that went before. Don't get me wrong."

"Yours is the story of a magnificent discovery," Clowes said. "A country doctor and his partner overcome enormous obstacles to bring their idea to fruition and save the lives of millions of people. This is a legend of heroes that the public will always remember.

I think that we should publish the results of your testing in a special issue of Dr. Allen's *Journal of Metabolic Research*. Your name will be at the head of the list of authors. Eli Lilly will bear the expense of distributing it through the United States.

You will get full credit for your work. This will also be a first step toward securing the Nobel Prize for you and your associates."

"The Nobel Prize," Banting said. "I'd be the youngest recipient and the first Canadian, too. I'd make history."

"Not bad for a farm boy from Alliston, Ontario," Clowes laughed.

When Banting returned to Toronto, he had lunch with David Robertson, and told him the good news. Robertson listened closely as Banting recounted every detail of his trip.

"Is that the same suit you wore when you met with the Hughes?" Robertson asked.

"It's the only one I have."

"I think it's time for you to remedy that."

When they finished their meal, Robertson took Banting to the most expensive tailor in Toronto.

"May I see your blues?" he asked. "Make this man a suit. And an overcoat, too. I'm not sure when he will pay for it, but I can vouch for him. He's as good as his word. This is a time for new suits and celebrations."

78

20
Containing a Hurricane

Upon his return, Banting continued to correspond with diabetics all over the world. He told them that relief was imminent and that they should not lose hope. He met with patients and prescribed the extract he received from Eli Lilly. Connaught Labs set up the vacuum still and produced its own.

Banting and Best had been calling the extract *Isletin*, but MacLeod used the term *Insulin* in the paper he delivered to the Association of American Physicians in Washington, D. C. on May 3, 1922. Jean de Meyer (1878-1934) first coined insulin in 1909. Edward Albert Sharpey-Schafer (1850-1935) used it in 1916 to name a hypothetical molecule, produced by pancreatic islets of Langerhans, that controls glucose metabolism.

Banting's name appeared at the head of the paper, but he did not share in the standing ovation MacLeod received after delivering it. He claimed that he was too broke to attend the conference. Others claimed he was in a huff because MacLeod was once again taking centre stage.

It would take a Nobel Prize Nominating Committee to apportion credit for the discovery of insulin. G. W. Crile (1864-1943) and Francis G. Benedict (1870-1957) nominated Banting as the sole discoverer. Crile, an American surgeon, was the first to succeed in a direct blood transfusion. Benedict developed a calorimeter and a spirometer used to determine oxygen consumption and measure metabolic rate. Professor G. N. Stewart (1860-1930) a formidable figure in American physiology nominated MacLeod.

August Krogh (1874-1949) nominated both Banting and MacLeod together. Krogh was the Danish Nobel laureate who discovered the mechanism of regulation of the capillaries in skeletal muscle. His wife had developed adult-onset diabetes and wanted to visit the discovery team on their North American tour.

Over dinner, Banting shared his theories with Krogh and MacLeod. By the time they finished their dessert, Krogh concluded that Banting could not have discovered insulin without MacLeod's help. Nevertheless, he decided that while consequent publications were the result of a collaboration among several authors, the prize should go to Banting and MacLeod.

John Sjöquist (1888-1957) appraised the physiological importance of the discovery, and J. C. Jacobaeus (1879–1937) assessed its practical application. Goran Liljestrand (1886–1968) wrote a special report on the insulin sessions of the congress at Edinburgh that both Banting and MacLeod attended. Each concluded that the discovery of insulin was worthy of a Nobel Prize.

Banting was livid when he found out that he would be sharing the award with MacLeod.

"Isn't it enough that Best and I spent that long, hellish summer making good on my idea while that son-of-a-bitch MacLeod was drinking whisky and playing golf on some bloody Scottish isle? Oh, he deigns to give me the credit for ligating the ducts on dogs to atrophy their pancreases, does he? Well, bully for him, the bastard.

Best, of course, has always been there for me. He may have questioned my science, but he never questioned my priority. He and I were together from the start. He and I are the only co-discoverers of insulin. All MacLeod did was stand in our way and oppose every step we took. And when he finally agreed to work with us? It was so he could horn in on the credit for my idea.

Him and that Collip are one and the same. Low men in high places, asserting their power over common foot-soldiers who slog it out every day in the trenches. I have to stand up for what is rightfully mine, or they will take it from me.

MacLeod is responsible for the credit brouhaha. He did nothing to retract the lies spread by Sir William Bayliss (1860-1924) from the *London Times* article, arguing that MacLeod wasn't receiving the full credit for his work. As if MacLeod would ever stand mutely by.

Lucky for me, he is not the only fellow with friends in the press. It took Roy Greenaway's article in *The Toronto Star* to shore up my defense.

Give Dr. Banting Credit for Insulin, his article begins."

"But the headline is misleading," MacLeod insisted.

"But your statement is unsatisfactory," Banting replied.

MacLeod stood up to Banting.

"I refuse to give you full credit for the discovery of insulin as it is now used in the treatment of diabetes. You were one researcher on a team. Your contribution is no more or less significant than others. We discovered insulin together. It was a collaborative effort. Yours was the beginning, but you could not have reached this point without us. You do not have priority."

"I think you and Collip have engineered this whole mess for your advantage."

"Don't be ridiculous, Dr. Banting. I am proud of my work. Naturally, I want credit for what is rightfully mine, but I do not need to steal anything from you. This discovery is so momentous that there is more than enough glory to share. We have changed the lives of millions of people. Because of our work, diabetics can now lead near-normal lives. They can have careers, raise families, and make significant contributions to society. That is what we have accomplished as a team. Let's not squabble over something as petty as credit."

Banting was not convinced. He viewed MacLeod as part of the problem, never as part of the solution. For one thing, MacLeod was initially reluctant to have Collip join the team. When he finally did, it was only after important advances had been made.

Charlie Best was caught between the two. First, he was MacLeod's student, and second, he was Banting's colleague. He took little part in the fighting between them, preferring to spend as much time as he could with his fiancée Margaret, minding his own business.

"We had the benefit of Dr. MacLeod's advice," Best said. "He gave us the opportunity to prove the efficacy of our extract upon diabetic animals, before others were allowed to participate in the work."

Best gave far more credit to MacLeod and Collip than Banting ever did. In separate accounts, the three shared their perspectives in writing about the discovery of insulin to Colonel Sir Albert Edward Gooderham, KCMG[10](1861–1935), member of the University's Board of Governors. However, he was unable to reconcile the differences in their accounts. The question of priority in his mind remained unresolved. He left that to the Nobel Prize nominating committee to determine.

Banting's ferocious hatred made MacLeod's life in Toronto miserable. Banting attacked him from every quarter. MacLeod was contemptuous of Banting as a researcher and did little to defend himself against Banting's accusations.

His scholarly record was unimpeachable. He was a kind and gentle man; a cautious and careful scientist; an internationally recognized scholar; and a teacher who protected his students from the full glare of critical scrutiny. He left Banting to his own undoing.

Banting and Best's work was criticized right from the beginning. Their own published evidence showed the incorrectness of their conclusions. The experiments they conceived were poorly conducted, and their results misinterpreted. Yet, the two of them proved that an anti-diabetic

---

10. Knight Commander of the Most Distinguished Order of St Michael and St George

hormone existed in the pancreas. It's not the first time that scientists discovered the truth despite themselves.

Banting and Best's mistakes enabled MacLeod, Collip and the rest of the team to take the next step. Their work was a necessary stumble toward the discovery of insulin. It was the first unaided attempt at research by a war-hero and a student who had not yet graduated with his Bachelor of Science degree. They worked on their own initiative. While wandering for a time along a wrong trail, they came by accident upon insulin. In time, Collip, MacLeod, and the others cleared up their mistakes.

In a presentation to the Association of American Physicians on May 3, 1922, the Toronto team made up of Banting, Best, Collip, Campbell, Fletcher, MacLeod, and Noble presented their evidence of the existence of insulin. On the basis of the authorship of this paper, each one of the seven was identified as part of the discovery team.

Banting's strength was that he had the faith to see the project through to its conclusion. MacLeod's tragedy was that he had to deal with Banting, his novice – untutored, insecure, and bull-headed. MacLeod could have dealt better with him, but he was no superman. He was an ordinary fellow, albeit a genius, trying to contain a hurricane.

21
A Most Reluctant Nobel Prize Winner

Banting drove from Alliston to Toronto on October 26th after spending a glorious day in the autumn colours with his parents. He arrived back at his office in the heartless centre of the university around 0900, another one of Banting's military affectations, using the 24-hour clock.

What a terrible place to spend all my time! He grabbed the morning paper, folded it under his arm, and made his way into the building. Opening the door to his office, he heard the telephone ringing. He tossed the newspaper on his desk and picked up the phone.

"Banting," he said as he pulled a whiskey bottle out of his drawer.

"Congratulations," the voice on the phone said. "Where have you been? Have you heard the news?"

"Who are you and what are you talking about?" Banting asked.

"My God, you damn fool! Don't you know that you and MacLeod have received the Nobel Prize?"

"What the hell!" Banting shouted.

He slammed the phone down on the receiver and opened the paper. There was the headline in all caps:

NOBEL PRIZE FOR MEDICINE AWARDED
TO DOCTORS BANTING AND MACLEOD

He couldn't believe what he read.

"I've won the Nobel Prize," he said, pausing to let the enormity of it all sink in.

Then, the thought of sharing the prize with that bastard MacLeod was so infuriating that Banting flung the whiskey bottle across his office. It hit a bookshelf and fell to the floor unbroken. Forgetting that MacLeod was still in England, Banting drove straight to Connaught Laboratories to tell him to go straight to hell.

Fitzgerald met him on the steps.

"Banting, old boy. Congratulations. I'm sure you're pleased."

He reached out to shake hands, but Banting ignored him.

"I refuse to accept the award," Banting bellowed. "Stockholm and Krogh can be damned for all I care."

Fitzgerald stopped him from entering the building and making a scene he'd later regret.

"Just talk to Colonel Gooderham," Fitzgerald pleaded.

"As Chairman of the Insulin Committee, he may have something to say."

"Like what? Name one thing MacLeod did with his own hands, one idea that originated from his head."

Banting was defiant and Fitzgerald did not have a chance.

"Please, talk to Gooderham before you do anything rash."

"Fine," Banting said. "I'll meet with the Colonel, but I do not expect him to change my mind."

He marched back to his car and raced to Gooderham's office.

"Yes. I'll see him right away," Gooderham said to his secretary when Banting arrived. "Send him in."

"Dr. Banting," Gooderham said. "Sit down. May I offer you a drink? I have a bottle from my private preserve that I have on hand for occasions like this. I'd like to be the first to congratulate you on this award."

Having received a warning call from Fitzgerald, Gooderham did not allow Banting to say a word. He wanted him to settle down before he blurted anything out.

"You are the first Canadian to receive this honour. The whole country is proud of you. Banting, I am proud of you."

Banting seethed, but he deferred to the colonel, whose calm and strong personality reminded him of his father.

"Colonel Gooderham," Banting said. He accepted the tumbler of whiskey.

"Cheers," Gooderham said.

"Cheers," Banting replied.

"Get on the first ship to Sweden," Gooderham said. "That's an order. Accept the prize. That's another order. I'll pay all your expenses. What would the people of our country think if the first Canadian to be awarded the Nobel prize were to turn it down? Swallow your pride. That's an order! Take the prize, Banting. Accept the adulation.

Think of your country first. MacLeod's a Scot. You were born here. This award is bigger than either of you. But it needs to be Canada's. Is that clear?"

Banting had no choice. How could he argue with the greatest Canadian philanthropist alive? Some are born great, some achieve greatness, and some have greatness thrust upon them. Realizing this, Banting relented.

"I feel like such an ass. I'll take the prize but share the money with Charlie Best."

"And MacLeod?" Gooderham asked.

"He can be damned to hell for all I care."

With that, Banting booked passage with a stateroom and ordered the most expensive tailor-made black wool suit that money could buy. He sent the bill directly to Colonel Gooderham, who paid it without question.

When MacLeod heard that Banting was sharing his portion of the money with Best, he decided to follow suit.

"Of course, I'll give half to Collip. I'll still have the honour of being a Nobel Prize winner, but the University of Toronto will be given a great deal of credit for this discovery.

Dr. Collip's purification of the extract was as important as Banting's idea. Without Collip, there'd be no insulin. Without me, this hodgepodge of researchers wouldn't have made any headway. I was the managing director who kept them on task. There'd be no insulin without my input."

Each man was right in his own mind: Banting, Best, Collip, and MacLeod. Others may have been involved in the discovery, but it was primarily a collaborative effort between these four. They were the principals who brought insulin to the world. Banting had no choice but to accept the Nobel Prize awarded to him and MacLeod. It became his mission in life to assert his right for the sole credit of the discovery of insulin. He was perhaps the most reluctant and belligerent Nobel Prize winner the world has ever known.

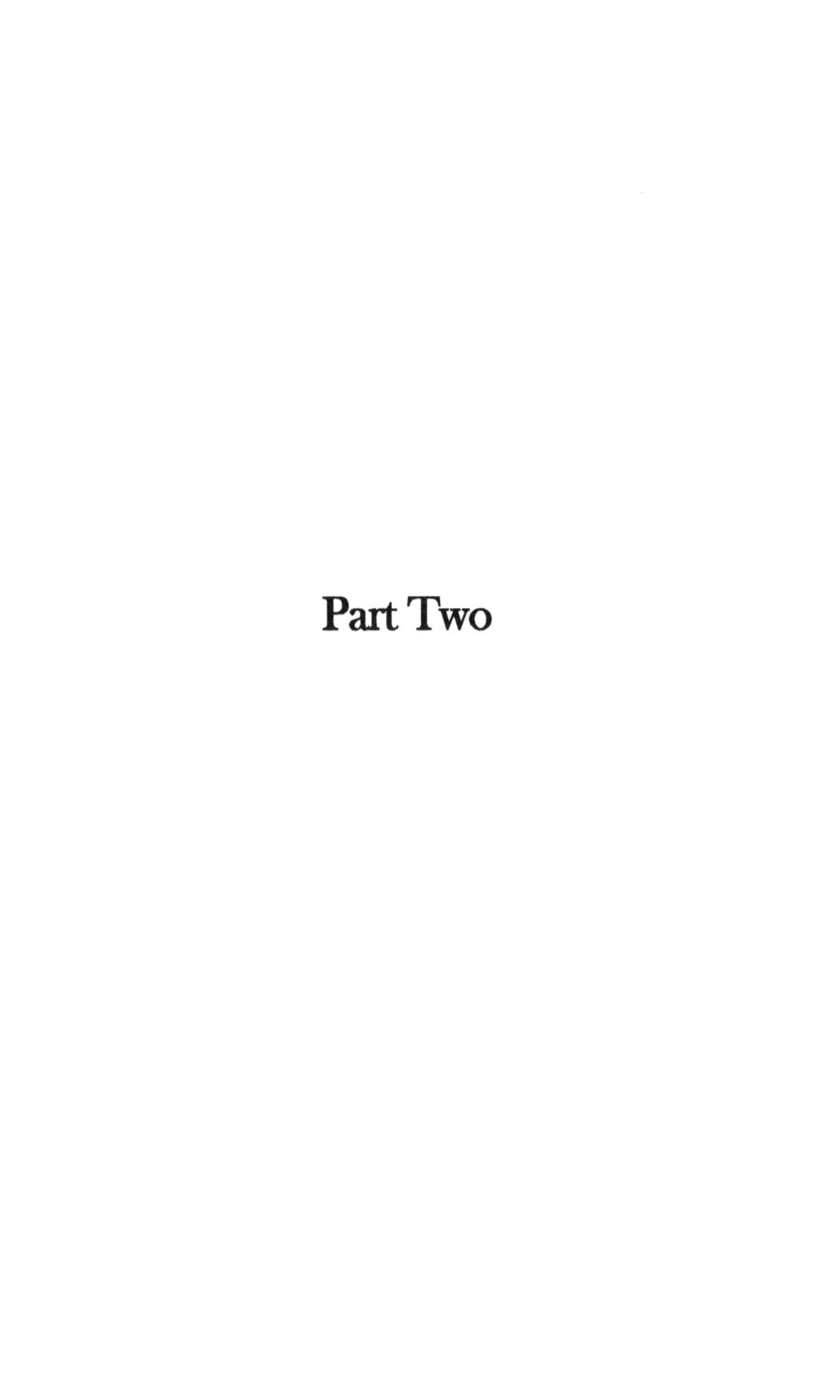

Part Two

22
Married Life

Over the long, slow years ahead, Marion came to realize that sex with Fred was a burden, and a duty to be endured. He was no longer a satisfying lover. For him, unbuttoning his fly was sufficient foreplay. For her, a lifelong process of being kind and gentle. Like he was in the early days of their relationship — someone who made her laugh.

Then, he changed. As their familiarity grew, so did his contempt. He became brusque. To his credit, Banting now changed out of his work clothes when he returned home from the lab.

The smell of dog made her gag. The thought that he killed animals for a living repelled her. He washed his hands before supper, but the words he spoke over the fine dinner she prepared were full of piss and stank of shit.

Marion wanted a man who would share his ideas with her, not catalogue the slights he endured through the day. She wanted a man who would dance her off her feet. She wanted a man who would spend his evenings with her — not return home late, eat a cold supper, and then retreat to his third-floor study, presumably to write down his drunken expositions on adultery as a virtue and a moral principle that could not be denied.

She wanted a loving husband and a house full of laughter. She wanted a housekeeper to clean up after them and a nanny to look after the children so they could go out in the evenings. She yearned for a happy life, not this solitary existence.

Marion hoped theirs would be a marriage of equals. Except it would never be. Fred would have been far happier with an Airedale bitch at his side, not a highly accomplished, well-respected woman in society.

It humiliated Marion that he couldn't keep up. Not in the ballroom, not in society, and certainly not in polite conversation. He stirred up controversy every time he opened his mouth. His unending dust-up with MacLeod continued to humiliate her.

"Give it up, Fred," she said. "What more have you to gain? How much more can MacLeod afford to lose?"

"His good name," Banting replied. "His soul, for all I care. I demand satisfaction."

"You have your supporters at the university and your devotees across Canada. The whole world adores you. Your animosity has cut you off from the medical and scientific community. You have much to offer them and they you. But your anger at MacLeod is isolating you. Can't you see that?"

Banting snorted with derision. He grew angry and clenched and unclenched his fists.

"What do you know?" he snarled, slapping her with cupped hands in places where bruises would not show and then rushed up the stairs to his study, three at a time, slamming the door behind him.

Marion slid to the floor and bawled.

"What the hell have I got myself into? Who have I married?"

She washed the tears off her face and brushed her hair. She clutched her side and went to the liquor cabinet and poured herself a whiskey. With Fred in his study all night, she had the main floor to herself. When he comes down in the morning, he'll be apologetic. She'll forgive him and say that she is sorry for provoking him. That she didn't mean to hurt his feelings. And then, he'll go to work in the morning and stay away all day.

When he comes home, she'll have to be more vigilant than ever. Because he angers easily and stays mad for as long as it takes for her to be cowed into submission.

"Marion Robertson Banting," she said to herself. "Watch your tongue, or your husband will have it out."

23
1925
Hart House Exhibit

Marion scurried to keep up with Fred's long forceful strides down the sidewalk. They were on their way to Hart House, for a showing of artwork from people affiliated with the university.

This would be Fred's first exhibition and he was in high dudgeon. He had to be there on time. He could not be late and if she didn't hurry the hell up, she'd regret it for the rest of her days. He seethed and she bemoaned her choice of shoes.

Their big, new house helped. It kept them out of each other's way. Except when they had to be seen in public. Then, she had to comply, for appearance's sake. So, she put her best face forward and Banting basked in the glory she received, not at all realizing it was not for him.

Fred on the top floor, forever in his study, Marion on the main. They slept in separate bedrooms with doors closed. She was too afraid to lock hers. They lived in an uneasy truce, an Armistice between edgy adversaries. Neither could claim victory.

Most importantly, she did not have to accept complete and total defeat. She would never capitulate to Fred's tyranny over her body or yield to his assault upon her soul. There was enough space in the house for them to avoid direct confrontation with each other. She could live her life out of his way. It was an accommodation of sorts.

He often came home brow-beaten and crabby from long days at the lab. She could hear him a mile off and would make a tactical retreat, so they wouldn't collide. It was safer to take the path of least resistance than to face him head on. Besides, she had subtler, more effective ways of getting him out of her hair.

I could almost feel sorry for the man, she thought as she let up the pace to catch her breath. Banting didn't slow down a whit.

The public has placed such high demands upon him that he could never hope to accept all the invitations they keep sending him.

He gives his lecture on following your dreams and never quitting until he is blue in the face. The public never tires of him delivering his tripe. But they waylay him with questions he cannot answer.

"When will you find a cure for cancer, Dr. Banting?" the halt, the sick, and the dying cry.

"What you've done for diabetics, surely you can do for us. Please, Dr. Banting," the death rattle weakening their voices.

But he couldn't do a thing, no matter how much he cared or how hard he tried. True grit and determination are not enough. He was given one chance for fame in his lifetime, which is more than most people could ever expect.

If he didn't hurt me so, I'd feel some sympathy for him. He's heading straight to a hell of his own making. I need to make sure that I am not damned along with him.

Building the house together gave us some reprieve from the unhappy state of our marriage. With his money and my good taste, our home on Bedford Street grew tall and magnificent. Its grand façade, however, belied a weak foundation. Like our marriage, she thought. It's a sham with a thin veneer of respectability. It's a house for show, not a home for living.

My advantage? He is in high demand on the lecture circuit. Of course, I have no intention of chaperoning him. He is constantly travelling. Every Martha, Rosemarie, and Suzette across the land wants a Nobel Prize winner on her playbill. And who am I to hold him back?

Go Fred, I tell him. "The world needs to hear what you have to say about the need for personal sacrifice in scientific advancement. Progress does indeed take long hours at the lab away from your home and family. Go Fred, I beg you. I'll make do until you return.

Don't listen to Sadie Gairns (1898-1986). She thinks all this gadding about is keeping you from your real work. She wants you to stay even longer in the lab, that the time you spend peering through a microscope is all that counts. But what does she know aside from filing? Whatever you do, Fred, don't pay her any heed. She's your administrator. If you stay huddled in the lab, you'll lose your soul.

You need to be among people who hang onto your every word. They energize you. The whole of Canada needs to hear you speak. The entire world waits with eager ears and grateful hearts for you to fill its lecture halls. Your best work is among the people across our great land, encouraging them to give their all in the pursuit of another scientific breakthrough.

Leave the drudgery to Miss Gairns. Your name alone raises money for medical research. You are an inspirational hero. Yes, I know how you hate the way the press hounds you and twists your words out of context. But you must be patient with lesser lights. They do not have the vision you do. Their limitations are the burden you must bear. Your cross is to be misunderstood."

Marion trudged on. Her heels were made for dancing, not keeping pace with her brute of a husband.

"For God's sake, woman!" Banting whispered loudly. "Hurry up. I don't want to be late."

She quickened her pace. Just a few more steps and she'd be through the front door. After he made his grand entrance with her at his side, he wouldn't give her another thought and she could be off.

He fumed at the foot of the stairs, waiting for her to catch up.

"This is a big day for me, can't you see?"

She reached him.

"These shoes aren't made for walking." She winced apologetically. "They're for show."

"Well," Banting said, slightly mollified now that he knew she was in pain. He took in a deep breath and exhaled slowly.

"Let's give them what they're all waiting for."

He opened the door for his gorgeous wife. The party could finally begin. Marion entered Hart House in all the glory it could muster. Maybe it wasn't Berlin, Leningrad, London, Paris, Stockholm, or Vienna. But it was her town, Toronto the Good, where she was celebrated, loved, and sinfully dreamt about.

At social events such as these, her husband trailed in her wake, grudgingly accepted for whom he had married. Not for what he had done, and certainly not for who he was. He may be the one who opened doors for her, but she was the one who received the invitations.

She had married Canada's most eligible bachelor. As a couple, they made the headlines. Without her, the newspapers would have soon lost interest in the dour, irascible Fred Banting. They would have filled their pages with hockey and British politics.

They might even have hidden on the back pages the newly won rights of women to vote and divorce men, on the grounds of simple adultery.

Instead, they mongered gossip and innuendo.

Fred Banting, she vowed to herself as the cameras flashed, you will pay for every slight and indignity you have thrust upon me. I just need to bide my time.

She smiled graciously when an entourage of her friends noticed her arrival. Walking towards them with open arms, she left Fred to his own devices. She knew this showing wasn't at the Louvre or the Tate. It was an exhibition of paintings by students and staff from the University of Toronto.

On the one hand, it was a pathetic show of artistic incompetence with a smidgen or two of promise. On the other, it was a grand occasion for her to have another night out. She could be the fetching Mrs. Banting, not the punching bag of a fighter about to lose his final round.

Banting also did not put much stock in this exhibition. It was the first time he had ever shown any of his paintings in public. He told her on more occasions than she cared to remember that he didn't have a very high estimation of his art.

Of course, she didn't let him know her honest opinion, no matter how confessional he was in his attempt to entrap her. It was that of a dilettante, not of one with any serious talent.

What he liked most was the process of production, not the finished canvas. He lost himself in the mixing of the paint, the physical act, not the actual conveying of an idea through images and hues of colour. He was not concerned that his work lacked depth and layering. He didn't know better.

Banting was captivated by Canada, this wild, inhospitable place, where people scrabble with the elements. Harsh winters; scorching, humid summers; black flies; life-resurrecting springs; and resplendent autumns. Who wouldn't give their eyeteeth to live out their days in its magnificence?

It seemed to him that Canada was a funny country to love — with her frozen north; her rocky, barren tracts; her mountains; and her lakes.

For Marion, it was a relief that her husband could love Canada without reserve. Especially if it led him to the land of pines, beyond where maples grow. Past the Canadian Shield to the vast prairies spread where lordly rivers flow to the sea. This land of hope for all who toil, the true north, strong and free!

That would suit her fine. The further he travelled and the longer he stayed away, the better.

Marion couldn't quite believe her ears when Fred told her that he was contributing two of his works for the show. She wondered what his real reason was.

"I'm doing this to demonstrate my willingness to contribute to the life of the university. After all, the value of this institution is more than the sum total of its research programmes.

The Arts transcend academic disciplines. They get to the core of what it means to be human. My paintings, flawed though they may be, are small steps toward what it means to be human.

True art represents the land and man's interaction with it. Mine is a representation of what I see and feel."

Then, Fred suddenly laughed.

"Besides, I heard that MacLeod has contributed one of his paintings to the show. I decided then and there: if he's showing one, I'm showing two.

24
Fit for Painting

With that remark ringing in her ears, Marion left Fred to hoist himself on his own petard. She had enough of him and was ready to enjoy herself. She hurried to her clutch of admirers.

"God," she said when she reached them. "I could sure use a drink."

Someone opened a flask and she took a sip. Smiling, she grabbed his hand.

"Anyone else care to go dancing?" she asked.

They all downed their drinks and followed her out to the street, breathless with anticipation.

Banting didn't notice Marion leave the building. He was too busy trying to ignore the discreet, admiring glances that people were giving him.

It is always thus, he sighed. I cannot be out and have a moment alone. There's always someone who wants to shake my hand or ask about a diabetic relative.

Don't they realize I may be the one who discovered insulin, but I am not a diabetologist? There are others better suited to the bedside than I. After all, I am a trail blazer. I lead the way to new breakthroughs. I am not a mere clinician.

Banting continued his search through the exhibition.

"Ah, there you are," he said. "Finally. I was wondering what corner they'd squeeze you into, you little bastard."

He cast a critical, appraising eye over MacLeod's careful, clean painting. It was an exercise in restraint. Traditional, kind, thoughtful, and sensitive. Muted, yet as vivid and as many-sided as MacLeod himself.

The old Scot had an engaging personality with the power to capture the interest of even the dullest of students. At the same time, he fascinated the most acute minds in any hall. His students delighted in the facility of his speech and the lucidity of his lectures.

He possessed to a rare degree the gift of attracting and inspiring students of promise and engaging those with minds as keen as his own. Wherever he worked, he drew about him a band of enthusiastically devoted pupils and collaborators. He gave everyone an immediate and engaging impression of his abounding grace and vitality.

His painting reflected the nature of the man himself as much as it did the well-tended, neat, and deeply plowed farmland of the Niagara Peninsula.

Of course, Banting didn't see any of this. He thought MacLeod painstaking and lack-lustre, a traditionalist in the worst sense of the word — a conventional bore.

This tired, old piece is obviously the work of a man who hasn't had a truly creative idea in years, Banting thought, smug in the success of his very singular and largely inexplicable accomplishment. A miracle of modern science.

Over the years of Professor MacLeod's long career, in addition to being a passionate educator and lecturer, he published eleven books and nearly 200 original papers. Various pupils, under his inspiration and direction, contributed about half as many more.

It was a record that Banting dismissed out-of-hand. He gets his ideas from students and staff under his supervision and claims them as his own. Old, arthritic MacLeod has nothing of interest to offer Canada. He should go back to Scotland.

With that, Banting strode further down the hall. When he saw Lawren Harris's canvas *Above Lake Superior*, he was arrested on the spot.

"God, what the hell is this!" He burst out.

He gaped open-mouthed at the highly formalized scene of rounded hills, barren trees, and stark landscape. In all his travels, he'd never seen anything like this before. The colours were rich, the effect sombre and foreboding.

"This doesn't make sense to me," Banting said in a loud voice. "Where's the lake? Where's the conflict? There is nothing natural about this painting. The hills are stark and bare. They are unworldly. It is not a landscape of the Canada I know and love."

"What's all the fuss?" Dr. James MacCallum (1860–1943) asked as he came up beside Banting. "What do you suppose? Maybe the subject isn't the rocks and the trees, or even the magnificent Lake Superior."

"Then what is it, Dr. MacCallum? These new glasses you've prescribed me aren't doing their job. All I see in front of me is a mess."

"Perhaps representation isn't the point."

"Why the hell would anyone paint a piece of garbage like this?" Banting asked. "Those brush strokes, the lighting. Those colours. I've been to Algoma. I know northern Ontario. This doesn't look like anything I've ever seen."

"Maybe the artist wants to evoke a visceral reaction from you? Not recreate a recognizable scene?"

"It makes me angry," Banting said. "Is that what he wanted?"

"Not sure. Perhaps I should introduce you? Have you met Lawren Harris (1885-1970)?"

"I don't know anyone outside the department of medicine or pharmacology. Marion's trying to socialize me, but it's no use. When I'm not in the lab, I'm alone in my study. Every time I go out, I'm on display."

"Harris is the prime mover of a new Canadian art movement," MacCallum said. "You've surely heard of The Group . . ."

". . . of Seven?" Banting asked. "His work is like nothing I've ever seen before."

"Mr. Harris and I put up the Studio Building that became the home for many of these artists. He even rented a shack to Tom Thomson for $1 a month."

"Who? Thomson? Oh yeah, the artist who drowned at Canoe Lake. I remember attending an exhibition. It must have been early 1920, wasn't it?"

"I was there, too," MacCallum said. "Funny we didn't meet. Thomson got me thinking that the rough landscape might be a fit subject for Canadian artists to paint."

"I heard about a scandal involving the Group of Seven. At last year's Commonwealth Exhibition in Wembley, was it?" Banting asked. "I didn't know what the fuss was about. Now, I have an idea. Some of their paintings were accepted, while many Royal Canadian Academy submissions were not. Sure attracted the scorn of many art critics."

"Their interpretation of landscape is a distinctly Canadian form of artistic expression; unlike anything the world has seen before. Except maybe Scandinavia. Their forests are as wild as our Canadian Shield."

" If this piece is anything like the others," Banting said, "I can understand the hostile reception."

MacCallum grabbed Banting's arm and pulled him along.

"Then I need to introduce you to Harris and Alex Jackson (1882-1974). The three of you will get along famously. I imagine they're having a drink somewhere. They all have flasks in their coat pockets should the opportunity arise."

They walked into a smoke-filled room and saw a group of men sitting around a table, laughing.

"There you are, Harris," MacCallum laughed. "You're the man I was looking for."

Lawren Harris stood and shook his friend's hand. "Why am I not surprised to see you here?"

"Have you met Dr. Banting?"

"No, but I've heard about him." He reached out to shake hands. "Dr. Insulin?"

"At your service," Banting laughed.

"Join us," Harris motioned to the table. "I didn't know you were interested in the Arts."

"I dabble," Banting confessed, "but nothing serious. Having a canvas in front of me and a brush loaded with paint fills me with hope. I'd love to be able to paint a sky with clouds or a patch of snow on a hillside. Then, I could die a happy man."

Harris laughed. "Alex here knows how to paint melting snow better than anyone I know. He has a canvas or two for sale that you'd love. Besides, he's always willing to take on an eager student. If you're interested, I could introduce you."

"What I'd really like to know, Mr. Harris, is how in hell you could paint those hills above Lake Superior like that. They don't look like anything I've ever seen."

"I try to express the life force beneath the surface of the landscape. It's hard conveying infinity with brush strokes and paint."

"Your work is so barren that I don't see any life in it," Banting said. "The lack of detail and abstraction makes me angry."

"What I attempt in art, you do in medical research. I take old forms and express them in new ways. You take old ideas, look at them from fresh perspectives, and work on them until something new emerges."

"You're right. The idea for diabetes came to me from out of the blue. I'd been preparing a lecture, then it hit me, an inkling that grew through fits and starts into an idea."

"I'm interested in the spiritual link between man and nature," Harris said. Your idea was inspirational, an emanation from the universal to the particular. In my work, I try to express the experience of that connection. The land will speak to us if we have ears to hear. And eyes to see?"

"Then you better introduce me to your A. Y. Jackson. I need all the help I can get."

25
A Sissy Game

"Ah, there you are," Alex Jackson said, breathing easily. He rounded a hill on the south shore of the Gulf of Saint Lawrence at Saint-Jean-Port-Joli, 60 miles east of Quebec City. A cold, north wind bore down on him.

He and Banting were on a sketching trip. This was the first of many the two would take together in the coming years.

"I've been looking everywhere for you."

Banting looked up from his wooden sketch box, his hands so cold he could hardly work. He was crouched behind a fence post, trying to stay out of the wind.

"To think, before I met you," Banting laughed. "I thought painting was for sissies."

Jackson tightened his scarf. "It's one thing to paint in a warm, glassed-in, well-lit studio. It's another when the wind is blowing straight down your neck from northeast Labrador."

"*En plein air?*" Banting asked with a snarly, awful French accent. "More like *en hiver gelée* — in frozen winter! Those French have a way of dignifying inhumane human experiences with their language, don't you think? Making it sound grander than it is! Exposed to frostbite in March and they call it — in the open air.

Me? I'm here, assaulting this salient like a soldier under fire, because you like painting melting snow in open fields."

"Just wait until the black flies come at you in June," Jackson replied. "Or the mosquitoes in northern Alberta. They're so thick, they gob up your paint. You've got to soldier on if you want to paint Canada."

"Good thing I got toughened up in the trenches before signing on with you," Banting replied. "Basic artist training should be a compulsory course for all soldiers. This is front line work that you've got me doing. Hand-to-hand combat with the enemy."

"Except the effects of this paint brush are mightier than those of a bayonet," Jackson said.

"The work I do today will last until my son goes broke and needs to sell a painting from his famous father's collection," Banting said. "I wouldn't be anyplace else."

"You have a son?" Jackson asked.

"Nah," Banting replied. "Not at the rate Marion and I are getting on. I was just hoping and dreaming."

He struck a match to his pipe. "I'm imagining the life I could have led as a humble country doctor. With a dutiful wife, who dotes on my every whim. A house full of children who spend all day outside, play-fighting Germans.

When they finally come in, all breathless and exuberant to sit down at the dinner table, their manners are impeccable. They eat their vegetables without complaint."

"Doesn't seem at all like the Marion I know," Jackson said. "You're more of a fool than I thought, if you married her to tend your home fires and all that."

Banting suddenly laughed. "You're right, Marion loathes me. She wouldn't sleep with me if her life depended on it."

"Well," Jackson quickly replied. "I think it's time for you to pack up your kit. The front is changing, and we need to get to where the action is. The Berubés are expecting us.

You'll like Monsieur. He drives a Dodge."

"A Dodge? As long as it's not one of those wretched Renault 6 CVs," Banting said. "If he's got a hot meal and a warm bed for me, I'll be a happy man."

"Don't lose heart, Banting. I'll make sure you're well fed."

"A Dodge you say?" Banting asked. "A Roadster?"

"Sorry, old boy. A four-door sedan."

"If he needs help under the hood, I'm the guy. I know how to get my hands covered in grease. I've owned a rattletrap or two, in my time."

"Sure a good thing you're used to toughing it out. That's why I invited you to join me."

"And that's why I'm going incognito. Fred Grant's my name, thank you very much. No, I'm not the Dr. Banting you're referring to. He's a distant cousin. That's why the resemblance."

"Art is warfare," Jackson said. "Do your duty and leave the heroics to others. True soldiering is on the ground, helping your mates. You go to war because you accept a call-to-arms. Nothing more, nothing less. The same in art. You paint what's in front of you."

"You're one of those commanders who leads by example," Banting said. "I'll follow you all the way to the North Pole."

"Out here, life is pared down to its necessities," Jackson said. "I have your back. In town in the company of women, you're on your own. If you want to paint with me, you have to meet Canada on her own terms.

You have to expose yourself to her charms, not coddle up in silk to a perfectly angled easel. Out here though? Do what you can to avoid the cold.

That's my advice. Hate to have your privates frostbitten, Captain."

Banting roared with laughter. "I can look after myself, don't you worry."

Struggling to his feet, he pulled out a flask of whiskey and offered Jackson a shot. "You're a good man, helping me put everything in perspective."

Jackson took a long drink, and the alcohol burned its way down. He shuddered at the taste. "You're not a Scotch drinker, Banting?"

"Wouldn't touch the stuff. I only drink Canadian. Gooderham four grain. You can have that imported single malt. I can't stand foreign swill."

"I'll have another try, if that's all you have." Jackson reached for the flask. "You know, it improves with each successive drink."

"Let me put my day's work away," Banting said. "I have a trick I devised that you need to see."

He broke a matchstick into five little pieces. Then, he placed one in each corner of the freshly painted board and the last in the middle, careful that the match sticks followed the direction of the brush strokes. He then placed an unpainted board on top of the match sticks and tied the two together with a cord.

"Those bastards back in Toronto who don't like me? They say after insulin, I won't discover a thing. Well, what about this?"

He tucked the wet board with its protective covering in his sketch box and latched the top shut. "I'm good to go."

"Artists the world over will acclaim you as their saviour," Jackson said. "Do you know the number of sketches I have ruined, trying to pack them up while they were still wet?

I destroyed many a masterpiece to escape the shelling when I was painting the front."

"Don't I know it?" Banting asked. "It's bad enough hauling a mortally wounded patient out of harm's way, let alone stowing away a piece of art that hasn't yet dried."

"We do the best we can with the resources we have," Jackson said. "Canada's climate makes it difficult to put into practice what we believe. However, let me say. The weather's not as bad as people think.

Many are cold but few are frozen."

26
Where Wildflowers Bloom

"All I know, Alex, is that when you and Lawren got me into the Arts and Letters Club, it was in the nick of time," Banting said. "I was losing all hope. I'll eat the food of rural Quebec and never get my fill. Just keep me out of that bloody city with its busy streets, packed tenements, and tramlines crowded with people.

It's so oppressive and stultifying, I'm ready to explode. Here, I feel like a calf bursting out of the barn on the first warm spring day, a colt frolicking in the spring sunshine. I'm a country boy, Alex.

Your introducing me to the Group of Seven has given me a reason for getting out the door. Here, I am as free as a young buck, kicking its heels in Alliston. What an idyllic life I could have led before all this hell broke loose.

Discovering insulin may be the greatest thing I have ever done, but it ruined my entire life. The public clamours after every word I speak. My wife turns on her heel the first sight she catches of me. At home or in the lab, I am persona non grata."

"Canada's soul is in the land, not on cobbled streets," Jackson said. "Her gold is in the soil. If you want to paint our country, you've got to escape the city. I'm going north on the Beothic this summer. I'll be painting the eastern Arctic. The ship's crew will be visiting remote northern communities, re-asserting Ottawa's sovereignty up there. I'll stick close to shore while it drops off supplies and people and takes on passengers heading south."

"Maybe I could come with you?" Banting asked. "Can you arrange something?"

"The *Beothic*'s an icebreaker, not a trans-Atlantic liner," Jackson cautioned. You won't be cruising the warm waters of the Caribbean. There's a chance we'll get stuck in pack ice. The ship could founder and sink."

"You mean, there's no first class for a Nobel Laureate?" Banting asked, jumping at the opportunity. "I'll have to requisition a parka from somewhere. I mean it can't get colder than where we are right now."

"You'd be bunking with me and that biologist. What's his name? Oh, yeah. Dr. Oscar Malte (1880-1933). He doesn't look to the sky or to the tops of mountains for his subject matter. He looks to the ground where wildflowers bloom.

If you want to know Canada, he says, look to your feet. Lower your gaze. Find her intimate places. Out west, up north, the vistas are so huge you can see the curvature of the earth.

You can't paint to the horizon. You have to paint a scene that's close at hand. Forget big ideas. Leave them to Harris. Grand and epic gestures. An enclosed space defined by a fence line, or a stand of maples is good enough for the likes of you and me. A strand of curled wire. An outcropping of moss-covered rock. A rivulet of water dripping from an icicle.

Have you ever painted a snowflake, Banting? Try that. Something temporal, ephemeral. Things that aren't meant to last. Things that signify nothing other than what they are. A patch of snow that is about to melt away.

Like rural Quebec. Like that cloud, dissipating in the wind. If you can capture the blue of that sky, you're a better painter than I'll ever be."

"I'd rather paint barns and outbuildings, sugar shacks, and privies than cathedrals in Europe," Banting said.

"Well, you're on your way then. One time, I was out with Lawren. His daughter begged him: 'Please Daddy, take a camera with you this time.'"

"Why was that?" Banting asked.

"So, she'd know what the countryside looked like. Lawren isn't exactly a representational painter, you know."

"I nearly throttled him when I first saw his painting above Lake Superior. Those rounded hills could have been anywhere."

"Lawren paints what he would like to see. The landscape may be his object, but the soul's journey is his subject. There is life in the land. That's what we're painting. It's the reason we work out of doors."

"Even when it's been ravaged by industry?" Banting asked.

"Especially so," Jackson replied. "There's nothing like decay and rot. Man's exploitation highlights the unstoppable drive for life. Survival demands that we adapt. That's what Darwin taught us.

The land and the seasons are never still. They will survive man's attempts to control the environment. Landscape is eternal. A human life is as long-lasting and impactful as a blade of grass — one short season and it's gone."

I should try to keep that in mind when I'm battling for what's mine in the lab, Banting admitted to himself. He didn't say a thing to Alex, who wouldn't have listened anyway. He reflected back on his on-going fight with MacLeod and got angry.

I may be an old fool, but I'm still not giving in to that bastard. He took what was rightfully mine. He deserves a punch in the face.

"If you want to paint the land," Jackson continued, not paying attention to whether Banting was listening or not, "we must find the small things that matter. Where is the struggle for survival in the scene before us? In the wars of nations? In the conflict between principalities and powers?

The struggle to survive the winter is all that counts. At least, that's what Thomson tried to teach me."

"I'm not really interested in people, you know," Banting said.

"Then you need to visit the North Pole," Jackson replied. "No question."

"And if I'm to have lasting peace at home?" Banting asked.

"Send Marion to Europe," Jackson answered. "Apparently, it's a nice place to visit now that the guns have stopped shelling the ground to smithereens."

27
Banting's Regret

That bootleg liquor from the Beothic was certainly working, Roy Greenaway thought as the train left the Kingston station. He resumed his seat beside the famous painter A. Y. Jackson, directly across from the greatest living Canadian: Dr. Banting.

"My article about your summer voyage on the Beothic should be in tomorrow's paper. Thanks for looking it over."

"It's a fine piece, young man," Banting said. "You've done a good job. The government doesn't want me to make any statements to the press without their approval. Nothing you've written will cause them any concern."

"The readers will be curious about your painting expedition to the north. It's such an inaccessible place; the ordinary person will never get to see the Arctic in person. You've opened it up vicariously for everyone."

"Hardly," Banting said, taking another long sip of whiskey from his flask. "There are far more qualified people than I to talk about the Arctic. This was my first trip north but hopefully not my last. I've barely scratched the surface. The man to talk to is Sergeant Joy (1887-1932)."

"Everyone radios Christmas greetings to him," Jackson said. "'Joy to the World,' he says when he begins his broadcast."

"For years, he's been The Mountie on the Top of the World," Banting said. "He came south with us on the Beothic. He is critical of Canada's Arctic expeditions, saying they're expensive and pointless. The supplies sent north are usually cheap and rotten.

He learned how to survive from the Eskimo. They are a kind-hearted and generous people. We southerners could learn a lot from them. The Arctic is the sort of place that will change you,

112

unlike anything south of 60. Mr. Jackson brought Canadian art within 10 degrees of the North Pole.

He's the one who should be congratulated. This is all his doing."

"The north is Canada," Jackson said, "and we've felt her to our soul. It is a looming and ominous presence. Full of foreboding, it's a holy place where angels tread in fear. I've never felt such awe before."

"Capturing the colour of an iceberg from a moving ship is no mean feat," Banting said. "There's nothing like the iridescent lavender white above the water and the aquamarine blue of the ice below."

"To think that 90% is underwater, and we only see the tip," Jackson said. "It staggers the imagination. I know of only one person who could paint an iceberg's latent power, and that's Lawren Harris. He captures the life force, and it emanates from his canvas.

If anyone can open the Arctic to the people of Canada and their collective imagination, he's the man."

"What I've discovered," Banting said, "is that there is no such thing as a still-life up there. Life in the Arctic is a moveable force. If something stands still, it freezes in place.

We walked along gravel beaches and saw where Franklin's ships were jammed in by pack ice. They experienced the Arctic at her worst and died because they were unprepared. We experienced her at her kindest and lived to tell the tale.

What is a miracle for southerners is day-to-day existence for the native people. You should see them skipping across slabs of ice floating free on the water. The only thing they fear is the polar bear, and yet they somehow survive.

They've worn fur and subsisted on a diet of blubber forever. The white man's food and clothing rob them of their ability to survive winter's blast and long nights on the barrens. They've become vulnerable to tuberculosis, measles, and influenza."

"All I can say," Jackson interrupted as soon as Banting took another drink, "is that those are thoughts you should keep to yourself. If they get out, you'll be pilloried."

"I admit that I'm no expert, but this is what I've seen."

Banting took another drink.

Seizing the opportunity, Jackson jumped in. "I have never seen such a stark, lovely, barren, and rich landscape for painting. At the Bache post, I painted the Beothic in the harbour.

Fog was enveloping most of the hills. The rocks, the windswept coves, and the bays. I'm never going to Europe again for inspiration. God, I love this country. It fills me to the brim. I am overflowing with pride."

When Jackson stopped for a breath, Banting resumed his tirade. "What troubles me, is the plight of the native people in the white man's north. How are they going to survive assault of modernism upon their world?"

"Are you talking about the Hudson's Bay Company?" Greenaway asked.

Banting shrugged.

"It has systematically taken possession of the entire north. They have men in every community who teach the people that the company, not the government, will look after them.

It will keep them supplied with food, woolens, tobacco, and alcohol. All they have to do is bring them furs and pelts for trade."

"No one knows how profitable the posts are," Jackson interrupted. "That's a company secret."

Banting raised his voice in anger. "All you have to do, however, is look at the miserable condition of the Eskimos to know who is profiting and who is suffering. They are poverty stricken and gaunt in their threadbare clothes.

The Canadian government needs to follow the example of the Danes in Greenland. Take over the fur trade. Use the profits for the benefit of the people who live there, not line the pockets of wealthy stakeholders in the south and over in Great Britain.

If the Canadian government doesn't intervene, the people of the north will soon be extinct."

"Why is that?" Greenaway asked. His notebook was out in the open for Banting and Jackson to see. He was writing furiously. The brass put him on the train to write a feel-good throwaway piece, to fill a column or two with some light reading in the Entertainment section.

Here, he had a real story happening. He wasn't going to let this opportunity slip away. If Dr. Banting had any qualms, he didn't say a thing. Greenaway did nothing to hide what he was doing. A man like Banting who was used to the scrutiny of the press must have realized what was going on. Greenaway was writing down his every word. The off-the-record comments would soon be front page news. Greenaway could already see the headline:

BANTING REGRETS HBC USE OF THE ESKIMO

There'd be hell to pay for Banting, but Greenaway had the scoop of a lifetime. The opportunity to write the truth about Banting would never come to him again. He had to make the most of it. This was his dream, writing newsworthy stories that made a difference. He wanted to write columns that people would devour. This one would garner him national attention, of that he was certain.

Except newspaper readers want snippets they can digest over their morning breakfast. They don't want long disquisitions and uncomfortable truths.

"The bastards trade baubles for furs and people are dying," Banting said. "The company wants them to devote all their time to trapping furs, not living their lives.

The fur trade is not sustainable at this rate. When it dries up, the traders will go back to their homes and carry on with their careers, wreaking havoc in some other distant land. The company has weaned the Eskimo off their traditional foods and has left them to starve. It couldn't care less about the people of the north. When the clothes on their backs are finally worn through, they'll have nothing because all the fur-bearing animals have been wiped out.

They who once were independent won't be able to clothe themselves because the women won't know how to tan the hides. They'll have lost the traditional knowledge they learned from their grandmothers.

You know, not one of those Hudson's Bay traders is Canadian. If they're not English, they're Scottish. Those traders should leave Canada to Canadians."

<h1 style="text-align:center">28
The Upper Hand</h1>

Marion poured herself another whiskey. *At least I'll get some reprieve when he goes on another painting expedition with Alex Jackson. The two of them deserve each other. Old boys rehashing war stories, drinking themselves into a stupor and freezing in snowbanks while they paint outside. They can have their manly time together, the buggers.*

But I won't be staying home while he's out gallivanting, let me assure you. I'll travel the world and visit all the European capitals. I will make my own way. And Fred will pay my bills. Of course, I'll get his permission. It'll be his act of atonement — him saying sorry until the next time he takes offence at my words, the way I butter his bread, or the outfit I have chosen for the day. He'll make his penance and for a short time, I'll be safe.

How can you love someone who hurts you when you don't give them exactly what they want, the way they want it? You can't. Sex becomes copulation at best, and rape at worst. Banting lords it over me, thinking he has the upper hand. Well, I have news for him. He will not get away with his mistreatment of me. I will make his misdemeanors known. I have to be patient and let him do the heavy lifting of destroying our already ruined marriage. It is only a matter of time before his pigheadedness pushes it over the edge.

The storm he caused after his return from the Arctic nearly set the house on fire. What was he thinking when he talked off the record to that little shit Greenaway? Sometimes Fred is so obtuse, he doesn't leave an unspoken thought in his head.

The whole thing was an embarrassment, especially when Ottawa called on him to make an account for what he said. By then, he was afraid that the Hudson's Bay Company would sue him for slander. Bully for them, I say. It's about time that he realizes that his words have consequences.

Good thing he had enough irrefutable evidence to back up his claims. The most famous medical doctor in the country laid serious charges against Canada's most prominent commercial enterprise. But he didn't capitulate. He made some conciliatory clarifications and adjusted his simplistic pronouncements.

He admitted that this was his first trip to the Arctic. He really didn't know what he was talking about. But it was enough to keep him out of the courts. This was a battle he knew he couldn't win, so he made a strategic retreat.

Good for you, Fred. It takes a strong man to realize you're wrong. Just don't take it out on me behind the closed doors of our beautiful house. The secret to a long and happy marriage? Being kind to one another.

I am tired of the way you treat me, Fred Banting.

29
Pipe Smoke

A two-decked sternwheeler with a steel-plated hull and a 14-inch draft poked its nose into the Athabasca River. The captain swung her wide out into the middle and she was off. The current pushed her north from Waterways near Fort McMurray and around the bend, past Fort McKay to Fort Chipewyan, 170 miles or so upriver.

The old HBC paddleboat steamed from daybreak until the sun dimmed over the horizon. At night, the passengers and crew camped on the shore, huddling in tents. Voracious mosquitoes were desperate to eat them alive.

Jackson yelled at Banting. "You in hell got any more of that repellant from Toronto? These mosquitoes, horseflies, and blackflies are killing me."

"You sure you want some?" Banting yelled, swatting another bug with his blood-stained hand. "All it's doing is making me more appetizing for these man-eaters."

He tossed the bottle to Jackson. "Keep it!"

"You two are a couple of sissies," Major James Mackintosh Bell (1877-1934) said, joining the fray. Mack was a consulting geologist for the Atlas Exploration Group sent north to look at their mining claims. He invited these two to join him.

"It won't be a lark," he warned. "Not what you're used to, a pansy-assed cruise where your eyes and arms are filled with fine-looking women and your bellies stuffed from a groaning board. It'll be a hardscrabble trip and will push you to the outer limits of your endurance.

Once we start there'll be no turning back. Are you man enough to join me?"

"You aren't the only one who has survived hardship," Banting said. "When I was at Cambrai..."

The Major raised his voice over Banting's and bellowed on. "While I was on the Russian campaign, seconded from the Canadians to work on a top-secret mission with the Brits, this would have been a Sunday afternoon stroll fit for a dandy and his lady.

You call these mosquitoes? The taiga is full of predators like this and more. Siberian tigers swipe men with their paws and carry them off to feed their young."

Mack pulled out his pipe. "If you want to survive the north, you have to carry a Webley .45 and make your own smudge."

He tamped some tobacco into the bowl, lit it, and filled the air with smoke.

"Ahh, that's better," he said. He tossed the bag to Captain Banting, who filled his bowl and then flung it hard at Private Jackson."

"Thanks," Jackson said, catching it easily. He was grateful for this temporary reprieve from the incessant bantering of his two senior officers.

All he wanted to do was find some open ground that he could sketch.

"I need space if I'm to paint Canada. In this bush, I feel closed in and claustrophobic. There's no perspective, just trees and shrubs blocking my view."

Banting swatted a mosquito as he pulled back on his pipe and exhaled a cloud of smoke. He'd have preferred to light up a Buckingham, but one look at the Major-Domo and he left the pack in his shirt pocket.

If I only knew then what I know now, he thought to himself. I wouldn't have come. I wouldn't have said yes and packed my bags and left my home with nary a goodbye to Marion.

I would have said, 'No, Mack, I prefer the frying pan to the fire.'"

Then, a sudden gust of wind blew smoke, soot, and cinders into his eyes. "God damn it all!" He cried. "This bloody place is enough to drive a man to distraction."

30
Not Half

As the boat pushed its way north, a bell would ring every couple of hours, signalling the Métis deck hands, whispering to one another in Michif and replying to everyone else in English, to pile more wood into the furnace.

The most multilingual people in the history of Canada: the Métis speak fluent Cree to the Cree, English to the English, French to the French, and Michif to each other.

Michif is an interconnected language with a complex intertwining of unrelated languages: French nouns, Cree verbs, and Algonquin syntax. Not poor French, not Creole, but a distinct language that adopted a consistent character over five generations.

The Métis danced and jigged to fiddle tunes, wore embroidered clothing with floral beadwork and quills, sashes, and shawls. Old people told stories to younger generations, intermingling traditional knowledge with Catholic spirituality, pilgrimages, wakes, holy water, tobacco, and *joie de vivre*. Life is festive and to be celebrated. But it is also hard and full of sorrow.

Métis are Indigenous and French, Scottish and English, the progeny of country brides married to Europeans, who left families back home and to whom they would return as soon as their contract with the Hudson's Bay Company was over. The traders took up with indigenous women to raise their status in the community. They married into established families from whom they were about to make their fortunes.

"I am not an Indian and I am certainly not white" Métis say. "I am the offspring of my ancestors, including the *Anishinaabe, Coureur de Bois, Dane-zaa, Dene,* fur traders, government administrators, *Nēhiyawak,* and *Nakoda.*

Métis are a people whose roots in this land are long and twisted. They are so deep that they cannot be pulled out and eradicated. They are not a crowd, a bunch, a mass, a throng, or a tribe, nameless, faceless, indistinguishable one from the other. They are one and not the same.

Men, women, children, one generation after the other, going on to the end of time. Métis have a language of their own, a culture, and a music, dancing, and laughter. They share a history of pain and hardship and a tradition of survival in a harsh and difficult land. Theirs is a community under siege and a religion that is both Catholic and Indigenous. Métis are a people unto themselves.

They are not in danger of extinction. They are brought to life in love, named with care, and destined to prevail. Each is completely whole in his and her own person, not half of anything. A treasured gift from the Creator.

"This is my home," they say. "I have no other. This is where my ancestors have lived, where I was born, where my relations struggle and thrive, where my children grow, and where I will die."

31

Men Among Men

As the young men stoked the fire, embers from the fresh fuel rushed out of the stack. Cinders and smoke were carried off in the wind or blew directly into everyone's faces and mouths. The smell of wood smoke from the fire enveloped those on the deck. First a wave of heat and then a wind from off the water that cooled them down and cleared the air.

The boat plied its way north, its passengers in comfortable discomfort, viewing the shore and the impenetrable bush from the safety of their deck chairs.

"This is a land you want to pass through," Mack said. "Not stay for long. It's one thing to travel downstream, but another to battle against it upriver. Going north is the easier journey, south the more difficult."

On the journey down the Athabasca towards the Arctic Ocean, the furnace would usually burn one to two cords of wood an hour but sometimes more. The riverboat captain would draw the boat near to the shore where firewood had already been cut and piled.

Slowly and carefully through one stretch of water at a time, the boat made its way towards Fitzgerald, the captain navigating more by instinct than anything. The shifting sand bars, the heavy current, the dead wood, the snags, the everchanging water course kept him vigilant. The last thing he wanted was for his hull to be stoved-in and his boat to be sunk in eight feet of water.

That'd be an ignominious end for his long career in this god-forsaken land. First, ferrying furs south for the Hudson's Bay Company. Now, transporting geologists and their famous friends to mining claims in the north.

The thing about paddle-wheeling is that it's dangerous and slow and dependent on water fluctuations. The best time to travel the river is in the winter, when it is 40° below and the ice is eight feet thick. Then you could drive on it, if your equipment can handle the extreme temperatures.

Mack knew that if Atlas were to develop its claims into full-scale mining operations and expect to turn a profit, it'd need a railroad that could be used year-round. Water and ice are not solid enough foundations for a profitable company to satisfy its shareholders.

"I've been studying this land for years" Mack said. "On the surface, it is nothing to look at, just scrub brush and muskeg. The natives can have all the surface rights they want. Let them hunt and fish to their bellies' content. I want what's underground.

All I need is the funding and the men to start digging, and railroads to carry the ore to market. There's money to be made, no question. Trains are ideal for transporting people and equipment to the north and raw material to the south. It'd open the north to the white man. These Indians have to adapt or die out, never to be heard from again. The old world is gone. The new one is pounding down everything in its way.

The natives are on their way out and I say good riddance. It is what it is. I have a job to do and a duty to fulfill. Besides, needs must prevail. Lives will be lost, but that is the price of progress. There is no other way."

"But what about the people?" Banting asked when Mack raised his half-full mug to his lips. "What's in it for them?"

"The only way for Canada to exercise its sovereignty over the north is to exploit its natural resources and build a network of railroads," Mack said. "If we want to do our part for the Empire, then we must become imperialists within our own borders. It is our duty to civilize this wilderness."

"Do we have to conquer the north to claim it as our own?" Jackson asked. "Can't we just paint it?"

"If we don't, the Americans and the Russians will," Mack said. "Look how the Danes claim that Hans Island is part of Greenland.

That is a foretaste of what is to come, if Canada doesn't get its act together."

"Maybe a fleet of icebreakers patrolling the Arctic Ocean and an extensive railroad across this land," Banting said. "Otherwise, we'll be asking Washington permission to visit what has long been undeniably ours."

"Have you ever been stuck in pack ice? Mack asked. "I have. Have you ever worked with permafrost? You can't.

It's not like the granite of the Canadian Shield. Muskeg can't bear the load of a train track, let alone a mile-long set of cars, each filled to the brim with 50 tons of ore, like they run near Lake Superior."

"I admit that a lot of engineering needs to be done before any real headway can be made," Banting said. "But the Canadian government needs to exercise its sovereignty, or it will lose the north."

"There's got to be another way," Jackson said, suddenly tired of all the politics and economic wrangling. "You two can blather into the long twilight of this summer day for as long as you care. I'm going to catch some shut eye so that tomorrow, I can use this brush to paint myself and this country into posterity.

The way to secure this land for Canada? Romanticize it. Paint its beauty and grandeur, so that people from all over the world will come and spend their money. Once they see and know, they will want to taste."

"Build up the demand and then, build railroads for freight and passengers," Mack said. "Commerce first and tourism second; that's the economical way."

"The artist, not the missionary, should be the first one to open up the land for colonization," Jackson said.

Mack smiled benevolently down upon the low-ranked private. "You use your brush and I'll use my hammer. Together, we can work as a team to bring civilization to this Land of Cain.

Besides, I want to make enough money to build a mansion back in Almonte. That's why I am here."

"I've won a Nobel Prize and lost all hope of ever living happily ever after," Banting said. "Be careful what you wish for. You might get your heart's desire. A grand house does not necessarily beget a warm and loving home. A beautiful wife does not guarantee a happy marriage."

Jackson walked over to the boat's rail, out of earshot. He needed time to think and too much gabbing drove him crazy. An artist needs time alone. He needs solitude if he is to create.

After Fort Chipewyan, the captain piloted the sternwheeler up the Slave River. When they docked at Fitzgerald, the three friends disembarked and bid the stalwart captain adieu. They completed the 15-mile portage to Fort Smith by motor vehicle.

They served in the war and were glad to tell their stories to like-minded fellows, who had ears to hear and enough war-time experience not to sit in judgement. This camaraderie of brothers was a welcome change from the tumult of their lives down south. Here, they could be themselves without fear or recrimination. They could drink down their memories in epic reminiscences of hard-won victories and near misses. They could disagree with each other; confident they'd survive any differences of opinion. They could be men among men.

32
Not My Kind of Story

Mack Bell served as second-in-command on the Canadian Geological Survey expedition. At the turn of the century, he was sent to the Great Slave and Great Bear Lake regions to conduct a geological and geographical survey.

During the war, he served with the Canadian Expeditionary Forces as an officer in France, where he suffered trench fever and was gassed. He travelled to Vladivostok. He knew war, he knew espionage, and he knew the north. He was here for the money.

Alex Jackson could hardly wait to get out of the boreal forest. "I need a sparse, clean country with open spaces. This bush is too dense. Look at these trees. Mostly birch, pine, spruce, and tamarack, and not a single maple to draw my soul. They don't speak to me. I don't know the language of this scrub. I certainly don't want to learn it.

This isn't a part of Canada that interests me. I want to paint a land that is about to be lost, not something that will swallow men whole. This bush is uncontainable. If I cannot control the scene in front of me, I cannot paint it."

"You can't expect to get the feel for a land if you travel through it on a paddle wheeler," Mack said. "You have to wear out your boots, walking its length and breadth. We chisel out its identity with hammers and carry samples back to our labs for analysis. Geology and painting are hard work. You have to dig down to the bedrock to find the good stuff. You have to start walking.

Don't get me wrong. I'm not saying you need to live here. That's for savages. This is wilderness that you should visit for a period of time to work, and then hurry home to a life worth the living. Man has a duty to exploit the north, not live in harmony with it. This is our dominion."

"All I know is that the bush is filled with muskeg, fens, and g-damn mosquitoes," Jackson said. "I'm here to paint Canada, but the swarms of those bloodsuckers gob up my paint. If you want me to sketch something, Mack, I'll have to use watercolours."

"Perhaps, we should leave you at Fort Resolution for a spell?" Mack suggested. "Give you more time so you can get a feel for the place."

"This country is so full on the surface that I cannot penetrate its density," Jackson said. "I can't see what's underneath. I want to make the invisible visible."

"It'd be a shame to go south and report that there are parts of the north that Canada's greatest artist can't paint," Mack said. "Is there is a part of Canada that isn't a fit subject for his art.

As your commanding officer, I order you to paint this country in its best possible light. I didn't invite you along for a lark."

"I'll paint the north," Jackson promised. "Just not this tangle."

"Then do your duty. We need a railroad here. With paint, you can massage the truth in such a way that we get what we want out of it. More money than you can ever dream."

"A man needs to know which way north is," Banting said. "Here, we're lost in the woods. It's terrible to lose your sense of direction."

"Just follow the river, old man," Mack said. "It's flowing straight toward the jackpot."

"Then, let's cross this lake and push north on the Yellowknife," Jackson said. "I want to get above the treeline. Surely, the landscape up there is more familiar than down here. Surely, there are fewer mosquitoes.

With the trees out of the way, I'll be able to see to the horizon. I hate it when they block my view."

"But the land can't be completely barren," Banting said. "It has to have something of interest. Something that defines it and limits its expanse. How else do you get a perspective on infinity?

You need to discover the limit to know where the threshold is. Break the rules of propriety to find your focus."

"But where are the people?" Jackson asked. "How can I paint the loss of an idyllic life when there are no signs of human habitation? No evidence of man's presence?"

"You're too late," Mack said. "The influenza epidemic nearly wiped everyone out. The Dene to the north and west, the Cree to the east and south. They normally meet at Fort Resolution in the summer to fish and hunt. In the winter, they go back to their homes, wherever in God's name that is.

This is a pleasant enough place for them to have a summer holiday. A happy breeding ground for kids. That's why they have such large families. Babies give them hope."

"And close quarters breeds disease, Banting added. "It spreads like wildfire."

"At least the bush is back away from the shoreline," Jackson said. "That way the people can spread out a little. There's a view, too. Something for tourists to see."

"Someone should build a hotel here, Mack said. "Southerners could go fishing on the lake or hunting on the land. Can you imagine the size of the moose they could bag and take home?"

The following day, the three boarded a scow pulling two canoes and headed across the lake. Towards mid-afternoon, a storm came up and they took shelter on a tiny island. They spent a wet, windblown night in canvas tents, listening to the lashing rain. Banting wondered if he'd ever have room service again. He remembered that Marion's idea of roughing it was not wearing silk.

Mack thought about the years he spent in New Zealand and vowed as soon as he returned home to read the story his sister-in-law wrote about him. He didn't think it'd be complimentary, so he put it off. "A Dill Pickle" by Katherine (née Beauchamp) Mansfield (1888–1923). He wondered how he'd get a copy. "Now's as good a time as any," he supposed.

Jackson, uncomfortable under his wet blanket, began to think that portraiture might have been a better career choice. He knew that painting en plein air had its disadvantages, but this was beyond the pale of decency. In the morning, they woke to the smell of coffee, sizzling bacon, and another feed of beans. Hope returned with a hot breakfast over a smoky fire.

Their Dene guide had made this trip many times before and knew what to expect. This inconvenient stopover was a matter of course. Besides, he planned for it when he felt the wind on his face. Just in case.

Sometime during the night, a Syrian fur trader moored his boat beside theirs. His beautiful, young wife lay huddled under some blankets.

"The waves were too high for us to continue," he said. "My wife is sick. Do you have any medicine I could give her?"

"We have Dr. Frederick Banting," Mack said. "Maybe he could treat her?" He looked to Banting.

"Who?" the Syrian replied.

"Dr. Banting, the discoverer of insulin."

"You're a doctor?" the Syrian asked. "Do you have any medicine?"

Banting examined the woman. She pulled a veil over her face.

"She has the flu," he said. "What she needs is rest and plenty of fluids. As soon as this storm lets up, get to land, set up camp, and stay there for a bit.

In a week or two, you should be able to start your journey again."

The Syrian thought he'd push on through to Detah once the weather cleared. His wife could heal up there while he continued to trade for furs. The more pelts he acquired, the more money he'd make. And the sooner he'd make his pilgrimage to the Hajj.

When they landed on the north shore, Banting took out a hammer.

"I've always fancied myself a bit of a geologist."

He went off on a bit of a hike. Once he rounded a knoll and found a bush for privacy. He squatted and had a long and painful crap.

"God," he said. "All this salt bacon and beans has given me the runs."

He cleaned himself up the best he could and rinsed his hands in a nearby stream. "There's gotta be a can of baking soda somewhere."

He strolled back to where Jackson was painting. He tossed the hammer back into the kit. "I've had enough of prospecting. I'm sure there's gold out there somewhere. But it's not at the end of my particular rainbow."

He grabbed his sketch box. "You know. There are fewer mosquitoes up here."

"I told you so," Jackson said. "Anything north of 60 is my kind of place. The vegetation is sparse, and life is hard won. That's my kind of story."

"Well, it's certainly not mine," Banting said.

33
1929
A Good Lay

Marion breathed a sigh of relief. Fred was finally done and rolled off her. As far as she was concerned, he couldn't have come any sooner. She reached for her smokes. Having endured this interminable one-night stand with her husband, if you could call him that, she was already filled with regret and self-loathing.

"It'll be good when he gets his ass out of my bed. I'm certainly never inviting him here again."

He'd returned from his trip out west with Alex and was confounded by the experience.

"Those black flies, Marion, the muskeg," he said. "And the distances you have to travel to get from one place to the next. It's unfathomable. The expedition had been a hard slog from the get-go. We two city-slickers had no idea what we were getting ourselves into. We were unprepared for the harsh realities that travel through the wilderness had imposed upon us. Some days, we walked 25 miles with 100-pound packs. The blisters, Marion. It was a hard trip."

To hear him wax so eloquently about the bush before he left and now to hear him whimper like a mama's boy on his return almost made Marion laugh. If she weren't so mad at herself for taking pity on him, she would have roared in wild abandon.

Serves him right, the bastard, she thought. He takes whatever he wants, whenever he wants, and gives nothing in return.

"You've got to become a bushwhacker if you want to paint Canada," Banting said before leaving on his ill-fated journey. "And a prospector. You've got to paddle a canoe, portage long distances, and make camp before the sun sets."

Unless you're up north in the summer. Then, it never does.

You've got to sleep out of doors and cook over an open fire. You've got to carry your sketch box on your back. To paint Canada, you have to hearken to the call of the wild.

I've heard that call, Marion. I am going into the heart of this great land. Nothing you can say or do will stop me."

"Maybe it'll teach you a lesson you won't soon forget," she said under her breath.

"Pardon?" he asked.

"Nothing," she replied.

He turned away from her, and then he was gone. Full of bluster and full of pride. Ready to take on the north, ready to conquer the west, and ready to bring civilization to the outer reaches of this great land. He didn't say goodbye, and she didn't wave him off.

Shortly after their wedding, he made it clear that he wanted an open marriage, without expectation or imposition of any sort from her. She was to have no real input into his life. She could not demand anything from him or expect anything in return.

Of course, he added that she could enjoy the same freedom as he. She could do whatever she wanted, with whomever she pleased.

That'll be the day, she thought to herself. He wants to catch me *in flagrante delicto*. Well, I won't give him the satisfaction of an easy way out of our marriage. He will have to take the lead in divorcing me. I refuse to have this dance with him.

I will not wive him the way his mother wived his father. She was not allowed a single choice in her life. She lived out her marriage under the caning rule of her husband's thumb. What was good enough for her is not at all what's good enough for me. I will not bend to his will or suffer his hidings.

"I don't know how they do it," Banting said, oblivious to his wife's thoughts. "The Indians," he added. "It's one thing to visit the north and travel by steamer, but another thing altogether to live every season there year in, and year out.

In the summer, they travel by open boats with small outboard motors and in the winter, with dog sleds and snowshoes. It's unthinkable how close to death these savages live, have their being, and die. I see no grace in the bush."

Much to her later regret, Marion listened sympathetically to his prolonged tale of woe. She commiserated with his despair. Her heart warmed to him. Before she knew it, they were in her bedroom, removing their clothes, hurrying towards an unthinking act of intercourse. They did not at all expect a return to the love they had long ago lost for each other.

By the time she had thought of gooping up her diaphragm, Banting was on top of her and there was no stopping him or her, for that matter. It had been a long time since she had sex. She wasn't going to jeopardize this opportunity, ovulation or not. In the lust-fuelled heat of that moment, an unplanned pregnancy seemed a small price to pay.

As he had un-husbanded her, so she had un-wived him, except she hadn't been unfaithful. Her situation was far more precarious than his.

She had to remain true to her wedding vows or lose every claim she had to their property. Theirs was a cohabitation based on convenience and appearance. She needed a roof over her head, and he needed a chatelaine.

The last thing she was going to do was move out of the house she had designed and decorated. He paid for it, his name was on the title, but she had dower rights. Thanks to Emily (née Gowan Ferguson) Murphy (1868–1933), he could not sell the house out from under her, abandoning her to the streets. This was her home and she belonged here, even if she had to consent periodically to a hurried piece of unlove-making.

Sometime weeks later, Banting came home from the university, gleeful and rejoicing. "That old bastard is returning to Scotland."

He was so lighthearted and happy he reminded Marion of the young man she fell in love with all those years ago.

Oh, God, how I burned for him! She admitted. He was so sufficient and strong and clever, an original man and a hero. No matter where he went, he was the centre of attention and I was there with him, on his arm.

First, there were the rumours of our friendship. We were the talk of the town. He was Canada's most eligible bachelor, and I was the luckiest girl in the world. Then, there was the announcement of our engagement and the heartbroken sobs of women across Canada.

I stole his heart, and he won my hand. We were a match made in the headlines. Our picture on the front page sold newspapers and that was all that mattered.

What a wedding we had and what a letdown our matrimonial bed turned out to be. I'll never forgive myself for being so stupid. I was completely gulled by this man, him and his Nobel laureate. He promised me the world and disappointed me entirely.

And now this? A moment's pleasure and an unexpected pregnancy. I was weakened by his vulnerability. He seemed so kind and needy. All I wanted was to love him again and enjoy a few moments of tenderness.

Who would have thought that our hasty moment of intimacy would have such a lasting consequence?

Banting threw the covers off the bed and planted his feet on the floor. He reached for his cigarettes. "Oh damn," he said. "I forgot. This isn't my room. I hope you enjoyed yourself, sweet Marion. I certainly did. There's no denying. You're a good lay. If you ever feel the need, I'm here at your service. You certainly won't find any better."

34
Un-Confession

Ten-month old William Robertson Banting (1929-1998) had finally fallen asleep in Marion's arms. All the mothers, grandmothers, aunts, and older sisters attending the Elora United Church breathed a collective sigh of relief.

The teenage boys and men hadn't given the young child a second thought. Instead, they mulled over how beautiful his mother was and how lucky that damned Banting was to bag the darling of Wellington County. The single men would have bartered their souls to change places with him, the married men their canines.

The church was a grand, brick building where people had been gathering to celebrate their faith since 1863. It had been Methodist until recently. For nearly 50 years, Methodists, Presbyterians, and Congregationalists in Canada had been exploring the possibilities of a union to bolster their flagging attendance.

By the 1920s, they realized that their polity and administrative differences could be resolved with some inconsequential compromises and concessions. The United Church came into existence on June 10th, 1925.

Most of the members at Knox Presbyterian in Elora, however, had voted against entering the union. The newly arrived Reverend Alexander Donaldson (1890-1957?) persuaded 125 members to vote in favour while 261 members voted against. Threats were made, aspersions were cast, and characters were sullied. The factions were at each other's throats and the local Presbyterians were divided over the formation of what was soon to become the largest Protestant denomination in Canada.

When Elora's Methodists heard about the difficulties that Reverend Donaldson and the pro-unionists were experiencing at

Knox, they immediately invited them into their fold and offered them sanctuary. Dr. and Mrs. Robertson, who happened to be Marion's parents, were treated warmly when they made the move. They responded in kind as they settled into their new church home.

Mrs. Robertson welcomed people to her table and fed them until they were bursting. When she succumbed to Bright's disease, her kidneys failing despite her husband's careful and attentive doctoring, the hearts of everyone in the congregation ached with compassion.

They attended her funeral, not only to pay their respects and lend their support to the family, but to ogle Canada's most famous son, Dr. Frederick Banting.

With her face veiled, Marion dressed in black and mourned the death of her mother Florence Adelaide (née) Wilson (1875-1930). Young William had been soothed to sleep by the gentle rise and fall and intertwining of the congregation's four-part harmony and awe-filled singing of Isaac Watt's "There is a Land of Pure Delight." The melody was a pleasing counterpoint to the sorrowful occasion.

Marion settled into the oaken pew and wept for the loss of her mother's companionship and wise counsel. She and her younger sister Vera sat on either side of their father and hooked their arms into his.

Dr. Robertson stared into the abyss of his wife's death and wondered how he would continue. Who would he whisper to at the end of each long day, their heads settling on the pillow as they were about to fall asleep?

Who would he voice his secret thoughts to now that she was gone? Share his burdens? Admit his true feelings about the people he had met throughout the day? His reactions?

Some good, some ill, some harsh and some kind, and still be loved? Who would he share his first coffee with and discuss the affairs of the day ahead of them? How could he go on? Would he be able to cope alone?

What would he do with her clothes that filled their closet? Her shoes and purses? Her brushes and makeup? Her dresses?

The two of them had never been apart in all the years of their long marriage. They'd been a good fit for each other, companionable and incredibly fortunate.

Dr. Robertson looked up and was thankful his wife lived to see the unveiling and dedication in December 1929 of the Memorial stained-glass window. The colours glinted in the sunlight.

With both his daughters and his sleeping grandson near him, Dr. Robertson felt he could withstand the storms ahead. Their presence at his side gave him hope.

As the congregation turned to the next hymn and began to sing, Dr. Robertson considered the words as they reflected his situation.

Rejoice for a wife and mother deceased. Our loss is her infinite gain. A soul out of prison released and freed from bodily pain! With songs let us follow her flight and mount with her spirit above. Escape to the mansions of light and lodge in the Eden of love.

"Goodbye Florence," he prayed. "I'll see you in the sweet by-and-by."

While Dr. and Mrs. Robertson were grateful for the good life that they shared, they were heartbroken at the marriage of their eldest daughter to that idiot son-in-law of theirs.

Poor Marion, shackled to a fool smart enough to win a Nobel prize, but dumber than a bull in winter, freezing its balls to the ground.

Dr. Robertson reached for Marion's hand.

"I'm here for you, dear heart, if you're ever in trouble," he whispered in her ear. She put her head on his shoulder, and they grieved together. They supported one another in this darkest of hours.

Banting, however, could barely hold his craw with the cloying sentiments of the hymns the congregation continued to sing.

I do not stand amazed in the presence of Jesus the Nazarene, he sneered. I am bored to tears with this facade. The words rankled to the very core of his common-sense, agnostic being.

Over the years, he had been withdrawing from the puritanism of his childhood. Sunday-school Christianity no longer made any sense to him. How could he ever again believe in God after the horrors he had witnessed in the trenches? He had seen man's worst and now, he had found a new way.

With A.Y. Jackson and the Group of Seven, he experienced luminosity in the rhythm and design of the natural landscape. He thought nothing was purer, higher, or greater than the environment. I am closer to God when painting in all weathers than when I am sitting in this uncomfortable pew.

He shifted in the seat and looked once more at his watch. The minute hand stopped dead. The verses of the hymn besieged his consciousness. He had no choice but to listen. He felt powerless and abused. The words were coming at him from all quarters. They were sung with the intent to bring comfort and succour, yet all they did was afflict his soul.

Death, like a narrow stream, divides this heavenly land from ours?

Give me some credit, Isaac Watts! Banting thought. "I am not a child any longer."

Trembling mortals fear and shrink to cross the narrow sea;
they linger shivering on the brink, afraid to launch away.

For God's sake, you bastard, he fumed. I'm a battle-hardened soldier.

Fear is a natural precursor to an act of bravery. If you're not afraid, you aren't apprised of the situation. The worst comes from not knowing what's ahead. Except I do. You need to channel your fear and act. I, for one, will not shrink from what's coming.

My mother-in-law is dead, dead, and gone. She is no more. She had one chance to live her life, for good or ill, and now it is finished. This priestly gobbledygook about Canaan land is putting me to sleep. I am bored in this pew and will never pine for a life beyond the grave. I demand what is mine and I demand it now.

The hymn I want to be sung at my funeral?

When we die? That's it.

If we are to know the limit, we must exceed the limit.

By living to the extreme, we know life in the mean.

By fighting, we know strife.

By striving, we know gain.

By losing, we know shame.

By dying, we know death.

From nothing we were born, and into nothing we shall return.

That's it.

I have done many things I am not proud of, but they have given me one thing of incalculable value: raw, human experience. I have robbed. I have stolen. I have born false witness. I have spent a night in the police station. I have committed adultery. I have coveted. I have been drunk. I have broken the Sabbath.

But I have not raped or murdered anyone. Other than those? I have broken every rule in the book.

Death, I do not fear thee. I will wring every ounce of life I can from my mortal body before I make that final crossing. Oh God, your Day of Judgement is of no concern to me. I will never surrender to death and find solace in you.

You will have to wrench me from all this bounty and good. I will feast at the table set before me. I will live my life in defiance of you and your priestly minions.

They are all hypocrites, each and every one, whited sepulchres who shove away the worthy bidden guest. Blind mouths! that scarce themselves know how to hold a sheep-hook! Wolves in shepherd's clothing."

35
Sleeper Awake

While the preacher went on and on about Mrs. Robertson's godly and faithful life, Banting's head nodded and dipped, jerked back, and finally slumped forward. He soon fell into the slumber of the dead.

Marion heard him snore and inched away from him. She was not going to rescue her husband from any embarrassment he was about to bring upon himself. She could already see the headlines in tomorrow's *Star*:

NOBEL LAUREATE ASLEEP DURING
MOTHER-IN-LAW'S FUNERAL!

"Could you not watch with me one hour?" She asked. Once again, she was disappointed in this man, who grieved her spirit, and claimed her body and soul as his own.

Banting would later recount over whiskey with his friends at the Arts and Letters club how that was the best part of the service for him. Sweet sleep had set him free from the droning of the preacher's sermon.

"Religion," he said, "is a man-made ritual, a selfish, self-seeking expostulation of introverted egotists. Baptism, marriage, burial, churches, and dogma are nothing but curses from the Middle Ages. If men and women are to live their lives fully, they need to cast off the shackles that keep them from experiencing all that life in the present has to offer.

From now on, I will live how I want — make love to whomever I want, whenever I want without regard for Marion or our wedding vows. They have lost their hold on me. I am my own man, and I will do whatsoever I please. My destiny is to follow my desire. If I want it, I will take it.

What harm is an extra-marital affair in a loveless marriage? None. The separation of hearts has already occurred, and the damage has already been done."

Lost to the world, Banting entered a dream where he and Tom Thomson were canoeing down a languid, lazy river toward the roaring, raging precipice of a cascading waterfall.

The organist pulled out all the stops, put his feet to the pedals, and the congregation, affirming its united faith in the risen Christ, let loose with their collective voices, the first verse of that glorious hymn, beginning "For All the Saints who from their Labour Rest."

Unsaintly, Banting started, awoke, and nearly had a heart attack. "What the hell?" He yelled, completely befuddled, not quite remembering where he was. Not yet hearing the words of the hymn that were resounding in his ears:

For all the saints who from their labours rest,
Who Thee by faith before the world confess,
Thy name, O Jesus, be forever blest,
Alleluia! Alleluia!

William squalled awake. Marion distraught tried to shush him. Completely rattled, he shattered his mother's already fraught nerves.

"Can't you do anything?" Banting barked.

"Damn acoustics," he said under his breath, suddenly conscious of the clarity of sound in the sanctuary.

The Elora town folk heard exactly what he did not mean to say. The farm folk knew exactly what he was thinking. They had all witnessed his descent into sleep and were eagerly anticipating his sudden awakening. They found it all so very amusing, the humiliation of Nobel greatness in their midst. City folk and their airs, they chuckled.

Banting and Marion were not a church-attending family. Sweet William had not yet been schooled in the art of sitting still for a single moment. His life had been completely free, and his mother doted on his every need.

Here, in this service to honour the grandmother he didn't know, he was constrained, pent up, and bursting at the seams. The congregants' vocal folds warmed, and their spirits invigorated, they sang the second verse with even more gusto than the first:

Thou wast their Rock, their Fortress, and their Might;
Thou, Lord, their Captain in the well-fought fight;
Thou, in the darkness drear, their one true Light.
Alleluia! Alleluia!

As the second alleluia rang out, William let out an explosive fart and filled his diaper with a piquant slurry. Everyone in close proximity to the mortified parents gagged, pulling out freshly laundered and neatly ironed handkerchiefs to cover their noses.

Indelicate bowel movements may not be conducive for numinous moments in sombre churches, but they do make for memorable funerals. This one became legendary and the telling and retelling of it went on for years to come. The details may have been muddied in the unfolding, but the smell remained as sharp and as nauseating as if it had occurred yesterday.

Marion was in distress and sobbing.

"You take him," she shot back. "This is my mother's funeral and I need to be with my father."

She placed the reeking child in Banting's lap and burst into tears.

There was nothing else to be done. Banting couldn't protest. Every eye in the church was upon him. He'd never seen Marion fly off the handle like this before. She took control and he had no choice but to obey.

The men in the congregation were curious to see how he'd react to this startling aspect of fatherhood they had never before considered. The women prayed he'd be an example their husbands could follow.

Banting's misery gave them hope.

Until this day, he had never cleaned up after his son. When William needed changing, he handed the boy over to Marion. She did the dirty work. However, given his extensive experience mucking dog shit that long, hot summer he and Charlie Best spent in MacLeod's lab, he was as qualified as anyone in the church to clean his son's diaper.

It then occurred to him that if he were ever to leave Marion, he'd have to learn about diapers and safety pins. Not only that, but the oaken pew had also grown harder and even more unforgiving. He couldn't sit still for another moment.

His son's shit became his redemption. It saved him in the nick of time. Banting decided he'd rather change a diaper than listen to another word of that god-awe-filled eulogy. He would father his son, like no father in this church had ever done before.

He gathered William's things and slipped to the outside aisle of the sanctuary. The last time he walked out of the church was on his wedding day. He had marched down the centre aisle with all the confidence and experience of a groom who'd been to the trenches and back.

Dressed in white, Marion was his new bride. He was eager to explore her nooks and crannies, her coves and harbours, her bights and white sandy beaches, and her gentle rises and falls. While he rued the loss of his bachelorhood, he revelled in the prospect of husbanding Marion and fathering-forth a son shortly thereafter.

As Banting carried William out of the church at arm's length, he wondered if there might be a more compliant woman back in Toronto, with whom he could enjoy raising a family. His life with

Marion left much to be desired. Then, he remembered the dirty diaper. Unsurprisingly, it stifled his desire.

The women in the sanctuary who witnessed all this with their own two eyes thought the world of Dr. Banting. Not only was he the discoverer of insulin and the saviour of many whose lives had been ravaged by diabetes, he was a fine and attentive husband who looked after his wife in her time of need. He was a jolly good fellow and worthy of their adulation.

The men weren't so sure.

Elora's boosters in the business community were pleased that Banting brought so much attention to their little community. Maybe there'd be an influx of people moving in and raising their families.

Newspapermen camped out for days, hoping to catch some candid photos of the couple and their young son. Even in mourning, Marion seemed at ease in front of the camera.

Banting certainly was not. He was an odd duck who never quite fit in. He was sociable and affable, yet awkward and clumsy. He was an ox of a man, with a beautiful baritone voice and a warm and hearty laugh.

As soon as the father and son escaped the sanctuary, Banting gave William a whiff.

"Phew, that's a ripe one, lad. Should I send a sample to the lab for analysis? There might be a correlation between the severity of a baby's diarrhea and the lack of trypsin in the stool. It's an idea worth exploring. Just don't pee in my face as I figure out how to clean you up. Sure was a good thing I saw those nurses change bandages in the war. Shouldn't be any more difficult than wrapping up an amputation, right?"

While William squirmed and wiggled, Banting wiped and swiped and smeared the excrement off the boy's bottom and applied some cream to the flaming diaper rash. With no small measure of aplomb, he somehow changed his son's diaper.

"Off with the old, and on with the new," Banting said triumphantly. "I deserve a medal for this."

He considered taking the dirty diaper to the lab, but quickly thought the better of it. It reeked to high heaven. He rinsed it in the toilet, wrung it dry, and tucked it in the bag. He wondered if the stained cotton would ever be clean again.

He'd seen the *Sacra Sindone* in Turin and thought William's soiled diaper a much worthier relic. Its negative image was redolent with the promise of a life to come, Christ's shroud a mere reflection upon a slow and agonizing death that occurred 2,000 years before.

Banting took his son to the foyer and laid a blanket on the floor for him to scoot around on. "You need freedom to grow. We should sell our house and move into the country. A young boy needs acres of land to explore and claim for his own. A grown man needs a mistress more than he needs a good wife."

36
1930
A Cheating Frame of Mind

"No, Sir William," Banting said. "This won't do. As much as I appreciate this honour, I don't want to dredge the whole controversy up again."

Sir William Mulock (1843-1944), the 80-year old Chief Justice of Ontario and the Chancellor of the University, wouldn't take no for an answer.

"The university wants to commemorate you as the discoverer of insulin. This small plaque in Room 221 of the Medical Building, where you and Professor Best did your ground-breaking work in the summer of 1921, testifies to that. It is an indisputable statement of fact."

"The battle over credit has been settled and the bloodied wounds we received have healed over," Banting said. "We've all moved on. McLeod has hied himself off to some sinecure in Scotland, Charlie has replaced him as Professor of Physiology, and Collip and I are back on speaking terms. The Insulin Discovery Team members had suffered enough. We worked out our differences and moved on to other things. We have new horizons that interest us."

"Dr. Banting, you are a Canadian who has done immeasurable service for all humanity. You put Canada and the University of Toronto on the map. You are worthy of this small honour. I will do everything in my power to make sure that you get the recognition you deserve. You're a genius in matters of research. You have an instinct for discovery and finding the right idea.

That notion about cancer that you're exploring? Not a problem. I want you to have the funding you need to hire a team of brilliant scientists who will do the work of seeing it out. Your name on the proposal is a guarantee for acceptance. You have powerful friends who are eager to support you. The university will reap great rewards from your continued association with it. It cannot afford to lose you, or the cachet associated with your name. That alone is worth millions."

"Charlie Best was with me each step of the way," Banting said. "I could not have achieved what I did without his help. He cannot be ignored."

"Yes, I agree. Best may have been your assistant, but you conceived the idea. Without you, he would still be a varsity athlete. Besides, you were born right here in Ontario. He's American. The last thing we need is another foreigner getting the credit for what should be Canada's alone.

At this crucial moment in human history, we need home-grown heroes more than ever. If we don't reward our citizens for their achievements, they will depart for lucrative positions south of the border. The Americans are stealing our best and brightest, and I for one would like to stop that exodus.

Many people in high places believe that you and Best alone should have had the priority in the discovery of insulin. They do not want the world to forget Toronto's role in providing you the opportunity to explore your idea. This plaque is a small step in that direction. What do you think?"

> In this room, in 1921, Banting and Best carried out the
> early experiments that led to the discovery of insulin.

"Hmm," Banting hesitated. "Let me think about it for a day or two. A more detailed wording might avoid putting people's noses out of joint."

"Don't wait too long," Mulock said. "Time is a-wasting. I have other projects in mind that need my immediate attention."

With that, Banting said goodbye and hurried home. He wanted to see Bill before Marion put him to bed. He better make a quick phone call to Alex, who had mentioned a bright, up-and-coming writer he knew. She might be able to advise him about the text on the plaque. Now, what was her name?"

The marriage between Banting and Marion was completely on the rocks. The only reason they spent any time together at all was to coordinate care for their son. Banting could no longer stand going through the motions. Marion stayed put because she had no other option. Young Bill may not have been the wedge that drove them apart, but he certainly wasn't the glue that held them together.

It was only a matter of time until they separated. Banting was bound and determined not to let Marion have custody. He refused to abandon their son to her care. Besides, the courts would decide in his favour. They were at an impasse of unholy waiting.

Banting proved beyond a shadow of a doubt back in Elora that he was as capable a parent as Marion. Besides, he could afford to hire a nanny if push came to shove. Not to forget, Marion was completely dependent upon his largesse. As long as he was paying the bills, she would have to put up and shut up. They both knew she couldn't survive without his backing. She needed to be more mindful of her place.

Banting opened the front door. He hung his coat and hat on the rack and took off his shoes. Growing up as a farm boy in Alliston, he never got used to wearing shoes inside the house. He placed his briefcase on the stairs up to his study and hurried into the kitchen, where Marion had finished feeding Bill.

"You're home early," Marion said, surprised.

"I wanted to see my boy before you put him to bed."

"Your supper's on a plate, warming in the oven. It's ready when you want it."

"I'll have a little tête-à-tête with Bill while you do the washing up. I'll eat my supper in my study and make a quick phone call to

Alex. I need his advice on something I am working on with Sir William Mulock."

"Sir William, how's he doing?" Marion asked. "We haven't talked in ages."

"As fit as ever. I hope to have as much energy as he does when I turn 70."

Marion turned to the sink. This was their norm. While Bill had his afternoon nap, she'd prepare the meal and feed him when he woke. She'd grab a quick bite on the fly. Fred's supper would be waiting for him if he came home that night. Often, he didn't. Then, she'd scrape his food into the trash. She'd tidy up the kitchen after she put Bill down for the night.

She had to admit, it wasn't much of an arrangement, this so-called marriage of theirs, but it did provide them with a façade of propriety. The appearance of good was of utmost importance in this city where a scintilla of virtue was more important than its reality.

Of course, the less time that they spent together, the less likely that they'd end up tearing each other apart. For the most part, they were reasonably civil to each other.

"I'd divorce the man if I could, but that would ruin my reputation whether I was the adulterous bitch, or he the bastard adulterer. The courts always side with the man. I may be a flirt and a tease, but I have not broken our wedding vows, at least not yet. But I make no guarantees.

It all depends on whether or not I meet someone who is in the right place, at the right time. If opportunity knocks, I may take advantage of it. I do have to be careful, though. Adultery is the only grounds for divorce in this country, and women don't have a hope.

However, the times are changing. It's been six months since the Privy Council granted women the right to be recognized as persons. Fred's word carries the authority, but I now have legal status. Besides, with the appointment of Cairine Wilson (1885-

1962) as senator, I have hope for the rights of women. The consequences are far-reaching."

Marion finished the dishes and hurried to rescue Bill from his father, who was about to lose his patience. "He's an impossible man with an impossible temper, that's even more impossible when he is hungry. I learned early in our marriage to feed the beast."

Once Bill saw her, he broke away from his father and toddled toward her as quickly as his fat little legs would carry him.

"There you are, my boy," she said, as she picked him up. "You need changing and a bath."

Banting clambered to his feet and tossed a few of Bill's toys in a basket. Marion could clean up the rest. He pulled his supper from the oven and hurried to the study on the third floor.

He locked the door behind him and poured a large tumbler full of whiskey. He needed to fortify himself before he phoned Alex about that woman. He was in a cheating frame of mind.

Part Three

37

The Whiteness of Snow

Alone in his study, Fred tucked into the meal Marion prepared for him. She wasn't much of a cook — nothing like his mother, whose meals were legendary. But he had to admit, she was getting better.

He picked up the phone. "Alex! It's me Fred. Remember that woman you told me about last week? The writer? Could you introduce me to her tomorrow? We could meet at the A&L and go someplace for a quick bite to eat."

Alex said he'd give her a call.

Fred hung up the phone, finished his whiskey, and put his dinner tray on the floor outside his door. Ever since he put a cot in his study, he didn't have to see Marion once he retired for the evening. He readied himself for sleep.

The next day, after a long and futile morning in the lab, Banting closed his office door. He'd been administering trypsin[11] to treat infant diarrhoea and had failed to bring any improvement in his young patients. He'd come to the disappointing conclusion that his original hypothesis was untenable.

"All the work I've done since insulin, and still nothing to show for it. I should have been a country doctor, toiling away in obscurity. Being chair of the Department of Medical Research is a nightmare."

He stopped by the desk of his well-organized and capable office administrator, Miss Sadie Gairns (1898-1986). "I'll be away until at least 1400. I have a luncheon appointment with Alex Jackson. It may take a while."

She smiled efficiently. "Certainly, sir, she replied. "I'll make a note of it in your appointment book."

---

11. An enzyme that aids with digestion

She was the gatekeeper who kept track of all his speaking engagements. Her official job was to keep the university's Nobel Laureate on top of his schedule and to deal with administrative minutiae.

Banting may have been the department's titular head, but she was the one who kept it running. Unofficially, she was the sounding board for the crazy ideas that he came up with in the middle of the night. The scientific rigour that Dr. McLeod put her through while she was his student kept her boss from further professional embarrassment. He needed her certainly more than she ever needed him.

She also parried his occasional sorties in her direction. Without her at his side, Fred Banting would have been a laughingstock.

He hurried out of the building and breathed a sigh of relief as he made his way to the Arts and Letters Club. It was a place of refuge for him, a sanctuary from the mounting pressures he faced at the university. He was desperate to make his life after insulin count for something.

He saw Alex sitting with a prematurely white-haired young woman. Not much of a looker, he thought as he watched her rise and reach out her hand to shake his. But not bad, not bad at all.

"Dr. Banting, I presume," she said, smiling.

He shook her hand, surprised at her forwardness. "Miss...?

"Davies," Alex said. "Blodwen Davies, the writer I was telling you about. Her work is published everywhere. She's made quite the name for herself."

"May I buy you lunch, Miss Davies?" Fred asked. "I have a document I need some help with. Alex, you too? I believe it's my turn."

"No but thank you anyway" Alex said. "I need to get back to the Studio. I'm meeting a fellow who wants to buy one of my paintings. I have the world's largest collection of original A.Y. Jacksons, and they're all for sale. Another time? Miss Davies, I'll leave you in Dr. Banting's good hands. He and I go a long way back."

"All that man wants to do is paint Canada," Banting said. "He's the one who came up with the idea of an out-of-door school of painting. When he saw Georgian Bay at the end of October with the colours past their peak and the winds stripping the trees bare, he found his oeuvre."

"If I'm not mistaken, Mr. Jackson and Tom Thomson shared a studio in the building that Lawren Harris and James MacCallum financed," Blodwen said. "They both had the courage to use purples and greens to paint the whiteness of snow."

"Miss Davies," Banting replied. "I know a little out-of-the-way place, a block or two from here. Shall we go for a walk?"

He pulled out the sheet of paper he and Sir William had been working on. "While we're waiting for our food, would you mind helping me with a new draft of this?"

"Certainly," she said, giving the paper a quick glance. "I have a few questions about the medical evidence surrounding Tom Thomson's death. Would you mind answering them?"

"I'll do my best, Miss Davies. I believe that we have quite a lot to talk about. Shall I order a bottle of wine?"

She could scarcely believe her good luck. They walked down the street. The most famous man in Canada is buying her lunch and wants her advice.

"What would her father say, if he knew what she was up to," she wondered? He'd have to admit that she had arrived." She was indeed making her mark. The Arts and Letters Club may be For Men Only, but she was confident that it would only be a matter of time until women could become members in their own right.

In the meantime, she'd write a biography of the virtually unknown painter who died under mysterious circumstances at Canoe Lake. Tom Thomson and Fred Banting. What a fond dream, that a woman could find her place in a man's world! If only she smoked a pipe. Then, it might come true.

38
The Devil Booze

"I've been thinking about what makes a man a hero," Blodwen said as she sipped a Gin Rickey at the Heliconian Club of Toronto on Hazelton Avenue. She and her girlfriends met there periodically to discuss their work. They conferred over the challenges they were facing in a world that favoured men and their pursuits over women and theirs.

They were artists in their own right and had to balance the demands of their craft with the expectations that society, marriage, and children placed upon them. Yvonne McKague (1897-1996) and Isabel McLaughlin (1903-2002) taught at the Ontario College of Art. Sometimes, the Group of Seven included them in their male-dominated exhibitions.

Bess Housser (1890-1969), a self-taught painter and a writer, was married to F.B. Housser (1889-1936) who wrote *A Canadian Art Movement,* which Emily Carr (1871-1945) called *The Book.* Carr was thrilled to meet the author's wife, whom she immediately recognized as a friend and a kindred spirit.

The women supported each other in the highs and lows of their careers and in their private lives. Today, the four were discussing men and how they were routinely rewarded for acts of bravery when they were away from home. This topic of heroic abandonment drove them to drink.

The building where they were meeting was designed along the Carpenter Gothic style popular in North America during the second half of the 1800s. It had a pitched roof and pointed arches, a board-and-batten exterior, steep gables with intricate decorative trim, and a bell tower without the bell. Reminiscent of stone Gothic cathedrals in Europe but built of wood and on a much more modest scale, the Heliconian Hall had high windows that filled the interior with light.

160

A group of women bought it in 1923 for $8,000 and burned the mortgage in 1931. It was a significant achievement that no man dreamed women could accomplish in such a short time.

Light poured through the rose-coloured stained-glass window above the entrance. A former church sanctuary with a soaring ceiling, the main hall felt like a sacred place. The club was founded in 1909 in response to the men's-only Arts and Letters Club that was formed in 1908.

Female musicians, artists, and writers needed a place where they could meet socially and engage intellectually without fear or intimidation. When they laughed from the heart, the entire building echoed with joy. When they cried, it wept.

"Since the beginning of human history, society has looked to men for its heroes," Bess Housser said. "This doesn't make sense to me, having lived with one for as long as I have. A hero is rarely recognized in his own home, I suppose."

Her table mates laughed, each thinking about the men they knew who didn't quite live up to their promise.

"The lustre rubs off more quickly with some than with others," Yvonne McKague admitted. "Then, there are those who shine all the more brightly as you spend time with them. They aren't all bad."

She raised her glass in a toast.

"To the men worthy of our loving!"

"And to those who aren't?" Isabel asked.

"Some men are foolish that way," Blodwen said. "Their egos keep them from becoming decent human beings."

"May they come crashing down and the women and children around them spared," Bess said. "A hero needs to be a spiritual being, up and away from the ordinariness of everyday life, a priest of a man, holding a transcendent light. Someone we can look up to."

"You mean you don't idolize Frederick Broughton Housser?" Yvonne asked. "The man whose book made you so very famous?"

"A woman's claim to fame should not depend upon the man she married," Bess answered. "Besides, Fred is too busy in the world of writing newspaper articles to make me delirious."

"My hero needs to be nearby and immediately embraceable," Yvonne said. "In a relationship proximity is critical. I don't want him up on a pedestal, where I can't reach him."

"Well," Bess said hotly. "Fred spends so much time away from the house, I sometimes think he has taken on a mistress."

Yvonne took a sip of her cocktail, a concoction made of equal parts gin, chartreuse, maraschino liqueur, and fresh lime juice. The bartender called it The Last Word. It seemed an appropriate choice since she hated backing down from any argument.

This time, however, she decided not to pursue the tack of this particular conversation any further. She might let slip something she'd rather leave hidden. In her more sombre moments, she knew that reticence is often a better virtue than a quick tongue. It's just one that is nearly impossible to practise.

The consequences of speaking the truth on this occasion were too dire for her to ignore. She better bide her time and hold her tongue. She prayed, to no avail, for a change in topic.

"I've always found it hard to understand," Blodwen said, "how women can break the bonds of sisterhood by having affairs with married men. Of course, the opposite is also true. How can men carry on with the wives of their friends?

Adultery seems the ultimate betrayal in a marriage of true minds."

"I suppose that's the catch," Bess said, 'being married to someone who is your equal. Love is not time's fool."

"It goes to show that for all our differences, men and women are essentially the same," Isabel said. "We think we can change someone instead of accepting them as they are. People who are desperate for love will go to any measure to find it. Loneliness is no respecter of persons.

All of us are guilty of wanting something we can't have. All have fallen short of the impossible standard society sets for us. It's a question of whose trust we are breaking, whether a marriage vow, business contract, or schoolyard promise."

Isabel sipped her tea, preferring it to liquor. She learned long ago that talking about men and drinking alcohol was a dangerous combination that was best avoided.

This was an afternoon for her to remain sober.

"That may be true," Bess said. "But for all our failures and shortcomings, women can be heroes, too. Flawed human nature does not preclude people from acting heroically. Look at the five women from Alberta, Emily Murphy (1868-1933), Irene Parlby (1868-1965), Nellie McClung (1873-1951), Louise McKinney (1868-1931), and Henrietta Edwards (1849-1931). They weren't perfect.

In the heat and turmoil of raising their families, they advocated for the rights of women and children. Because of them, women now have legal status as persons. They were cracked vessels and the light shone through them."

"Don't forget Bobbie Rosenfeld (1904–1969), the Olympic Gold medalist," Yvonne said. "The best Canadian female hockey player there ever was."

"Sexual differences may prove you wrong," Blodwen said. "Men seem more capable of winning things by barrelling through. Women need a more tactical approach."

"Foot size is not an indication of heroic ability," Yvonne said. "Every farm wife on every quarter section across this land has proven that. From the milking of cows in the morning to the turning down of the coal oil lamp at night, they work marathons. They do what needs to be done."

"It is their good and faithful service to their families that holds society together," Blodwen said. "The war showed what women are capable of, when men were slaughtering each other in the trenches."

"What I meant to say," Bess said, "is that heroes need to be elevated. They cannot be ordinary people. They have to accomplish something that makes a significant contribution to society at large. It can never be for personal aggrandizement. What is the point of risking everything for the thrill? You have to do something important."

"But what happens when the ordinary and commonplace are ignored?" Isabel asked. "Like giving birth?"

"There is nothing more extraordinary or exceptional than that," Blodwen said. "What more do women need to do to gain the recognition that they deserve?"

She sipped her Gin Rickey. "Look at Mrs. Wilson, who raised eight children. Now, she's Canada's first female senator."

"It should have been Mrs. Murphy who was nominated," Isabel said. "Except she's a Conservative and Mrs. Wilson has a long history with the Liberal Party. Mackenzie King (1874-1950) could do no other.

He chose Mrs. Wilson because of her friendship with Mrs. Zoé Laurier (1868-1919). Liberals must appoint Liberal senators. That's how it is.

Men make political decisions and women are forced to comply. We have no choice."

"Regardless of how she was selected," Blodwen said, "Mrs. Wilson's appointment will do wonders for the lives of ordinary Canadians. I know she favours the new divorce legislation that is in the works. Once it is passed into law, it'll give women more rights and independence.

If men say that they honour women and motherhood, they should respect the struggles they face putting food on their tables and making careers for themselves outside the home."

"Take Emily Carr in Victoria, for example," Yvonne said. "It's easy for men to dismiss her. She doesn't fit their standard for beauty."

"She doesn't meet the standard women set for each other," Blodwen said. "Her female critics are just as vicious."

"That and the fact that she is a fearsome opponent to anyone who crosses her," Isabel said. "Her irascibility goes beyond feisty, pretty, and adorable, all the way to alarming and dangerous. She is not a person men can ignore. If people threaten her, she fights back."

"That's so unwomanly," Yvonne laughed.

"The struggle she's endured has given her the independence she needs to survive. It's made her resourceful. She is fierce. It was that or go begging to her sisters. She lived hand-to-mouth and was unrecognized in the art world, until Lawren Harris embraced her: 'You're one of us, he said.'"

"It's almost as if his male seal-of-approval gave society permission to see her as a gifted artist," Blodwen said. "If Mr. Harris hadn't been so gentlemanly, she'd still be left out in the rain."

"The last thing I want is to lose the scant freedom I have to decide what is best for me," Isabel said. "I prefer to live in a world where I can make decisions that are the best, as far as I can tell, for my life.

No man will take that away from me."

"Now, if you ask me, Mr. Harris is a man worthy of my worship," Bess said. "But you won't catch me in his bedroom."

"Especially with Trixie on the lookout," Yvonne said.

"Honestly, I don't know what he ever saw in that woman, other than her gorgeous eyes, kind temperament, and staggering bank account," Bess said.

"Maybe her gypsy spirit?" Yvonne suggested. "I hear that they're packing up their current place and moving into another mansion."

"Isn't the one they have grand enough?" Isabel asked.

"Apparently not," Bess said.

"My glass is empty," Yvonne interrupted. "Is it too early to order another one?"

"Not if I can have a refill," Bess replied.

"I'll stick with tea," Isabel said. "You have always been more inclined to the world of spirits than I.

My feet need to be planted on the ground. I'm tipsy from this heady conversation. I don't know how you can hold your liquor with all this talk."

"Pacing yourself darling. That's the secret. Just like with men. You don't have to drain the glass with the one you are holding in your hands. Sometimes a sip or two is all you need. Other times? Oh, what the hell, and you empty the glass and call for seconds."

"And live a lifetime of regret?"

"There's nothing like a one-night stand to strip away your dignity and self-importance," Yvonne said. "Just blame the devil booze, sister."

39
An Unsung Distinction

"The problem with men is that they think only acts of bravery on the battlefield are heroic," Blodwen said. "But what about heroism away from the front? The kind of heroism that interests me does not make headline news.

An ordinary person who does something of extraordinary benefit for the community is my kind of hero. Canada's short history is full of people who have sacrificed their all, so that their children could have better lives than their parents or their grandparents. My dream is to tell their stories."

"But who will read them as long as men hold the purse strings?" Isabel asked. Canadians and Americans want self-made heroes, who accomplish great things on their own coin. Look at Roald Amundsen. He paid his own way. People love that man because of his accomplishments."

"But what about the furor he caused across the British Empire?" Blodwen asked. "He sailed through the Northwest Passage in a 70-foot, shallow-draughted sloop the *Gjøa* with a crew of six men. When she was trapped in the ice, he skied 500 miles to Eagle City in Alaska to be the first to tell the world of his accomplishment.

What woman wouldn't linger with him the whole night through? It took him months to make the return trip. When he and his crew finally arrived in Nome, it was at the end of August."

"Did you read about the welcome he received when he arrived in San Francisco after the earthquake?" Yvonne asked. "Americans loved him so much they invited him on the lecture circuit where he made a fortune that funded his next adventure.

Heroism doesn't mean you have to be nice, faithful to your wife, or even keeled. You need to finish what you set out to do."

"And make sure no one steals the credit for your achievement," Bess said. "Apparently, Amundsen had love affairs with three married women. People see what they want and turn a blind eye to things they don't. His reputation remained untarnished."

"What ruined him here in Canada is that as a Norwegian, he horned in on our territory," Blodwen said. "The north is Canada's. Exploring it is our birthright. Sir John Franklin put a love for the north into our national consciousness. It is a magnetic land of snow and ice and holds our imagination.

The tough Norseman stole the priority from Canadians. He is lauded everywhere in the world, except the British Empire."

"He used trickery and deception to make it to the South Pole five weeks before Scott, who died on the return trip," Isabel said. "Poor old bugger breathed his last less than 12 miles from the next food cache, knowing he had been bested. What a horrible way to die — in disappointment.

Nevertheless, his failure in the Antarctic transformed him into a hero. Statues were erected across Britain because of his bravery. He was lionized in spite of his failure and became an inspiration to all."

"Amundsen won the trek to the South Pole because he was better prepared than Scott," Blodwen said. "During the two long winters he was stuck in the Arctic, he learned from the locals how to survive blizzards and live on the land. They hunted animals and ate fresh meat to avoid scurvy."

"From what I heard?" Yvonne said. "Amundsen and his men wasted no time in spreading their seed among the Nitsilik women, who warmed their beds at night. I wonder how many blue-eyed, blond-haired babies they left behind as they continued their journey westward?"

"Isn't that typical of male heroes?" Yvonne asked.

"They carry onward in their quest to do battle and leave the mess of victory for their abandoned women to straighten up."

"Infidelity, so they say, may be in man's nature, but it doesn't justify his acting upon it," Bess said. "Men need to be responsible and respectful of women."

"True gallantry is domestic and ordinary," Isabel said. "Heroism benefits people in their day to day lives."

"Like Fred Banting?" Blodwen asked. "God, how I adore that man. He is strong and brave, and determined to act. He will do his duty no matter what. The fact that his idea about insulin came to him out of the blue attests to his superhuman nature. A divine spark touched him. He is more than he seems. He is a hero of exceptional talent. I wish more men were like him, quiet and forceful. Bound and determined to make his own way, yet conscious of his duty."

"Shouldn't we all be free to follow our hearts and fulfill our bodily desires without fear or reprobation," Yvonne said. "A society that restrains its people keeps them from realizing their complete selves. If people are to live full and happy lives, they need to be set free from a thin, hollow morality that does not touch the heart or the spirit."

"You've been reading too much Walt Whitman (1819-1892)," Isabel said. "It'd be much easier if you lowered your expectations."

"This life we live is an organic cycle of birth, growth, reproduction, death, and regeneration," Bess said. "The spiritual force within each of us is unstoppable. We need to loosen the ties that bind us and chase after the freedom that calls us."

"Give me liberty and the autonomy to live how I choose," Blodwen said. "I will pursue my destiny, regardless of the cost."

"Sounds like you better not get married," Bess replied.

"I want to live with my soulmate," Blodwen said. "Whether we marry or not is immaterial."

"Without marriage, you have no rights," Yvonne said. "Do not give your body to a man before he marries you. Such a relationship will end only in heartbreak. Read the news. Men routinely abandon women who bear their children out of wedlock."

"You will be sorely disappointed if you have an affair with a married man," Bess said. "However, that could be the beginning of your spiritual journey. Lose everything in this world that you hold dear. Then, pick up the pieces and start over. That is the hero's journey."

"Women who are bound in marriages can never be free, unless they are of independent means," Isabel said. "A room with a view is important but having one's own livelihood is even more important. Nothing speaks equality more than having complete access to a full bank account."

"It all depends on what you are willing to sacrifice for your art," Blodwen said. "Love, marriage, children, financial stability. It is hard work being a hero.

For women, life as an artist is almost always an unsung distinction. No one ever said that the independent life would be easy. Or fair. Nothing is."

With that, the four women finished their drinks and paid their bill. They stepped out of the hall and walked down the street, hurrying to catch a tram that would carry them into the city.

Suddenly, a cloudburst soaked them to the skin. They laughed until they cried, and they laughed some more. As they waited at the stop, the sun came out and warmed their smiling faces. For the briefest of moments, they felt like young girls again.

They breathed in the fresh clean air and were filled with hope and desire. The rainfall revived their spirits, and the world was once again theirs for the taking.

40
The Idiot

Marion took off her coat and hung it in the closet, then she removed her hat, and placed it on the rack. "I cannot go anywhere without people whispering and gossiping behind my back.

Really Fred? You are up to no good and I know it. Your sins will be shouted from the roof top. I will be vindicated.

Now, my friends tell me that you have been seen out and about with that Miss Blodwen Davies. Apparently, she's writing another biography on poor Tom Thomson.

Her first was a pamphlet. I doubt she'll find a publisher. There isn't much of a market for Thomson's paintings. Besides, it's only because of his death that people are giving his work a second look.

Fred's giving Miss Davies medical advice. She questions the conclusion of the coroner's report that Thomson drowned and suggests that something nefarious happened to him. She thinks he was murdered.

I imagine MacCallum and others like him welcome this new controversy. Nothing raises the value of a piece of art like an uproar, the hotter the better. Can't she see the real reason Fred's helping her? He has a vested interest in getting her into the sack. Why else would he bother?

All I know is that he is done screwing with me.

Miss Davies wonders how such an experienced woodsman as Tom Thomson could die in the shallows of Canoe Lake. For her, suicide is out of the question. It was too unmanly for him to take his own life. Therefore, she comes to the obvious conclusion that he must have been murdered. Obvious to her, but to the rest of us? A leap of logic.

Someone gashed him on the side of his head with a paddle. He was knocked senseless and died before he hit the water. His lungs were still filled with air when the coroner examined the corpse that had been submerged for a week.

At least, that's the conclusion my husband has drawn from the papers he has read. Miss Davies believes him because of the authority his discovery of insulin has bestowed upon him.

What she doesn't know is that my husband has a habit of shooting off half-cocked. He routinely makes pronouncements on subjects he barely knows anything about. Just another example of him being a blowhard.

If anything, the scandal she's formulating about Thomson will make her equally infamous. It's all a matter of marketing, I suppose. And her affair with my husband? If it comes out, it'll make her a household name across Canada. Her book will sell like hot cakes. The little minx.

Fred spends his evenings ostensibly up in his study reading. In reality, he is formulating a justification for adultery. He thinks that I don't know. One morning, he forgot one of his notebooks at the kitchen table. I gave it a quick peek before returning it to his office.

The man is so much more a fool than I dreamed possible.

I hope it soon all comes to a head. I can see no other way for me to get out of this miserable marriage. He is bound and determined to commit adultery. My poor sweet William — my son; my darling, what a mess you've had to grow up in.

Perhaps there's still time for you to have some joy in your sad childhood. I'll do whatever it takes to save your life from the hands of this idiot."

41
The Curtains Drawn

Blodwen found tremendous comfort in her friendship with Fred Banting, the wonderful discoverer of insulin. He was her kind refuge in a world of predatory men, where she was trying to make a name for herself. She wrote stories about Canada's romantic cities, villages, and places.

"I may be a travel writer now," she vowed. "But I have dreams of something grander. One day, I will be Canada's social historian. My work on Tom Thomson is just the beginning."

Banting showed genuine interest in her ideas and feelings. He made her laugh with pleasure, and she loved being with him. She idolized him. The thought that he valued her work made her love him even more. He did not dismiss her on account of her sex.

In fact, he chose to be with her when he could have had any woman in the city.

Fred respected her and allowed her to be herself. She didn't have to pretend to be someone she was not. Blodwen worshipped the man Marion Robertson Banting despised.

"What woman couldn't help but love a man like Dr. Banting," Blodwen asked herself over and over again. He never said anything untoward to her or did anything inappropriate that made her feel uncomfortable. He respected the boundaries she set early in their relationship. That made her love him even more. He was a perfect gentleman and she felt completely safe in his presence.

After those men at the Fort William newspaper where she began her career, Dr. Banting was a dream come true. He wanted her to succeed and encouraged her to fight the good fight.

"Miss Davies," he said, "if I can make it, you can too. This world is yours for the taking. But it demands hard work and determination. You and I are one and the same, fighting against opponents who are mightier than we could ever be. I fought with a gun and then, struggled with an idea in a lab.

You are fighting in a petticoat and with a pen. Yet, you are better prepared than I ever was. We are the little people standing up to powers and principalities. If we don't take them down, they will destroy us."

Blodwen was a vulnerable young woman and Banting had the good grace to show her that she could overcome any obstacle in her way.

"You have insight," he said. "You have the power within you to achieve far more than your detractors ever could. Your idea about the evidence surrounding Thomson's death suggesting murder is plausible from a medical point of view.

It has merit and cannot be dismissed out of hand. If Thomson had drowned, there'd be water in his lungs, but the coroner's report says that bubbles of air issued out of his mouth. He died while he was breathing. That implies someone killed him before he hit the water. The only questions that I have in my mind are who knocked him unconscious and where is the murder weapon?"

Blodwen was so very pleased with the comforting words the great man spoke to her. He validated her opinion like no other man ever had. If he weren't already married to the utterly beautiful Mrs. Banting, she'd give him her heart, soul, and body.

But Blodwen couldn't betray another woman. A bond of sisterhood between the two compelled her to respect the vows of fealty Dr. Banting had pledged to his wife on their wedding day. She would never be that other woman.

Besides, the connection that she shared with Dr. Banting transcended mere physical sexuality. Theirs was intellectual, spiritual. She'd been reading Arthur Avalon's[12] writings about tantra and was getting to know the mythology of the Far East from Pierre Bernard (1875-1955). Their ideas made sense to her.

––––––––––––––

12. See Sir John George Woodroffe (1865-1936)

Her relationship with Dr. Banting was spiritual in nature, and there is no infidelity in a meeting of true minds. If they didn't touch, didn't copulate; and kept their clothes on, she reasoned there'd be no sin. They wouldn't be committing adultery.

But there's no harm in sharing sublime thoughts, is there? After all, what could she offer Dr. Banting that Mrs. Banting had not given him on their honeymoon? Slim ankles and gorgeous eyes, a full bosom and a radiant smile that melted hearts. Mrs. Banting was easily the sexiest woman in Toronto. Her dance card was always full when she went out and she always went out. She had no shortage of admirers.

Blodwen, in contrast, was slight and stooped and white-haired. She was not much of a catch and felt it to the very core of her being. However, Banting was attracted to her clarity of thought, her insight, and the quality of her writing. Or so he said.

"Men like women with style, and I have style. Just not the kind that lures men to bed. My prose is translucent and clear. It's my most attractive trait," she rued bitterly. Banting loved her writerly self and Blodwen was happy he did. "I'll take what I can get."

As far as she was concerned, Mrs. Banting could have all the attendant problems of living with the man. She could deal with his dirty shirts and wash his dishes. She could keep their house, raise their son, and keep their larder full.

Blodwen was no chatelaine, but neither was Mrs. Banting — an uncomfortable truth her unfaithful husband was soon to learn.

Blodwen kept the best part of Dr. Banting for herself. He was thoughtful and encouraging, kind and respectful. He honoured her and she adored him, this discoverer of insulin. His idea was truly transcendent. The heavens opened up and showered him with a grace no one else deserved. Now the world is a better place.

"Fred Banting is my hero," Blodwen said. "I love him with all my heart.

Mrs. Banting, you can have his body. I want his soul."

———

Then Fred and Blodwen, through no fault of their own, had sex one day. It was a sudden encounter that changed everything. A wonderful beauty had been born.

They'd been so pure and so chaste in their relationship that they were beyond reproach. They met in public places and coffee shops. They dined at the best restaurants with their bohemian friends. All were writers and artists who raged against the stifling norms that made their city so good. They took the ferry to Toronto Island and strolled the promenade.

Theirs had been a good and honest relationship out in the open, for all to see, not hidden under the sheets in a room with the curtains drawn.

That is, until they met in her apartment one afternoon to discuss the Thomson mystery in detail. They wanted to go over Dr. Banting's writing, and to meditate on the role of the artist in civilizing society.

Blodwen accidentally brushed against him as she was clearing the table. He laid his hand upon her wrist. That's how it all started.

Before she knew it, they were kissing and undressing each other — eagerly, excitedly, not daring to pause or come to their senses. They hurried so guilt wouldn't catch them and stifle their desire. They stumbled toward the bed, laughing nervously, and fumbled their way into wild passionate lovemaking.

There was nothing tantric about their heat-filled sex. It was pure physicality, lusty, intimate, and delightful.

And when they were finished, they were both warm and glowing and happy.

"My God, this feels good," she whispered breathlessly into his ear. They shared a cigarette and rested beside each other, half-covered with the sheet, and at peace with the world.

They finally became lovers and there was no turning back.

"We have to get Marion out of my life, so that I am free to marry you," Banting promised. "But there's only one way for me to divorce her. I need proof of her committing adultery. Someone needs to catch her in the act. We need to introduce her to someone stupid enough to desire her."

"Do you know any charming, single man who would dream of having an affair with the divine Marion Robertson Banting?" Blodwen asked.

"Alex Jackson?" Banting suggested.

Blodwen burst out laughing. "He's probably the only hot-blooded male in Toronto who wouldn't. He may be incorrigible, but he is certainly not the cheating type."

"The two of them would be fighting before the night was out," Banting said. "Neither knows the first thing about compromise. She needs a young guy who can't keep his pecker in his pants. But who?" he asked.

"I have an acquaintance. He's a Director of the Department of Mental Health and a member of the Arts and Letters Club."

"Donat LeBourdais (1887-1964)?" Fred asked.

"You know him?"

" We've had dinner at the club on several occasions. His ideas about improving mental hygiene would make a huge difference in the treatment of Canadian veterans, still beset by the fears and horrors they experienced in the war."

"He also has a reputation for being a flirt," Blodwen said.

"A womanizer? Marion wouldn't risk her reputation with a known philanderer."

"He's very discreet," Blodwen answered. "Women do enjoy his company, though. He makes them feel good about themselves."

"And you?" Fred asked.

"He's not my type," Blodwen answered, giving him a light cuff.

"How'll we get them to meet?" Fred asked.

"It shouldn't be too difficult. I'll have a dinner party at my apartment, a cozy affair, the four of us. I'll invite him. You bring Mrs. Banting, and we'll go dancing afterwards. Let nature take its course. They'll hit it off. They're both caring professionals.

They need time together. We'll eventually have the proof we need. The challenge is not to rush in like fools, but to wait until they make the first move."

"She's a tease and he'll fall for her."

42
Music Where There was no Music Before
January 2, 1932[13]

When you stand straight and tall
Talking gently,
Your long fingers stressing what you say,
And speak of dreams and works, and lives saved by the
uncountable scores
And show me the narrow path by which you rose out of
the darkness of your unhappy loves
Why then in spirit I am crouching at your feet in worship
Because you are my god.

When you sit by the light
Urging and leading me and showing me the stars of effort,
Drawing from out my sleeping soul the stuff with which
we shape our gifts to destiny
Believing in me, driving me, dreaming with me.
Then, dear love, you are my father.

When you come, kind and gentle, firm, insistent,
Stroking my hair, talking of ancient days and glories of the
past,
Of beauty gone and beauty yet to be, of sunsets, dogs, and
war,
Of friendships, travels and adventures, opening the
corridors
of your past and bidding me to wander in at will
Ah! then, how sweet you are my husband.

---

13. See the Banting Papers for the typescript

When in the dusk you lean and seek my lips
Hungry for yours,
When your strong arms enwrap me and press me
Throbbing to your breast
And all is lost, forgotten, in the white flame that wraps us
round
Ah! then you are my lover

When softly by I come and take you in my arms,
Draw your dear head upon my shoulder,
Play in your soft, pale hair with yearning fingers,
Until you close your eyes and rest unmoving there.
When soft I lay my lips against that broad, white brow
As though a sleeping child lay on my breast,
Know you not, then, you are my son?
When in the darkness all around grows still
While the old clock ticks stoutly on
And by the fire you sit, dropping your ashes in a green
bowl,
Reading slowly from a book, pausing to praise or blame
or disagree
While I sit leaning by your shoulder, journeying far in the
train of immortals,
Then: dear, you are my friend.

Blodwen Davies

43
Second Thoughts

Months later, Blodwen could not believe her good fortune — still not pregnant. Banting's condoms really do work. He told her that it was something he learned from the war. The army distributed them freely. To keep the men from contracting gonorrhea and syphilis.

But to be in bed with the man of your dreams and not worry about having a baby. He is so damn fine, Blodwen thought, as she snuggled against him. I do worry about him forgetting, though.

Elizabeth Bagshaw (1881-1982) caused quite the stir in Hamilton, telling women to take charge of their reproductive destinies. The same with Margaret Sanger (1879-1966). They say a cervical cap doesn't require a partner's cooperation.

I better not depend on Fred. It is a duty that I owe myself.

Fred is so accomplished and young at heart. I cannot imagine my life without him. He'll undoubtedly slay another dragon singlehandedly in medicine, while I finish my book about Tom Thomson.

That is, if I don't become pregnant.

Frederick and Blodwen Banting. I don't care if he's branded as a divorced man. It's the price I'll gladly pay to live with the man I love.

Fred lit a cigarette and shared it with Blodwen. "Have they made it in the sack yet?" He asked.

"Mrs. Banting and Mr. LeBourdais?"

"Surely, they've had enough time to be tempted beyond that which we were able." Banting gave Blodwen a kiss. "What's it been? Four months since we celebrated the 11th anniversary of My Idea? That's more than enough time for them to become intimate. The concerts they've attended at Hart House. The long evenings they have enjoyed alone at my place while I've been up in my study, ostensibly working, but in reality, staying out of their way, so that they could go at it like rabbits."

"Have they spent the night at his apartment?" Blodwen asked. "I can't imagine them making love in your house. Does she tiptoe into her room late at night?"

"Not as far as I can tell," Banting replied, "but then, I sleep with my bedroom door closed. They're too damned discreet for such a blatant transgression."

With that, the two got out of Blodwen's bed. She tidied up the room while Banting dressed. He needed to get home to Marion for supper, and a long evening in his study.

"If we want our plan to work, we have to stay out of their way," Blodwen said. "You cannot let down your guard, Freddy, and say anything that you'll later regret. Bide your time and let them come together in their own sweet way."

"You're right, Blodwen. The less time I spend with her the better. When she falls into my trap, I'll go at her with both barrels blazing. I learned in the war that if you want to win, you take no prisoners. I'll give the two of them the hell that they deserve."

"And once your divorce is through, we'll marry and live happily ever after?"

"Absolutely," Banting said. "Marriage, then family, and a happy home. We'll get a nanny and a housekeeper, and you can keep writing."

Blodwen smiled happily at the delicious prospect of having a space of her own for writing her heart's desire.

"And then?" she frowned. Being a mother and the keeper of her husband's home didn't exactly square with her dreams of being Canada's most famous female writer. A sense of foreboding crossed her mind, but she dismissed it out of hand.

This is an inconvenient time for second thoughts.

While Banting hurried home to his wife, Blodwen sat at her desk. She reviewed her notes about Tom Thomson's death. She had all night to go over what she had written and all day to sleep while Banting toiled away in the lab. She'd welcome him tomorrow afternoon, fresh and lovely, and smelling of lavender soap.

44
Breaking Glass

While Blodwen fleshed out the details of Tom Thomson's death with Fred at her side, their plan for Mr. LeBourdais and Mrs. Banting went swimmingly. He was an accomplished dancer and led her on the dance floor until she had no choice but surrender to her chair, collapse laughing, and take a tall drink from his hand.

They went to concerts together and enjoyed each other's company. At New Year's, everyone assumed that Mr. LeBourdais and Mrs. Banting were a pair when, in fact, Dr. Banting and Miss Davies were the ones who danced the night away.

They met again on New Year's Day for tea.

Mr. LeBourdais and Mrs. Banting were slowly and delightfully falling in love but hadn't yet crossed the point of no return. His heart hadn't quite left the fold of the love of his mistress whose identity he steadfastly kept secret, although he was circling ever wider and further away from her arms.

Mrs. Banting was thrilled to have a vibrant social life again. Always dour and still smelling of dog, Fred was no fun to be around.

"Blodwen can have him," she said.

On the evening of February 8th, 1932, Mrs. Banting stood up from the desk in Mr. LeBourdais's apartment.

"Your script, as usual, is thought provoking and interesting," she said as she put on her coat. "I wish someone from the government would listen to your Saturday morning radio show."

"The trauma those men faced during their time in the trenches still haunts them and will for the rest of their lives," Mr. LeBourdais replied. They may have demobilized in 1918 and 1919, but they and their families are now engaged in a battle that will certainly destroy them if they don't receive the help they need."

184

"Psychological wounding is as invidious as physical, but not as immediately obvious," Mrs. Banting said. "Unfortunately, mental illness is stigmatised, and hospital staff aren't prepared to treat injuries they cannot see."

Suddenly, there was a knocking on the door and the sharp sound of shattering glass.

"Someone's breaking in!" Mr. LeBourdais yelled, grabbing a poker from the coal bin beside the heater and rushing to the door.

A gloved hand whacked broken glass from the pane and reached in to turn open the door handle.

Banting burst into the apartment and slammed Mr. LeBourdais against the wall, knocking a crystal vase filled with fresh-cut flowers to the floor, the glass exploding into a thousand shards.

Marion began to scream. "Fred, what are you doing?"

"You whore," he replied.

"You son-of-a-bitch," he said as he throttled LeBourdais. "I've finally caught you in the act."

"Sir, unhand me! I have done nothing of the sort."

LeBourdais struggled to free himself from the much larger, stronger Banting. "We have been talking about my radio script."

"Shut the hell up!" Banting roared.

"Stop it, Fred! You don't have to do this," Marion cried. "Let's talk."

One of the detectives pulled Banting away from the shaken LeBourdais.

"You can't take a dead man to court, Doctor."

Banting let go of LeBourdais, who was gasping for breath.

"Please, Fred," Marion said. "I beg you."

He pulled a piece of typed paper out of his pocket.

"Sign this, you bastard." He shook the document at LeBourdais.

"I've caught you having an affair with my wife."

"Fred," Marion pleaded. "Calm down. Get control of yourself. Give us a few minutes?" she asked the detectives. "Please."

They forced LeBourdais to his feet and escorted him from the room.

"Mr. LeBourdais and I haven't done a thing. I was here reading the script from his Saturday morning radio broadcast. Which, as you know, I wasn't able to listen to at home. I was with you, looking after Bill."

"Get off it, Marion. You've been having sex with this sorry-excuse-of-a-man ever since the first time you laid eyes on him."

"Don't be ridiculous Fred. He's Miss Davies's friend. The two of you introduced us. Remember?"

"No court in the land will let you weasel out of this one. You've been making a fool out of me ever since our wedding. Everyone knows you're a slut."

"I'm not listening to anymore of your insults, Fred. I am innocent of whatever vain imagining you think I am guilty of committing. If anyone has jeopardized our marriage, you have. I know that Miss Davies isn't your first diversion."

Banting raised his hand to hit her and then thought better of it.

"I'm divorcing you for being unfaithful to me, Marion. I now have all the proof that I need."

"But we haven't done a thing," Marion insisted. "As God is my witness."

Banting hurried to the door.

"Let's get out of here," he yelled. The detectives chased after him.

Marion hurried to Mr. LeBourdais. He wrapped his arms around her, while she sobbed uncontrollably.

"I didn't sign that ridiculous paper of his," LeBourdais said. "You and I have done nothing wrong."

Marion pulled away.

"I need some time to think. There's no use talking to Fred when he's like this. There's no saying what he might do."

"It's not safe for you to go home," LeBourdais said. "But you can't stay here. You should take a room at the Royal York. Make that idiot pay for humiliating you."

"No, I better talk to Sir William Mulock. He's the Chief Justice, the Chancellor of the University, and a close friend. It's only 8:30. He won't mind me dropping in unannounced. He'll give me the advice I need. And a room for the night. I don't want to exacerbate what is already a nightmare."

LeBourdais walked with her down to where her car was parked. When she drove off, he hurried back to his apartment.

"What's all the ruckus?" Mr. Bartsch the building manager asked, as LeBourdais climbed the stairs.

"A huge misunderstanding," he replied. "I'll get this all fixed up tomorrow."

He found a piece of pine board and screwed it across the broken panel. "This'll do until the repairman arrives."

He made sure the door was locked, and he straightened out the mess. He swept the glass and gathered the pages of the script that had been strewn across the floor.

It wasn't too late for Marion to call on Sir William in her distress. She knew that he would welcome her into his home. They were family friends. He waited for her to explain what happened.

"This is a scandal that'll blow up in everyone's faces," he said. "No one will emerge unscathed. If word gets out, even if you aren't the guilty party, your reputation will be ruined. We have to keep your name out of the papers at all costs. Let me call Bill Blatz (1895-1964). You can see him in the morning. But you better spend the night here. It wouldn't be wise for you to go home tonight."

"Thank you, Sir William. I was about to ask."

"No need," he said. "What are friends for, but to help each other during times of need? You are always welcome."

Early the next morning, Marion met with Dr. Blatz, the director of the University of Toronto's Institute of Child Study.

"There's only one way for this to go away without it getting into the papers," he said. "You must accept a no-contest divorce."

"You mean admit to committing adultery when Mr. LeBourdais and I did no such thing?"

She couldn't quite believe her ears.

"Let me remind you, Professor Blatz, Dr. Banting has sinned far more against me than I ever have against him."

"But no one will believe you, my dear. Dr. Banting is loved and revered the world over. His word is pure gold and yours is tarnished silver. He could probably get away with murder and no one would think the worse of him."

"What a travesty," Marion said. "He is the guilty party. I am innocent."

"A no-contest divorce is the only way you'll survive this scandal. In exchange, we'll get Dr. Banting to agree to a financial settlement. Of course, you'll get the house, custody of your son, and monthly support payments."

"Do you honestly think Fred will comply with them?"

"He has his reputation to think of and that of the university. He is well known across Canada and will not want his name to be pulled through the mud."

"I'm afraid that he will do something foolish and make this worse than it need be," Marion said. "He always does."

45
The Defence

Dr. William Robertson, a worthy citizen of Elora, Ontario, kindly physician, and Marion's father, flew into a rage when he opened the newspaper to the Classifieds section. He was so upset that he spilled his coffee.

"Vera! Get me a cloth! Where are you, Florence, when I need you?"

His youngest daughter handed him a tea towel, and he soaked the coffee up. "What has that damn fool gone and done?"

"What do you mean, father?" Vera asked. She hoped against hope that it wasn't her brother-in-law he was raging about.

"Blown the whole thing completely apart! Look here!"

He shoved the paper toward her. "The idiot put in a notice that he won't be responsible for any more of Marion's debts. Then all our effort to keep this sorry mess under wraps has come to naught."

Vera took the towel from father and rinsed it out in the sink. She handed it back to him and he continued wiping the table.

"What he's done is confirm the front-page news in the *Toronto Star* about their marriage troubles and the raid upon Mr. LeBourdais's apartment."

"Poor Marion," Vera said. "Now the whole world will assume that she is the adulteress because the Discoverer of Insulin could never be so vile."

"Her decision not to defend herself in the divorce proceedings is an admission of guilt," Dr. Robertson said. "They all say she is a trollop, who could never stay home where she belonged. That she was always the flighty socialite out on the town while her husband toiled the evening hours away in his study, making the world a better place."

"She's been found guilty," Vera said. "Any question of her innocence has been dismissed out of hand."

"They're implying my daughter was never fit enough to marry the great Frederick Grant Banting. He did not deserve the ignominy she has brought upon him."

"I understand her reasoning for not wanting to defend," Vera replied. "She didn't want to upset the delicate financial terms they had decided upon. After all, Banting agreed to give her the house, car, pay her $250 a month, and grant her custody of young Bill."

"Do you honestly think that fool will remain true to his word?" Dr. Robertson thundered. "Don't be so naïve! At the first opportunity, he'll refuse the terms and renegotiate. He is too pig-headed to let this whole thing disappear into the good night."

"Fred will have his pound of flesh," Vera agreed. "That will be the undoing of us all. You know as well as I that he doesn't act rationally."

"As long as we have known him, his first instinct is to explode, wreak havoc with everything he says and does, and then to brood angrily until another thing sets him off. Sober second thought has never been his forte."

"Marion has to think about Bill, Vera said. Could you imagine growing up in a house with a father like that? She has to protect him and get out while she still can."

"She is strong and capable," Dr. Robertson said. "Your mother and I raised both of you to be independently minded. Marion will make her own way once she gets her feet on the ground."

"Then you better talk to Mr. LeBourdais. He was trying to protect Marion when he agreed not to defend himself against Banting's ridiculous charges. Talk to him, father. If he stands up for himself, maybe Marion will have a chance. Maybe we can salvage your grandson's childhood and give him a legacy that will make him proud."

With that, Dr. Robertson took leave of his younger daughter. He put a notice on his office door, cancelled his appointments until further notice, and drove into Toronto. When he got into the city, he phoned Mr. LeBourdais and made arrangements to see him.

"I refused to sign Banting's ridiculous statement," Mr. LeBourdais insisted. "He doesn't have any proof. Those detectives lied in their testimony. I didn't defend myself because that's what Mrs. Banting wanted. I hoped to save her reputation. She doesn't deserve any of this. That bastard Banting and his mistress Davies set us up, I'm sure. They duped us.

When the detectives shattered the glass in the door to my apartment, Mrs. Banting was standing at my desk. She was putting on her coat and was about to leave. That she and I were on the couch, with her dress above her knee and my fly unbuttoned, is a complete fabrication.

They embellished their testimony so that Banting would get his money's worth. He must have paid them handsomely to perjure themselves.

At no time have Mrs. Banting and I ever had improper relations. She came over that evening to read the radio script for my broadcast. We enjoy each other's company, but Mrs. Banting and I are not intimate.

I have a wife I do not love in California, and a lover here in Toronto I adore. While I couldn't care less about the first, I would never cheat on the second. If I could, I'd marry her tomorrow, but the Church forbids divorce.

Mrs. Banting is a good friend and I feel sorry for her. Her husband is a beast of a man. I cannot bear how he treats her and would do anything to protect her. Even risk my reputation so that she could be safe."

"Have you been reading the papers?" Dr. Robertson asked. "Roy Greenaway now has it out for Banting, and that cub reporter Gordon Sinclair (1900-1984) is digging up all the muck he can.

They will do everything they can to destroy Banting's reputation. The rest of us will be taken down as well."

"I heard that Sinclair tried to interview Banting while he was up on a ladder, painting his house. Banting almost hit the cheeky kid when he flung a pail of paint at him. Then, Sinclair tried to interview Banting at a football game practice. The players circled Banting and little Sinclair thought better of asking any more questions. He hightailed it out of there before he was tackled and thrown to the ground."

"All I know is that Marion's reputation is ruined and there is no recourse for her, but to escape Toronto," Dr. Robertson said. "She needs to start a new life, where the divorce isn't the talk of the town. She could go back to her maiden name.

Mrs. Robertson doesn't have the instant recognition that comes with continuing as Mrs. Banting."

"Perhaps she is reluctant for Bill's sake."

"Young Bill growing up with the stigma of divorced parents. He'll have a rough go of it."

"He's not the only one."

46
A New Day

Marion and her sister Vera were seated at a table in the Arcadian Court, an Art Deco restaurant on the eighth floor of the Simpson's Building in downtown Toronto. The restaurant held 1,300 people on the main floor and in the mezzanine. It had wrought-iron railings around the gallery, where businessmen struck deals, drank whiskey, and smoked fine cigars.

The main floor where women were allowed to dine without escorts was decorated in beige and turquoise. It had 40-foot ceilings, tall colonnades, arched windows, and huge chandeliers. It was a glorious place for the two sisters to mark the end of a terrible period in their lives and the beginning of something new.

"Such a grand place," Vera said. "And affordable. I hear the chicken pot pie is marvelous. We should eat here once a week."

"We could," Marion said. "As soon as I get my first paycheque. Fred promised to support Bill, but I don't trust him to keep his end of the bargain. He has a long history of reneging on past agreements. I need to pay my own way."

"It's a matter of honour, isn't it?" Vera asked. "Him paying his share? It's his duty as Bill's father."

"There is no honour when he gets into one of his rages. A smart woman should have a career before she walks down the aisle. A bank account in her name will give her the freedom to choose what she thinks is best for her and her children. A woman without means has no choice at all."

"Men in poverty also have no choice," Vera said. "Look at the soup lines. Nearly everyone is unemployed."

"People need the dignity of a living wage," Marion said. "Work is good for the soul. A paycheque that puts a roof over one's head and food on the table is an incalculable treasure."

"Aren't men supposed to be the sole breadwinners for their families?" Vera asked.

"That's what they keep telling us, but I'm not so sure. What happens if the man gets laid off, or becomes sick, and can't work anymore? Two salaries are better than one, good insurance when hard times come."

"But if a woman brings home a paycheque, won't she displace her husband as the head of the family?"

"Not necessarily," Marion said. "Besides, two heads are better than one."

"Men are supposed to be spiritual leaders whereas women and children are to submit to their authority. Isn't that what they teach in the church?"

"Depends on who is doing the teaching," Marion said. "All I know is that it is never good for a woman to be entirely dependent upon a man. Only if she has the means to support herself financially can she be an equal partner. Free choice and treating each other with kindness seem like good theology to me."

"Can you quote chapter and verse?"

"No, but it is common sense."

"If the husband works, the wife can stay home to create a nurturing atmosphere for the children."

"In this time of low pay and long hours?" Marion asked. "Then the man is away from home too much. Dr. Blatz says that both parents are essential for providing a child with the security he or she needs to grow into an independent adult.

It takes time together to raise healthy children. One parent always away is never a good thing."

The sisters watched couples chatting happily and dreaming about long lives together. Smartly dressed sommeliers opened bottles of wine. Beautiful servers carried orders to tables. Young bussers cleared away dirty dishes and glasses, laid fresh table linens, and reset the tables in a friendly, but efficient manner.

"The world should run so smoothly," Marion thought.

The sisters forgot their troubles and enjoyed their brief reprieve from the dark world around them.

Caught between her father in Elora and Marion in Toronto, Vera couldn't be in two places at once. At home, she helped her father, who was shaken from the Court's decision to side with Banting. Here in Toronto, she listened to her sister sort out her problems.

"Of course, I can't go back to working as an x-ray technician like I did when I was single," Marion said. "After the divorce? The hospital wouldn't have me."

"It may have abandoned you, but not a single one of your friends has. We know Fred too well. You are not alone."

"I have Bill for the week. Then, it's okay. It's on weekends he's away that I'm the worst."

"You'll just have to come to Elora, or I'll come here. Together we can get through this."

"Dr. Blatz says that couples shouldn't stay together for the sake of the children. Strife and conflict are never good. Lasting differences cannot be resolved through bickering. Strife ruins the magic of childhood. Kids need to play outside exploring ravines and woods. They need to catch frogs and kill ants with magnifying glasses. They need to fill their lungs with fresh air and ride their bikes pell-mell down long hills.

They do not need angry parents being mean to each other. It's no way to start your life, being afraid of what your parents will do behind closed doors."

"So, you're taking the job then?" Vera asked.

"I think so. Simpson's has offered me a position in customer service. If I know anything, it's how to make people feel good about themselves. That's the first step in finding solutions to problems. Take people's minds off the difficulties they're facing, even if it's just for a moment. Give them space to breathe and help them settle down. Then, work towards a solution."

"There's no telling which way you'll go, Marion. The world is yours if you're brave enough to go out and get it."

"The manager says there's lots of room for advancement. Once I learn the ropes here, I'll be next in line for a promotion. A position heading Customer Service may be opening in Oakville. They've ear-marked it for me if I want it."

"And your home on Bedford Street?"

"I've had enough of all it represents. I'll sell it. The last thing I want is to end up like Miss Havisham, pining for lost love."

Vera signaled to the server. They each tallied their share of the bill, put their cash on the table, and made their way out of the restaurant.

Marion adjusted a blue scarf over her shoulders. She stepped into the sun that had stretched out over the long afternoon she and Vera spent together. It was now dropping into the western bay. Tomorrow would be a new day and she was ready to face whatever came before her.

47
Starting Over

"Damn, she's a beautiful woman," Fred Banting thought as he gave Dr. Priscilla White (1900-1989) a long and savouring assessment. She looked good both coming and going.

Banting first met her in Boston while visiting Elliott Joslin (1869-1962) at his diabetic clinic at the Deaconess Hospital. Dr. White was in her late twenties — pretty, with a fine figure. She was interested in everything he had to say, unlike his two-faced bitch of an ex, whose eyes would immediately glaze over as soon as he opened his mouth. Or Blodwen, who reminded him of everything he was not. Her fawning had become so sickly sweet, he could hardly stand to be around her anymore.

After the divorce, Banting needed some time alone, so he went on a sketching holiday to the Massachusetts coastline. He briefly considered inviting Alex Jackson to join him, but immediately thought better of it. In spite of their long friendship, they did not indulge in each other's inner turmoil.

Theirs was a gruff and manly camaraderie that never got to the heart of the matter. They rough-and-tumbled through life together and shared rollicking good times as mates — drinking whiskey and roaring, not whimpering like those limp-wrists they saw at the university and despised.

The sea, sky, and sound of squawking gulls along with the crashing of waves along the Atlantic coast, were a welcome relief from the cacophony that assaulted Banting back in Toronto. He breathed in the ripe, fermented umami of the briny, sour sea air, and failed once again to paint the landscape that surrounded him. "Where was Jackson when he needed him?"

It felt good to be alive again and freed from the shackles that bound him to Marion. He mixed his palette with greys, blues, browns, and dull greens, and found some solace in the tumult of his life. He loved being in complete control of the empty board on his easel.

When he was ready to be around people he knew, he dropped in on Dr. Joslin and then, the lovely Dr. White returned his gaze. He decided to stay put for a while, even though Dr. Joslin's brusque manner was rather off-putting.

Observing Dr. White's high-heeled clicking efficiency and encyclopedic knowledge, Banting thought immediately of the flat-shoed and sensible Sadie Gairns. Dr. Joslin used Dr. White as a ready reference for everything, the way Banting depended on Miss Gairns for organizing his personal life and career.

Dr. White reappeared a year later in Montreal. Instead of attending the seminal paper that Israel Rabinowitch (1890-1983) delivered on gas toxicology, Banting took her sleigh-riding. Oh my, the fun they had together.

"Dr. White," Joslin later said. "A word to the wise?"

"Certainly, sir."

"He's not the man you think he is."

"Pardon?"

"Haven't you read the papers? What would the hardworking, thrifty, no-nonsense people back in Boston say about you wasting your life on him? That you should be ashamed of yourself! That's what they'd say. He's damaged goods.

That's what they think. Banting's on the rebound from a painful divorce and he will ruin you. That's what they'd warn you."

Dr. White was dumbfounded. She had fallen for the charming Dr. Banting because he had given her young diabetic patients the prospect of long and happy lives. Without insulin, they would have starved to death.

She loved him for the contribution he made to medical science. He made millions of lives all the better.

"If you value your career, you better forget about him," Joslin said. "He'll ruin your reputation if word gets out."

Joslin was morally outraged at the thought of a Nobel Laureate being found guilty of infidelity. Even if Banting were innocent, he was still responsible for the failure of his marriage. Mrs. Banting would not have cheated on her husband if he had loved her completely. Now that Joslin saw Banting chasing after a woman half his age, he knew beyond a doubt that Banting was the guilty party.

Besides, Dr. White was a charge under his care. He had to look out for her best interests. Heaven knows what she'd be up to without him.

It had never occurred to Priscilla that Fred's flirting with her might jeopardize her work with patients. He flattered her and was interested in everything she had to say. It felt good to be taken seriously and not treated as an underling.

However, she worked too hard to get where she was to consider any more toying with him. She had a duty of care for her patients that she could not ignore.

If Dr. Joslin thought Banting an incorrigible reprobate, she better pay attention. He was her supervisor, and she valued his opinion. Besides, he signed her cheques and she needed to make a living.

She had no choice; Dr. Joslin laid down the law. Banting would have to look elsewhere for love and happiness. She was not to be had, even if the briefest of these pleasures had been entirely of her own choosing.

Banting had abandoned Edith for Marion, Marion for Blodwen, and now was hot on the trail for Priscilla. It was a pattern that became abundantly clear when he returned to Toronto.

When Blodwen realized that he would not make good on his promise to marry her, she took matters into her own hands. She may have been an idiot to fall for a married man, but she was not the first nor would she be the last.

Falling in love is a visceral response that sometimes should be acted upon. Other times not.

48
Blodwen

After Banting, Blodwen hoped she'd be a more discriminating lover, but wasn't so sure. She had responded emotionally to him. Next time? She'd follow her intellect. She wouldn't be fooled again. Once was enough. She learned her lesson.

She looked at the cheque that Freddy had cut with her name on it. Knowing what she now knew about him, she hurried to the bank and cashed it before he had second thoughts and cancelled it.

With Priscilla ignoring his calls, Banting had tried once again to reel in Blodwen. He gave her a bit of money to help her through a rough patch. She kept it, she wasn't that stupid, but she showed him the door.

Banting paid her off with the proviso that she kept her mouth shut. And she did. She had an idea of what to do with the extra money in her account. Invest it in her career and enjoy a welcome return. Wise is as wise does.

"I am broken-hearted and filled with so much pain that I never want to see you again," she said to Banting. "Nothing that I have received from you compensates for the misery you brought down upon me. You know how to seduce a woman, but you do not know how to love her.

Why have you punished me for loving you? How can you be so cruel? I gave you my heart and you took advantage of me. Please do not try to see me again. There is nothing you can say or do that will make me change my mind."

Banting elbowed his way through her outpouring of grief, but she gave him no quarter. "Blodwen," he said, reaching out to touch her.

She slapped his hand away, infuriated with the man.

"You are tone deaf," she said. "I will have nothing more to do with you. I know better than anyone else the humanity, awareness, intelligence, and latent power that is within you. I idealized you as a great man. I thought you were tempered by wisdom, gentleness, and human richness.

Insulin has given you the authority and opportunity to influence the hearts and minds of people all over the world. But you have blocked the channels of your intelligence with your grudges and rancour. You are less than you could be.

You are easily angered and slow to forgive. There is so much more that you could do if you showed grace and kindness to friends and strangers.

Try to make peace with those around you, Fred. You might not have this chance again."

Of course, Banting did not listen to Blodwen. He walked out of her life, and she slammed the door on his heels. She escaped to Buffalo and New York to get away from the press and find some peace of mind for herself. She needed to immerse herself in her work.

She visited the Library of Congress in Washington, DC where she discovered the letters of Margaret Congalton Hall (1799-1876), wife of Basil Hall (1788-1844), a Scottish naval officer and politician who kept journals that formed the basis for a series of books about his travels.

While Basil Hall's writing was published in 1829 and his work later housed in the Library of Congress, Margaret Hall's letters were passed down through the family from generation to generation. Stored in trunks and attics, they eventually ended up in Washington, where they caught Blodwen's attention.

"Here's a woman living in the shadow of a great man," she said. "Her story needs to be told."

Margaret Hall's letters differed from her husband's, in that she named people and places that he referred to guardedly and obliquely. He had to be politic because he was writing for posterity. She did not. Her work was a private reflection that she thought would never see the light of day.

Mrs. Hall was a woman of fashion and *au courant,* a welcome relief for the lonely wives consigned to the colonies because of their husbands' postings. The letters of introduction that Captain Hall carried with him guaranteed a warm reception from Upper Canada's ruling class. Mrs. Hall saw the country from a woman's perspective.

She and her husband were devoted to one another and were the best of companions. Their journey through Upper Canada was a prelude to the years of travel that they would later take. Packing children and servants, they wandered like aristocratic gypsies from the Mediterranean to remote German principalities, back and forth across a restless Europe in the 1830s.

Her letters give her a niche in history as an observer of royalist and republican sentiment. They are as important a contribution to the social history of the first 50 years of Upper Canada's history as those of Elizabeth Simcoe (1762-1850), Susanna Moodie (1803-1885), Catherine Parr Traill (1802-1899), and Anna Brownell Jameson (1794-1860).

The appearance of "Margaret Hall Discovers Upper Canada" in *The Canadian Geographical Journal* was Blodwen's first publication after her affair with Banting.

Resettling in Toronto, she struggled to find a publisher for her biography of Tom Thomson. Of course, no press wanted to touch her. She sullied the reputation of the most famous man in Canada. Now, she wanted to ruin the reputation of an obscure, if influential, Canadian artist.

"Don't be absurd! Let Tom Thomson rest in peace," the publishers told her when they rejected her book. "He died of natural causes at Canoe Lake."

They insisted that he was not murdered, but that he drowned unseen. "Don't go digging up his skeleton. Hasn't the family suffered enough? Leave his good mother alone.

We won't encourage your nonsense with our coin," they all decided, closing ranks, and shutting the voice of another good woman.

"No one wants to read another rehash of an old story, poorly told," they said.

Thomson may have been mentioned in Fred Housser's *A Canadian Art Movement,* but he was not a household name. Besides, the Group of Seven was embroiled in a scandal of its own making.

Lawren Harris ran off with Bess Housser, when she discovered her husband was having an affair with her best friend, Yvonne McKague. Rumours reverberated throughout the town with talk of the realigned couples sharing a house together.

"What on earth is happening to this world?" everyone asked. Tom Thomson was old news, and this scandal was too hot for the press to ignore.

Blodwen Davies reminded Toronto the Good of the shameful pleasure it had in reading about the moral failings of artists and scientists alike. They savoured each dollop with a spoon and sought God's forgiveness in church on Sundays.

Torontonians could easily forgive Banting for having an affair. After all, he was just being a man, but not Miss Davies. That she wasn't the most beautiful woman in the glamour pages testified to her diabolical powers.

"If she could bring down the good doctor, what could she do to mere mortals?" The men were enthralled, the women mesmerized.

Blodwen used Banting's pittance to pay for the self-publishing costs of her 1935 book. Where else could she get the money? From her income as a freelance writer paid in pennies? Her father? Hardly.

Blodwen Davies may have been naïve in the ways of married men and their mistresses, but she was not stupid. Her affair with

Fred Banting did not ruin her life. It hurt her, but it did not prevent her from finding her own way.

She survived the foolishness of youth, went on to do her own work, and live her own life in her own way because she was a responsible and determined human being.

Banting never had any intention of marrying Blodwen. To him, she was an available skirt when Marion refused to return his affection. She stroked his ego, but he soon tired of her devotion. She was worse than a soppy lap dog.

Now that he was free to look elsewhere, he wasn't going to settle for a transcendental theosophist, whose single-minded ambition was to write about Canada. He wanted someone who would bear him a houseful of children. He had a son, but he wanted daughters. Lots of them. And he couldn't wait any longer.

He needed a dutiful wife who would be a loving mother to his children and was willing to overlook the fact that he was a divorcee.

Blodwen did not fit the bill.

Part Four

49
A Murder Mystery

After Banting, Blodwen turned her attention to Tom Thomson and his death at Canoe Lake. Here was a man whose memory will live on in Canadian history. She would make sure of it.

What I know for certain about Tom Thomson is that he painted in Algonquin Park during the spring and autumn. He fished and canoed in the summer. He drowned in Canoe Lake on July 8th, 1917, at about 1:00 P.M. in the afternoon.

The facts, as spare as they are, are indisputable. However, they leave enough room for speculation and interpretation. I can tell my own story, not his. The mystery of his dying has made his death memorable. His work depicts the struggle to survive. It tells the story of Canada.

While at Canoe Lake, Thomson often stayed at Mowatt Lodge, which Shannon and Annie Fraser managed. He helped Mrs. Fraser with the laundry, cleanup, and some of the cooking. "He is a useful man to have around," Mrs. Fraser said as her husband snarled and deducted a percentage from his bill.

Shannon preferred customers who paid the going rate, but when the lodge had rooms to spare and no one to fill them, a discount for services rendered was better than nothing. On the rainiest of days, half-full was preferable to half-empty.

In good weather, Thomson usually camped at Heyhurst Point. In bad, he busied himself around the Lodge, doing whatever needed to be done.

Mark Robinson (1867-1955) the assistant Park Superintendent said that Thomson had been painting a daily record of the weather that year. A sketch a day, from the middle of April to the middle of June. He had to quit when the black flies were at their worst and the trees were fully leafed out. There may be a thousand shades of green in summer, but it makes a pretty dull painting.

In art, there must be contrast. In contrast, there must be drama. And in drama, there must be struggle . Without struggle, there is no interest. Without a clash of wills there is no story. That is the heart of the matter. That is the mystery I need to uncover.

Thomson was a great fisherman, expert paddler, strong swimmer, and experienced woodsman. He knew how to survive in the bush. He couldn't have drowned in that shallow, calm lake.

He and Robinson were vying for the big trout they had seen at the foot of the Joe Lake Dam. It eluded both of them. They wanted more than anything to have the bragging rights for catching it.

On the morning of the 8th, Thomson rose rather late and breakfasted with Mrs. Fraser at Mowatt Lodge. She thought him the handsomest thing she'd seen in a long time. God, she would have bedded that man in a heartbeat, if only he'd asked. But he didn't. He was as skittish as a colt when it came to women.

He was in good spirits and came in freshly shaved, his hair brushed and shining. He sat with her at the table, eating and talking in a leisurely way. Then, he lit a cigarette and wandered out while Mrs. Fraser returned to her duties, washing up and kneading dough.

Thomson and Fraser walked over to Joe Lake Portage to have another try at landing the trout before Robinson caught it. Again, they failed. By then, it was nearly noon.

"I know what I'll do," Thomson said. "I'll portage over to Gill Lake and get a big trout and lay it on Mark's doorstep, so that he'll find it the first thing in the morning. He'll think I've beat him. What a joke that'll be."

After he and Fraser returned to Mowatt Lodge, Thomson put his canoe in the water. Fraser went up to the Lodge to fetch him a freshly baked loaf of bread. Thomson stowed it away, with a can of corn syrup, under the bow of the canoe. He took no other provisions because he intended to return to the Lodge later that day.

Thomson left Mowatt Lodge dock around 12:30 P.M. that Sunday. He paddled down the lake, just off Little Wapomeo Island where there was an unoccupied cottage just back from the shore. He then paddled into the stretch of water between Little and Big Wapomeo.

Nine days later, searchers found his canoe and pulled his body from the water. His watch had stopped shortly after 1:00 P.M. It was not a ten-minute paddle from Mowatt Lodge dock to the place where his body was found.

On Monday morning, Martin Blecher, the German-American who spent several summers with his family at Canoe Lake, reported that he had seen a green canoe floating between the islands on Sunday afternoon at 3:00 P.M. He didn't report it because he thought it was one that had drifted away from Joe Lake Portage and belonged to Mr. Colson from the Algonquin Hotel.

However, it was a wood-canvas Chestnut canoe. Thomson's friends recognized it as his when Mr. Blecher commented on the metal strip on its keel. A search party went out immediately.

No one believed Thomson could have drowned. He was a powerful swimmer. He had been traveling in a light east wind with a gentle rain. They assumed he went ashore and had fallen and injured himself. That seemed the most logical to them.

Robinson tramped the woods for seven days, whistling and calling, thinking Thomson was laid up somewhere near the shore. The Blecher family searched the lake from Mowatt Lodge to Tea Lake Dam.

Dr. Goldwin Howland (1875-1950) of Toronto arrived a day or two after Thomson's death to occupy the Taylor Statten cottage on Little Wapomeo Island. On Monday morning, July 16th, he discovered Thomson's body when it became entangled with his fishing line. He informed the authorities who towed the corpse to an isolated spot near the shore on Big Wapomeo Island and anchored it there until the coroner could arrive and complete his examination.

Dr. Ranney (1876-1944) the coroner from North Bay was notified. A train was scheduled to depart on Tuesday at 14:10 and reach Canoe Lake at 21:12, seven hours later. He packed an overnight bag.

On Tuesday morning, Robinson removed Thomson's decomposing body from the water. Dr. Howland made an examination. In a statement he provided to T. E. McKee (1873-1943), the North Bay Crown Attorney, he wrote that an undertaker had arrived from Kearney. The body was embalmed on the island and transferred to the mainland on Tuesday morning, where it was buried on the side of a small hill.

When Dr. Ranney arrived later that evening, he was surprised that the burial had already taken place. Before departing, he had wired his arrival time at the Canoe Lake station. Those in charge were unable to find any trace of such a message being filed, and the telegraph files for that year have since been destroyed.

No one knows if that telegraph was ever received, or if it was, why someone would not act upon it.

It added to the mystery surrounding Tom Thomson's death.

The inquest was held in the Blecher home instead of in the hotel. The Blechers showed their German hospitality by serving beer and cigars to those who attended. When Robinson realized that George Rowe (1883-1969?), who had towed the body to shore, had not been summoned to the inquest, he paddled across the lake to get him.

Nothing later came out at the trial of the violent quarrels between Martin Blecher and Tom Thomson. Thomson had written to his friend Arthur Lismer in Halifax about his strained relationship with Blecher, but the letters have not been preserved. Thomson was unhappy — he had wanted to enlist but had been turned away. It rankled Thomson to no end that Mr. Blecher was a draft-evader from the States. Being German in British Canada didn't help Blecher either.

Thomson's friend, the Toronto ophthalmologist Dr. James MacCallum, had pressured Tom not to enlist. He was becoming celebrated as an artist and MacCallum knew that he would soon be a legend. He could not be lost, battling in the trenches. He had too much to offer as a living, productive, and innovative painter of Canadian landscapes. "It's not your death that counts, but the life of service you lead while you are alive," MacCallum said.

Martin Blecher is the one who originally said that Thomson's legs were bound together with a piece of rubber. This statement is untrue. He also stated that Thomson's body was cramped and rigid, which is also untrue. He is a liar and should not be trusted.

The chief fact that prevented a suicide ruling was the four-inch bruise along the right side of his temple. It should have been obvious. Within ten minutes of him leaving the Mowatt Lodge dock, just out of sight of the cottages, he was struck over the head with a weapon that caused blood to ooze from his ear. Corpses do not bruise, and they do not bleed. It would have only come about while he was still alive.

The waters of Canoe Lake are mild enough for swimming all July and August. Yet Thomson's body, which should have floated to the surface in two or three days, was still submerged nine days later.

The only explanation is that someone tied a trawling line around his ankle and anchored it underwater.

Thomson was buried on the edge of a sandy hill, not far from Mowatt Lodge. A few days later, his family ordered Franklin W. Churchill, the undertaker from Huntsville, to exhume the body, seal it in a metal casket, and transport it to Owen Sound.

Churchill arrived but Robinson was not informed until later. He rose at dawn, went to the cemetery, and discovered that Mr. Churchill had already tidied the grave site up and placed the body in the casket.

Robinson doesn't believe that the body was ever disturbed. It seems impossible that a single man could do that much work in such short order. Even the flowers that had been laid on the grave at the funeral had not been moved.

George Rowe accompanied the undertaker to Mowatt Lodge. He recalled the undertaker being anxious to be alone and refusing all offers of help. Shannon Fraser, who delivered the man and the casket up to the spot, arranged to answer the undertaker's signal when he finished the exhumation.

He recalls that he was not long back at the hotel before he heard the gunshot and returned at once to load up the casket.

None of those at Canoe Lake believe that Thomson's body was ever removed from the grave. There is no variation in opinion in any of those who have been questioned. Under the family's directive, however, Thomson's sealed casket was loaded on the train and transported to Leith, where it was buried in the family plot.

Even though a stone has been erected over the grave, no one knows for certain whether the body is buried there or at Canoe Lake. The family's refusal to have the grave opened up has made Tom Thomson's death an enduring mystery.

I would like to investigate the death and tell the story of Tom Thomson's life.

The burying place at Canoe Lake is not a consecrated cemetery. There is room for six or so graves. I believe that Thomson was buried outside the fenced area. There was no room for his body in the enclosure.

Everyone who knew Thomson at the time of his death is still living. His family are aware of the circumstances. They debated taking action to clear up the situation, but it would have disturbed their aged mother. They decided to let the matter drop.

The quarrelsome Blechers are still in the same cottage at Canoe Lake.

I believe that the opening of Thomson's original grave at Canoe Lake would lay to rest the persistent rumors that claim he still lies there. His family must now regret his removal to Leith and would have preferred knowing he had not been disturbed. Any action that proves Thomson died as the result of foul play would remove the stigma of suicide from his name.

Martin Blecher is responsible for spreading those rumours. The people who knew Thomson would never believe that he killed himself. He was a sensitive and lonely soul, who was passionately devoted to the wilderness. If he had been in a mood to take his own life, he would have gone off on a trip into the wilderness, never to be heard from again.

It is utterly at variance with his character to suppose that in a fit of depression, he would have tried to commit suicide ten minutes from his own camp.

I am certain he was murdered.

50
His Mantle Blue

"I'm here," Tom Thomson shouted into the wind. "Do your worst, you fury. I'll not be cowed by you." The cold rain lashed down hard upon him.

He settled in the lee of a giant stump from a blown over maple, a defiant fist-less arm raised high, truncated, and broken; silent and stubborn, a furious shadow of what once was; but still a thing not to be ignored.

A force in nature.

Tom Thomson, Lawren Harris, and James MacCallum had come to Cauchon Lake in northeast Algonquin Park to paint, but a storm blew in. They had to take cover in an old cabin.

MacCallum went immediately to the stove. "This'll need cleaning before I can use it."

He found a shovel, whisk, and pail, and got to work emptying the ash-filled fire box.

Thomson dug out his paint box that held three 8 x10-inch panels of birch. He used its lid as an easel to hold a panel upright, and the lower part of the box as a palette. He checked his fishing creel to see if he had the paints, thinner, and brushes he needed.

"What are you waiting for, Harris?" He asked. "If you want to paint your Canada, you need to expose yourself to the wind and rain. Let's go!"

"But the rain's pelting down," Harris protested.

"Soldiers in the trenches are slogging through mud right now and you're worried about a little shower? Come on, man! You need to toughen up. We're fighting the elements, not the Bosch. Don't you ever forget this! Ours is a battle. We cannot cower inside where it is warm and comfortable. It's to the breach or die."

Harris wasn't convinced. He liked to paint in his studio while wearing a suit, tie, and brogues. The sunlight soaring in from the ceiling-high windows and alighting softly upon his canvas. A bird easily frightened off.

Much to his wife Trixie's[14] dismay, he played Edvard Grieg, Fritz Kreisler, and Jean Sibelius at full volume on his phonograph. As recordings improved in quality, he kept up to date with the latest, newest, and loudest. He played his records louder and louder and forced Trixie to build bigger and grander houses.

She had to get away from that man of hers. He drove her crazy with his art and bohemian friends, and that infernal racket he called music.

"At least we can wait until the rain stops," Harris said. "Dr. MacCallum brought some fine whisky for us to enjoy."

"Are you kidding?" Thomson scoffed. "It's in the storm that we hear the still small voice whispering the truth we need to hear. Stay inside, you pansy-ass! I'm heading out to capture the moment. I need to hear Nature call my name."

Not wanting to be thought the fool, Harris reluctantly gathered his things.

"This'll give me enough time to cook up a stew for us to enjoy when you get back," MacCallum said. He was glad that he had come along as chief cook and bottle washer. He'd stay warm and dry while they battled the elements. He didn't have to suffer for his art.

Good thing there was an armful of dry wood in the box near the stove. He'd have it swept out, the fire banked, and the stew simmering in no time.

Harris followed Thomson out the door.

"I'll go this way," Thomson said. "You go that. Respond to what you feel, not to what you see."

Harris reminded himself that to refuse an adventure because of hardship was poor form. Canadians do not back down because of the weather.

---

14. 1885-1962

"Yes," he muttered. "Yes," he swore under his breath.

"Yes, for Christ's sake," he shouted into the wind. Then, a thunderbolt landed so near, he almost died.

He found a spot close to the shore under an overhanging rock. Whitecaps crashed against the beach.

It's a good thing they hauled the canoe up high onto dry land and tied it to a tree. When the weather breaks, they'd have a way out of this wilderness that does not suffer fools lightly. She exacts a heavy toll upon all who venture into her territory.

That's what Harris learned from his travels. It's one thing to visit forests, mountains, and deserts in good weather, but you sure don't want to be there when it turns bad.

He looked across the small bay and saw Thomson painting while leaning against a wracked stump. The weather roiled around him, but he kept daubing his brush and laying it on the board. He painted like a wild animal in a frenzy. He had no plan, no idea where he was going, or what he was doing. He painted. Furious and rabid, he could do no other. He was as intense as the storm.

So very unlike Lawren Harris, a man who planned everything down to the smallest detail. A sharper contrast could not have been made.

Thomson did not work out ahead what he wanted but painted what he felt in the here and now. He did not hold deeply held convictions that hobbled his every action but discovered his subject while he worked. He was intuitive.

"I need to paint the truth as I see it," Harris said as he looked at his nearly empty canvas. "It has to be in this expanse of whiteness somewhere."

After his time in Palestine with Norman Duncan, Harris vowed always to take charge. He would no longer wait for someone else to get things going. He would never again subject himself to another's incompetence. Duncan was too much of a drunkard to think things through.

Harris could see the big picture. He could visualize a project from start to finish. Going on an expedition required the same sort of attention to detail that building a house does. You have to be sober and plan properly.

Lawren Harris could do that. He could be trusted to finish what he started. He was a facilitator and an organizer. If you wanted something done to the best standard that was humanly possible, you called him. No one else.

Harris sheltered under the overhang of a rock, safe from thunderbolts and falling branches. He was as dry as dry could be in a torrential downpour, plotting a sketch of the scene in front of him. He did not hurry. He painted with care, one fastidious stroke after another.

He saw Thomson across the water, stalwart in the storm, a tree of a man, fully limbed: hemlock, yellow birch, and sugar maple.

Tree-cleaving thunderbolts flashed across the sky.

An unmerciful God ruled from on high, snapping, crushing, and boot-heeling sacrificial lambs and scapegoats into the granite and the duff and the detritus of the forest floor — uncreating the creation that had brought the world into being.

God of wonders, God of might, all this undoing is yours. Your un-mercy is an unconscionable unmaking.

Here we cower, weak and infirm against your might, unable to paint that which is before us. Poor miserable creatures without hope, yet who persist against all odds. Why do we keep on in this world where innocent lives are in jeopardy through no fault of their own?

Harris didn't know the answers to the questions that bedeviled him, but he made his way through the best he could. There was nothing else for him to do. His paintings were designed for the stage. Theatrical set pieces with the drama in the foreground and the mystical, ploughed down and hidden in the back, unformed and nebulous.

Thomson, in contrast, painted in a spontaneous rush of creation, each brush stroke surging forth in a world without end. He was in his element.

Harris? Ha! He would rather be home, warm, and comfortable.

Unhappily married but fathering forth, loving his children, sipping bone-dry Rieslings, easing open, yellow-labelled bottles of Veuve Clicquot, the most famous champagne in the world, and celebrating the good life that he had been given.

That's why he built mansions. He was an heir to the Harris farm-equipment fortune and could afford to keep Trixie's attention elsewhere. To keep her distant. To keep her otherwise occupied, without him in her sights.

"If it works, I'd do it again, just to keep her out of my way. So, I can heed my calling. To paint something important. That's why I am here, at this lake with Tom Thomson. Him, whisky-soaked and me stone-cold sober and wet through.

I like my art neat and my liquor dry. He'll drink it any which way he gets it. Bottoms up and straight from the bottle.

Thomson roughs it, wearing hob-nailed boots and mackinaws. He paints life amid wrack and ruin. He paints as if this is his last day on earth. For him, the struggle is all.

For me? I am now painting through a glass darkly. But I need the clarity of clear vision."

Then, straight out of a patch of blue in the centre of the storm, came a lightning bolt. It split the stump where Thomson was hiding. The sky cracked and the earth shook.

Thomson rose and waved and twitched his mantle blue.

"Now that's a voice I can hear," he shouted.

51
My Canada

Camp cook and bottle washer; the flashy, unconventional, and eccentric son of a Methodist minister, Doctor James Metcalfe MacCallum is now known in some rarified circles as the Father of Modern Canadian Art. He was passionate about the wilderness and a big-hearted supporter of destitute artists living in Toronto.

He moved among Toronto's medical elite and its bohemian underbelly. He was an ophthalmologist, researcher, and patron of the arts. He bought art without haggling over the prices the artists set. He supported those men whose work he liked for a year, so that they could get their start and stay in Canada.

"It's not charity," he said to Jackson in 1913. "I want you to paint the wilderness. That means you'll have to get out there in all kinds of weather. En plein air just above zero may be inhospitable for wimps in silk but is essential if you want to paint our nation. Are you man enough?"

"Of course," Alex replied. "I can do anything I want when I set my mind to it."

"Then you'll give my Canada a go?"

"I will, sir. That's a promise."

"You'll celebrate its north?"

"I'll paint its praises."

"Then we have a deal," MacCallum said. He shook Jackson's hand and gave him a year to work full time at his craft.

In this manner, a group of artists came into being, painters in the foreground, upfront and making their mark with MacCallum behind the scenes, not quite calling the shots, but enabling them to put on canvas the vision he had for his country.

MacCallum's group eventually included Frank Carmichael (1890-1945), Alfred Casson (1898-1992), Lemoine Fitzgerald (1890-1956), Lawren Harris (1885-1970), Edwin Holgate (1892-

1977), A.Y. Jackson, Frank Johnston (1888-1949), Arthur Lismer (1885-1969), J. E. H. MacDonald (1873-1932); and Frederick Varley (1881-1969). Varley, however, refused to feel beholden to MacCallum whose wallet snapped shut more quickly than Varley could finish a bottle of whiskey.

Sight unseen but ever-present, of course, was the overwhelming influence of Tom Thomson, who was with them in spirit, if not in body.

They would not have had the impact on Canadian art had MacCallum not bought their work when they were flat-broke and covered their expenses when they needed help.

MacCallum was the catalyst that brought the movement into being. Lawren Harris organized it, and Fred Housser wrote its manifesto.

MacCallum was an avid outdoorsman. His father's parish included the east shore of Georgian Bay, where he grew up hunting, fishing, canoeing, snowshoeing, and traversing the wilderness. He went for morning swims, slept under the stars on clear nights, and huddled in canvas tents during stormy weather.

If he had worn a mackinaw, he would have been the quintessential Canadian outdoorsman. Instead, he chose a rakish hat, waxed his moustache, and sported fine clothes. Not particularly rugged, he nevertheless engaged in manly activities that distanced him from aesthetes like Oscar Wilde and such others.

He chummed with the lads, talked intelligently about their art, and attended boxing matches with them for the sporting fun of it. They had a blast. "Those fighters are in fine fettle!' MacCallum exclaimed.

One day, the young Frank Carmichael took his girlfriend, Ada Went (1891-1964) on a date to the ring. It didn't go as he intended.

"They are wholesome bouts," Frank said to Ada. "There's nothing more exciting."

"I'm not so sure," Ada replied. "I've read the reports in the newspapers about the injuries these poor men sustain for your entertainment."

"They are physically fit," Frank insisted. "No one is ever seriously hurt, though some do get knocked out."

"Come on," Ada said, pulling Frank away from MacCallum and the others, changing the subject. She realized she wouldn't win this particular sparring match, and knowing that if she did, it would be a hollow victory.

Some battles are fought with bare knuckles, some with kid gloves, and others with soft words. Besides, she had something far more important on her mind.

A boxing ring was not it at all.

"How about a visit to your studio?" she asked.

Frank flushed red. He thought of the empty paint tubes, the ashtrays piled high with cigarette butts, the sink filled with dirty dishes. He and Tom painted there. They couldn't be bothered to clean up after themselves.

It was a pigsty. There were empty liquor bottles everywhere. His mother would be horrified, and Ada would never talk to him again.

"It's not a place for tea and tangoes," he said. "We meet there to paint, talk about our work, and critique each other's efforts. We don't socialize, much in any way."

"I suppose someone would have to tidy it up first," she replied. "To make it fit for a lady."

"Tom isn't the best of housekeepers, and I can't keep cleaning up after him, can I? I wouldn't get any of my work done. You must give Tom and me warning. Don't show up unannounced," he pleaded.

"In case I surprise you?"

Frank breathed out a sigh. He was getting very uncomfortable with the tack this conversation was taking.

"Women visit the building occasionally," he admitted. "But they never stay over," he added.

Ada arched her eyebrow and Frank realized he wasn't going to get out of this one. He turned beet red.

"What I meant to say is..."

She gave him a hug.

"You're cute and naive," she said. "Just the way I like you. But, if you want me, you'll have to let me enter your studio. There can be no hidden rooms, separate lives, or locked doors between us. Your art and our life together need to be one."

He exhaled and hugged her back.

Suddenly, he decided to go for broke, and he dropped to his knee.

"Want to get married?" he asked.

"Perhaps," she said. "There is one condition, though."

"Which is?"

"Take me to your studio."

"Why yes, of course!" he yelled. "Just not tonight."

He sprang to his feet and charged off down the street and then ran back to her. "I've got to clean the place up first, but I've got to buy a ring." He turned in circles not knowing which way to go next.

She stopped him in his tracks. "Let's go someplace where we can be alone. We can talk this through."

Frank smiled and grabbed her hand, and they half-ran downtown. Laughing and happy, they were two lovers at the beginning of a long life together.

He hoped she'd forget about the studio until late tomorrow afternoon.

52
West Wind Island

One day back in 1911, MacCallum came upon Jim MacDonald's solo exhibition at the Arts and Letters Club.

"They are full of natural poetry," MacCallum said. "You're painting the Canada I know — rocks, pines, ice, snow, stormy lakes. I've built a cottage north of Penetanguishene. Come to Georgian Bay and put on canvas my feelings about the landscape. Bring your wife and children. There's lots of room for them to holiday and for you to paint."

"I'm not sure," the soft-spoken MacDonald replied. "Joan and I have a ten-year old son, Thoreau. He's a handful."

"My cottage is on a 27-acre island, three miles from shore where he can run and play until he's ready for lunch; and then off again, until supper, exploring its length and breadth; and then back again, before dark, ready for a snack and bed exhausted.

I'll put you up in a houseboat and moor it off Split Rock Island. Your wife could relax and regain her strength. I know she's ill. The forest is as good a cure as anything I have to offer."

"How could I ever repay you?" MacDonald asked.

"With a couple of your sketches," MacCallum said. "I'll buy your finished paintings when you offer them for sale. I'll do what I can to support your work. It won't be charity. You need to keep painting. Our country needs men like you."

Broke, MacDonald took MacCallum up on his offer. It was a lifeline.

That same summer, Lawren and Trixie, with one-year-old Lornie, were renting a nearby cottage that Doctor David Gibb Wishart (1859-1934) owned. He was an otolaryngologist[15] from Toronto. His son D. E. Staunton Wishart (1889-1958) specialized

---

15. A specialist who treats the ears, nose, or throat

in the problems of deaf children. During the war, he distinguished himself at Gallipoli, Balkans, and Egypt.

Lawren heard about the new cottage that Dr. MacCallum had built on Island 158 and wanted to have a closer look.

"You're out of your mind," Trixie said. "There's no way I'm canoeing in that choppy water with you and our son. I'll stay here, thank you very much, and look after Lornie when he wakes. You know what they say about curiosity? It killed the canoeist."

"Don't you mean cat?" Lawren asked.

"You're the one going out for a paddle in these whitecaps, thinking you have nine lives, not me."

Lawren gave his adorable new wife a hug and kissed their son.

"I'll be back in a couple hours. Maybe then we can go cliff jumping into the water below."

"I'd rather we while away the afternoon in our room with the curtains drawn," she said.

Lawren stepped into the centre of the canoe, settled himself in place, untied the painter from the wharf, and pushed off into the wind. It felt good to free himself from worldly matters.

Georgian Bay is a huge body of water. Its waves, despite Trixie's misgivings, were nothing he couldn't handle. He paddled his way into open water. Soon, he crossed the three miles to Island 158, which MacCallum had renamed West Wind. He looked back to where Trixie and Lornie were playing on the beach and lifted his paddle to wave.

Watching him through a pair of binoculars, she waved back and relaxed with Lornie.

He paddled into the shallows near MacCallum's spacious Arts and Crafts cottage. When the prow touched the shingle, he jumped out of the canoe and pulled it up on the shore well away from the water. He grabbed his ever-present sketch pad and walked towards MacCallum.

"Dr. MacCallum, I presume?" I'm Lawren Harris.

And that was just the beginning.

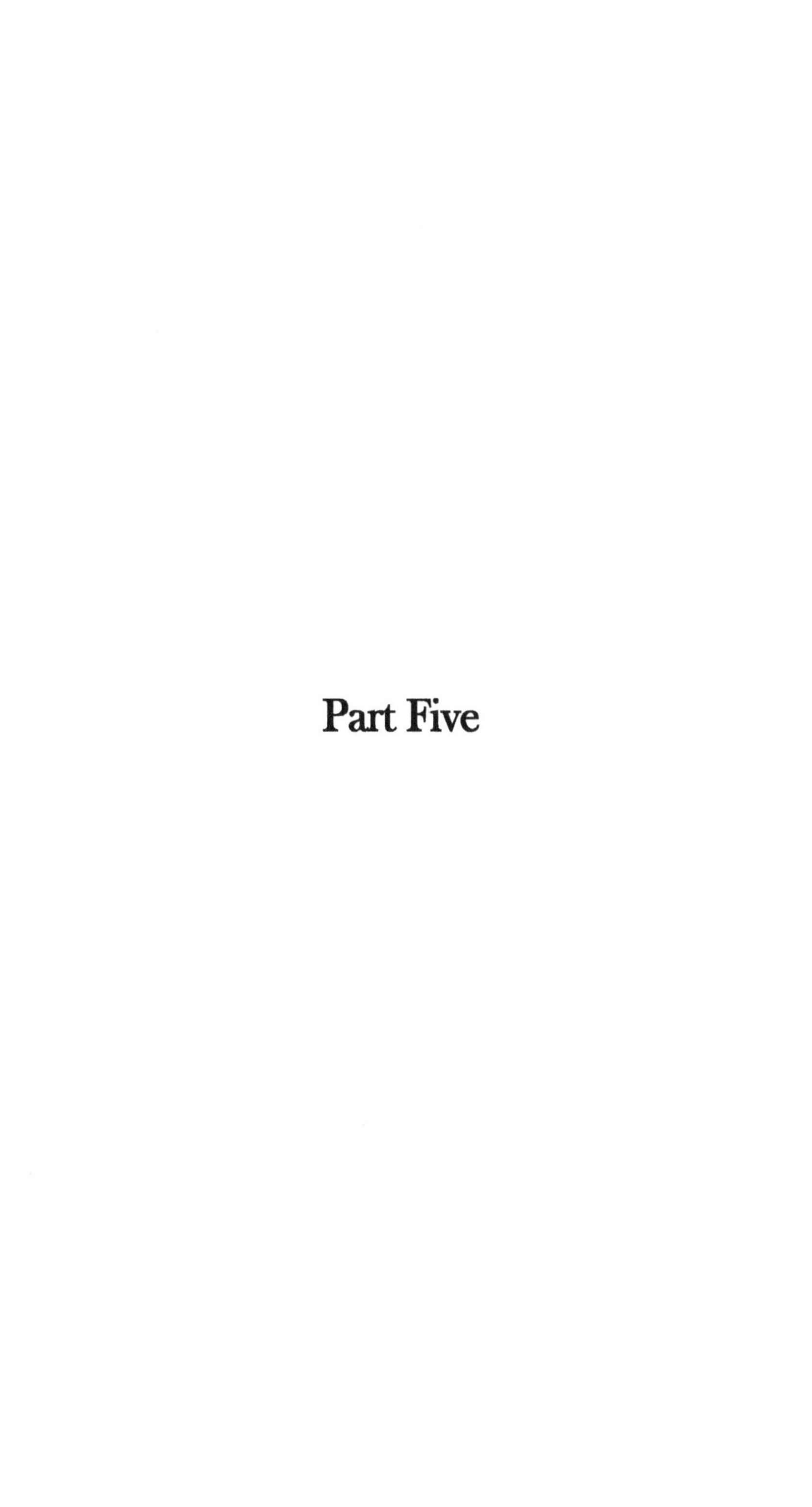

Part Five

54
The Brook Trout

A regal brook trout, lord of the deep, rose slowly to the surface of Potter Creek below Joe Lake Dam in Algonquin Park. The big fish opened its mouth and gorged on newly hatched midges swarming on the water.

It was during that golden, shimmering space of time on a late mid-summer evening when the sun has set below the horizon, but the sky is still full of brilliant, conjuring light. The trout flexed its powerful tail and surged out of the water. Then, it splashed down and swam away.

The living was fine for this mighty fish, king of the undercurrent, and the food abundant. Its life was long. He fathered-forth without care — realm-ruler, wave-rider, ready for battle. His sovereignty stretched as far as he could swim.

He did not suffer interlopers gladly but routed them from spawning beds. He mated at will and was sire overall.

From hard experience, this lord of all he surveyed, knew truth from falsehood and an angler's lure from a meal worth the eating. Imitations did not tempt him. He was nobody's fool.

Two fishermen on shore caught sight of a flashing of olive green, red, brown, black, and silvery white when the Brookie jumped.

"It's after stoneflies," the one said. The other thought midges.

"Let's see who's right", they decided, each tying new flies on their tippets.

And so, the competition between friends began. To catch the largest fish that they had ever seen below Joe Lake Dam.

"Must be fourteen pounds," they guessed. Or more, each privately hoped without saying a word. With that, they shook hands and cast their lines. "May the best man win."

It was July 1917 and while the trenches in northern France were hell on earth, this was paradise. The two men counted their lucky stars.

Mark Robinson diarist, Park Ranger, and Vimy Ridge survivor, limped with his leg shattered. He soldiered on, an officer's whistle on a lanyard hung around his neck.

In a mostly happy marriage with Emma Jane Webb (1875-1939), Robinson was completely devoted to his wife and children. He came home from his brief but deadly stint in the war, haunted and horror-struck. A shell of a man, shocked to death and dragged back to life, his heart and soul emptied of all that was good.

He needed refilling.

Algonquin Park nursed him back to health. Before long, he was hearty and hale, except for his hobbled leg and broken spirit. This north country man was at home in the bush, and he would never leave it again. His life depended on the land.

Emotionally, he was as fragile as a seedling in snow, yet as tenacious as a jack pine on the water's edge.

He refused to die.

Tom Thomson, tall, angular with a shock of black hair, was spared the horror of the trenches. He failed the physical.

Women loved him when he wasn't painting. What wasn't there to adore? Funny, thoughtful, intelligent, and generous, he could bed or wed anyone he chose, and they would have cried yes, all the night through.

He was a man whom women enjoyed and he them. Their company was always welcome and so was his when he wasn't painting and especially when he wasn't drinking. But when he was, he was a man possessed and in need of exorcism. The bottle was his downfall, the canvas his salvation. When he painted, he illuminated the unseen, brought the unknowable into the light, and made the ineffable plain.

He didn't have room in his soul for any distraction, two-legged or otherwise. Short tempered, raw, and sensitive, he wore his heart on his sleeve to be pecked at when he was slighted.

He was what he was, a dangerous man to love.

"Who could live with such a man?" All the women in his life asked.

Woe to the unfortunate soul who comes between him and his work. He was a loner, best side-stepped, and avoided. But who could resist him? Honestly?

Everyone learned the hard way to let him be and that was a good thing, especially for those who came after. But for those who lived in his wake, he was a challenge, a devotion, and a sacrificial calling. They were expected to love him without expectation and then to be slighted and cast off without warning.

No wonder the American romance novelist Alice Lambert (1886-1981) laughed when he proposed to her in Seattle. It wasn't at all malicious, just an involuntary reaction. She loved him with all her heart. But to be his wife, day in and day out?

"You've got to be kidding!"

No sensible woman would say yes to such an accommodation. You'd have to be mad. And she wasn't. She wouldn't hide away in an attic, safe from his canvas on easel, paint board on lap, brush in hand, and whiskey Whaddya Call. She wanted a life, not a white-knuckled ride through wild water.

His taste on her tongue made her yearn for more, but her mind made her turn away.

So, she laughed at the absurdity of his proposal. Of course, she wasn't going to marry him. Love him; have sex with him; she'd compromise her morals for a quick dalliance in darkened inns. All he'd have to do is ask.

But put up with him every living moment for the rest of her life? Entwine her destiny with his? That'd be putting her own dreams and aspirations in jeopardy. Something she wasn't prepared to do, so she laughed instead of saying no.

And he tore off in a rage back to Canada with his pencils, crayons, inks, and pipe dreams all in stipple. He returned home, shy and broken, embarrassed and seething.

Alice stayed in Seattle, ruefully, wistfully regretting the day she let him go, but honestly, gratefully, and single-mindedly getting on with her work. She knew that living with Tom would be like fighting on the front in France, always having a hair-triggered rifle aimed at her head, her heart, and her gut.

She escaped him to write, and he escaped her to paint. It was a close call for the two of them.

Then, there was the lovely Elizabeth McCarnen (1871-1957?). She chose to care for her ailing parents rather than loiter around with the turbulent Tom Thomson. Theirs was a fleeting affair that she barely escaped.

"It was the only sensible choice," she later said when she came to end of her long confinement in her parents' home. But by then, it was too late. Tom was dead and gone. She'd done her duty and was now abandoned, mulling over what might have been. He was no longer there, and her heart was broken.

Thomson retreated into the bush. He canoed on lakes and rivers, searching for that one true thing that would make sense of this dark and wearisome world, where nothing was as it should be. It was as if he knew his days were numbered. He had to get his work out before it was too late.

He finished an epic, recording the return of spring to Algonquin Park. A tree here, a vista there, a patch of snow in some scrub. He painted the force of life nosing its green-shoots through the decay of the forest floor to the sky and wind-thrown clouds above.

His was a tossed and tumbled view of the world, untamed, scarred, and cut to the quick. Newfound life emerged between stumps and fallen timbers. It was not ordered or safe, but full of furious thunder, a battlefield bombed out and winter-killed, yet reborn, year after year. Emerging from death to new life.

He painted skies, clouds, and star-filled or moonlit nights like no other.

He found light in darkness.

When spring's subtle colouration was blown away by summer's green exuberance, Thomson's subject matter was overrun and blocked from view. He put his palette and brushes aside. He picked up his fishing rod and went out on the water to think.

He needed the empty wilderness to quieten his soul. Its will to survive resonated deep within him. It spoke and he listened.

Having regained his composure, he returned to painting, furiously and in haste. With broad brush strokes and bold colours. He intermixed a palette of hues, gobs of paint, and knifed them on the canvas; smears of bloodred yellows; golden browns, and blues; blood-orange whites, and grey mauves.

Dappled, brinded, stippled, tackled and trim, fickled and freckled deft touches here and there. He expressed the spirit and the nature of the thing. Its riot under the surface. The deep sprung of the world below him was his desire and his truth.

That's what spoke to Tom Thomson. Life birthed and lived out, breathing the air, surviving the elements. Then dead, buried, and born again — cycled, and recycled in an orgasmic gyre.

He preferred to paint the struggle of nature, not its boastful green. His subject matter was the instinct to survive. Beauty at its most tangled. It was the basic structure of life that he was after. Life's hard return from winter's death knell.

From death in winter comes newborn life in spring. Tender shoots in rocky crags interested Thomson, seeds strewn on stony ground. Cast offs were a mystery worth the brushing, not those carefully sown in cultivated fields.

He left the tamed, the bridled, and the saddled-up for European masters and Canadian studios, specializing in worn-out clichés and tired images.

Thomson's subject was singular. His eye caught the cosmic spectacle of new life rising above the chaos. Shooting upward, springing from loss, living was his only concern.

Such is the irony of what it meant to be Canadian. Snow-bound and vibrant with four distinct seasons, the most habitable of which is the least paintable.

Thomson was in his element. He did the hard work of painting the wilderness, his fingers frozen and the paint in its tubes stiff from the cold.

When it was too hot, and the black flies were too thick, he put his paints away and went fishing. He sketched on small boards in the spring and fall, fished all summer, and developed full canvases in his shack behind The Studio Building during the winter. He was a man for all seasons.

Like Thomson, Mark Robinson fished while the world went to hell. He knew exactly what was happening in the trenches in France, the horror on the Eastern front, and the nightmare in the Austrian and Italian Alps.

He fished to forget. And didn't care if he caught a trout or not.

They both had enough of killing.

55
Catch and Release

The next morning, Thomson enjoyed one of Mrs. Fraser's famous Sunday breakfasts. After a plateful of eggs, fried potatoes, and her matchless Irish beans, he and Mr. Fraser — the Lodge's proprietor and primary reason it was tottering on the brink of insolvency — sat in the sun on the porch and smoked.

"The Brookie is the biggest I've ever seen," Thomson exclaimed.

"You know, Gill Lake has bigger fish than Canoe," Fraser declared. "It's not nearly as frequented by anglers. You could easily catch a big one there."

"And pass it off as the Joe Lake leviathan?" Thomson laughed, doubling over at the thought. To play a joke like this on his best friend would be better than catching the fish.

"You could land one from Gill and leave it on his doorstep."

"And let him jump to his own conclusion? I wouldn't have to say a thing."

"We should try our luck at Joe Lake Dam one more time," Fraser suggested.

"It's a bit of a walk," Thomson replied.

"But I'm too full to paddle my canoe," Fraser complained. "I need to stretch my legs. What do you say? Let's go for a saunter."

"I can hardly wait to see Mark's face when I show him the fish I've caught."

"I have some silver spinners that might do the trick, better than those flies and that floating line of yours," Fraser said.

So, they gave it a go, walking on a lark to Joe Lake Dam to try their luck in the midday sun. But the trout wasn't interested. It stayed submerged in deep cold waters and fed on nymphs and larvae.

"Them and their flash," it said. It couldn't be bothered.

235

Trounced, Thomson and Fraser wound their way back to the Lodge, the old trout following at a distance. He wasn't going to let that tall bastard out of his sight.

"Come back to try me a second time?" This made him seethe.

"That will not do," it said. "You will not do."

"Perhaps I can catch it while trolling through deep waters," Thomson thought as he hurried to load his canoe. His rod, his line, his net, a blanket, some canvas, a cast-iron frying pan, and some bacon for the grease. He stowed away a bag of rice, some flour, potatoes, maple syrup, and jam. Food enough for a couple days.

"I may or may not spend the night, but I'll be prepared," he said. "It all depends."

He glanced up from the path and tripped on a root.

"Damn it all to hell," he said. Pain shot up his leg. Rather embarrassed at his clumsiness, he tried not to hobble as he strode to the canoe. He found some copper trawling line at the dock.

"This'll do nicely," he said. He wrapped a length of it around his twisted ankle. "It's as good as a cast," he thought.

Settling into the middle of his dove-grey, top-of-the-line Chestnut canoe, he paddled off. He looked back to the shore and bid everyone nearby adieu. He stretched out his injured leg and hugged the shore for a bit. "I'll have better luck out in the middle."

Once he made it into deeper water, he attached a sinker to his line so that the hook would troll well below the surface as he made his way towards the Gill Lake portage. "You can't catch a fish if you don't have a line in the water."

As he headed towards Little Wapomeo, the fish trailed behind him.

"You never know," Thomson said to himself. "Stranger things have occurred. I might catch the biggest trout in Canoe Lake. At the very least, I must try."

The trout, however, had other things in mind.

"I need him to have the hope that he can catch me. A tug here, a sparkling of colour there. His ill fortune depends on the line he has cast upon the waters. He fishes so that he may live to tell a tale and I will die. Except his time has come, not mine.

He will not live to see the setting of this day's sun. I catch but do not release."

Thomson pointed the canoe into the waves. Resting the paddle on the thwart, he stood to unbutton his fly. He needed a piss and couldn't wait any longer.

Then, he noticed a tug on his line. "Damn it," he said as he finished his leak. He grabbed the rod and gave it a backward jerk to set the hook in the fish's mouth.

Startled by the sharp mouthed pain, the Brookie took off, first in one direction, then another, the line spinning off the reel. Thomson used his hands as a brake to keep the line from free-wheeling and snarling into a mess. Except he wasn't quick enough.

The fish led and Thomson followed in a candome, habanera, mazurka, milonga, polka, schottische, and waltz— luring and dancing, angling him until he was dizzy.

"I'll fill him with desire but deny him the performance," the fish scoffed.

The line that could have become a noose, a hang man's rope — not to swing Thomson high, but to hold him down, snagged on a branch, low and submerged. Until the breath expelled from his lungs and water rushed in.

Except he died before he drowned. A freak accident, something that could not have occurred in a million years.

Thomson turned to face the fish and kept the rod high, making sure the line didn't go slack while being dragged under the canoe. When the fish pulled, he released the line. When it swam towards him, he reeled it in.

He stepped forward and back, twisting and turning, reaching the end of the rod over the bow of the canoe, then over the stern. Time and again, the fish circled back and forth, trying to dislodge that damned hook from its mouth. But to no avail. Thomson had set it for good. The barbs held tight, and the fish grew furious.

Thomson reeled the line in and kept it taut while the trout tested its strength and grew tired in the effort.

"I won't let you go," Thomson vowed.

"I won't let you net me," the trout replied.

They both fought for their lives, knowing this was a battle neither could lose.

The boon of incompleat anglers drifted in close to the canoe, its bulk rising to the surface.

"My God, you're big," Thomson said as he raised his rod with one hand to pull the fish in. He reached with his other for the net. Teetering and unbalanced, the canoe caught the wind, turned, and wallowed into a trough as a fatal and perfidious wave rocked it sideways, knocking Thomson off his centre, his weakened ankle collapsing under the strain. He released his grip on the reel. It spun free.

The fish, sensing the line go slack, surged under the canoe, and pulled the line with it. Thomson dropped the net and began to haul the line in. Then, the reel loosened from the rod and fell to the floor of the canoe. Thomson shifted his weight and used his hands to yard the line in. It pooled in whirls, whorls, and crow-nesting tangles at his feet. He turned. A felon wave rocked the canoe. Thomson lost his footing and slid off balance.

The fish gave a final tug and broke free. A strand of line trailed from its mouth as it swam away. Thomson fell forward. His ankle screamed in pain.

He hit his head, an innocent blow to his temple, a slight tap on the gunwale of the canoe. It knocked him out. He stopped breathing and tumbled headlong into the water. His body twisted and turned as it plunged below the waves. The line tangled around his ankle and snagged on a submerged log. It held fast. Already dead, his lungs were full of air.

He died while fishing, while having the time of his life. He wasn't painting. He wasn't drunk. He was sober. Tears of joy filled his eyes. His heart was full of laughter. He had so much more to say, so much more to paint, and so many more trout to catch.

"His loss is ours and we grieve his death," later generations said. "Tom Thomson, we weep for you."

He had hardly begun and now, his life was over. His chances for love and happiness were gone. Those he left behind were broken-hearted. His loss became their loss. His death, theirs.

Mournful, they lived one sad day after another. Woe overcame them.

Tom Thomson died alone on a shallow, northern lake. Without a word, the wilderness took him as he was, unlord and unmaster of all that he could no longer see. It unrealmed him and set him adrift on a course of undoing.

56
Code Breaker

The next morning, there was no sign of Thomson, but none of his friends were worried. They were used to his disappearances. With his canoe laden with provisions, he could live off the land for days and weeks at a time. And then he'd come home, freshly shaven, as bright as a robin in spring, as if nothing had happened.

They went about their business, knowing that he was about his. Not necessarily painting but thinking and absorbing the wild as it entered the deepest part of his soul.

They knew he needed time to mull things over. To fish, to build a fire, to sleep in the rough. To cook a meal over banked embers. Smoke wisping and flavouring its way through the ingredients in the pot, melding everything together into a complex palette of flavours.

Cooking and painting have much more in common than people think. They involve design and balance, nuance, and layering. Cooks savour a dish the way artists savour a painting. One slow and thoughtful mouthful at a time. A lingering gaze.

The response to the food on the plate or the image on the canvas is involuntary. It is an immediate visceral reaction. You love the work or hate it. There is no telling why.

Thomson's friends at Canoe Lake understood this angle of his life, but not his art. They kept their distance, off to the side, so as not to interrupt him. In case he had a fit and flew off the handle, sharp-tongued and angry. Later, regretful for what he said.

They didn't want to endure another one of his shame-faced apologies for once again letting loose his hell dogs. He was so damn meek and kind and generous when he wasn't painting, and such an ass when he was.

They let him alone when the paint escaped the confines of his palette and found refuge on his pine board.

Except for Winnie Trainor. She had a love for that unreasonable man when he was painting that knew no bounds. She adored him and that made all the difference. When he wasn't painting, he was magnificent, rough-hewn, and ready. When he was, she trod softly.

A white-tailed deer, skittish on a forest path, drawn through shadows to rich leas and salt licks. She couldn't stay away. She hung around whenever he was near and missed him when he was away. Spring, summer, and autumn — she lived, loved, and flourished. In winter, she pined and wasted away, hibernating until the sun returned and Tom came back to Canoe Lake.

This time, however, he hadn't adieu'd her when he left. He went his solitary way. She had been in Huntsville, busy with her bookkeeping. When she returned, he was gone. Then, her mind was unsettled. She missed this sometime lover of her soul.

"Where was he? Had something untoward happened?" Her mind assumed the worst. It was her way of coping, being prepared for the cruellest turn of events that she could imagine.

The longer he was away, the more agonizing her days became. How much more of this torture could she endure? She wasn't sure.

"Where are you, Tom? Why aren't you here? Why haven't you married me? The gulf between our families makes the prospect of marriage impossible."

For Winnie, this was a time of Adventless waiting. For that which will never be. Waiting for a proposal that would never be offered, waiting for vows that would never be broken, and waiting for the blessing of a long life, lived together. That would never be.

"I would gladly bear his children and give him the space and time he needs to do his work. Bring him home safely, oh God," she prayed. "I don't know how much longer I can endure.

This man not painting is my life. Him painting is my cross, a cup that I do not want taken from me. Him drinking is my Gethsemane."

Then, Ed Colson from the Algonquin Hotel dropped in to Mowatt Lodge for a chat.

"One of our canoes is missing from the portage at the foot of Joe Lake Dam. The wind must have carried it off. If anyone sees it, I'd be most grateful."

That Monday morning, Martin Blecher, Jr. reported seeing an upturned canoe by Little Wapomeo on late Sunday afternoon.

"Might be Colson's," he surmised from a distance. He hurried home and promptly forgot about the canoe and its unusual dove-grey colour. That it could have been Thomson's didn't occurred to him until Monday morning.

When he made the connection, he ran like hell to the Lodge.

The news that he found the canoe exploded like a bombshell, and everyone crawled out of their frontline trenches and scrambled into No-Man's land. A blast wave had stripped the landscape. It was barren. Tom Thomson was missing and there was no telling where he had gone or what had happened. Thunder clouds hung like a shroud over their hearts.

"I need to paddle off some steam," Charlie Scrim said. "I'll go investigate." He hurried off towards the overturned canoe, floating in the middle of the lake. When he saw that it was Thomson's, he panicked.

The water was dead calm. He paddled back to the lodge as hard as he could. When he landed, he babbled breathlessly.

"I thought that Tom was on the shore hurt. I hurried back to get help." He was afraid of the worst and could not cope with the unimaginable.

George Rowe and Larry Dixon grabbed a tow rope, determined to continue the search.

"My God, what happened?" they asked. "Tom, where are you? You haven't drowned, have you? Are you hurt and laid up somewhere?"

They tied a painter to the bow and towed the canoe to shore.

"If he's not here, where is he? He must be close by. Where's his signal fire?"

Those at the dock were also puzzled. "Had something happened? Did Tom have an accident and the canoe capsize? How is that possible?"

Not Tom. Strong-armed swimmer. Painter of wind, earth, and waves. Tree-recorder. Fisher of trout.

"He's got to be somewhere out there. We better find him. The wind and waves must have freed the canoe while he slept. It drifted off and now he's stranded. He needs our help."

Shannon Fraser sent a telegram to the Thomson family in Owen Sound and Dr. MacCallum, saying that the canoe had been found, but that Tom was missing. Mark Robinson spent the next several days and nights looking for Tom, limping through the bush, blowing his officer's whistle, calling out for his fallen friend. He waited and waited and waited for an answer that never came.

At Vimy, "I didn't leave my comrades behind. I'm certainly not doing that here." He soldiered on, marching and sore, worried as hell. But not giving up. His friend needed help. By God, he was going to do the best that he could.

"I'm here for you, Tom," Robinson said. "You and I have a lot more fish to catch before our time is up."

George Thomson (1868–1965) arrived on Thursday to investigate the matter of his younger brother's disappearance. He assumed Tom would turn up. As a favour, he took the epic of spring sketches that Thomson hung to dry in Winnie Trainer's cabin back to Leith.

"He's resourceful if he's anything, that brother of mine. Maybe this'll teach him. Him going off on his own, it's never a good idea. Maybe he'll learn this time. The bush is no respecter of persons. Capable or not."

That following Sunday, a long, hot summer's week later, Dr. Howland took his daughter Margaret out trolling. She felt something heavy on her line. Her father took the rod and began to reel in the dead weight. When he saw a body rising slowly to the surface, he let the line slip back into the water. He quietly returned to their cabin so his daughter would not see the corpse.

He asked George Rowe and Larry Dixon to secure the body in the water off Big Wapomeo, cover it with a blanket, and keep vigil until Dr. Ranney arrived.

The two men spent the night watching the body and drinking, waiting for the morning. They kept a fire burning bright. A beacon and a funeral candle, lit in memory. In that long, black, and hateful night.

Under the authority of George Bartlett,[16] Superintendent of Algonquin Park, Robinson made plans to have the badly decomposed corpse buried as quickly as possible, in a grave on the rim of a sandy slope overlooking Canoe Lake.

"I cannot allow my friend's body to suffer any more indignity," Robinson said. "This is the last good thing I can do for my fallen comrade. He and I were soldiers together. This wilderness was our battleground. Me to keep it safe, him to get its message out. Tom Thomson: code breaker, voice-giver, paint-thrower. Now dead and gone."

---

16. 1852-1939

57
The Forgotten Woman

Winnie Trainor stepped off the train at the Canoe Lake station. She was a tall, slim woman. Strong and vigorous, strait-laced, tight, and trim. Dressed in a subdued beige outfit, jacket, and hat, with a pair of sensible shoes. Her thin, light brown hair was braided, restrained, and pulled into place.

She was the very model of a deeply saddened yet dignified young woman. She knew her place in society and what was expected of her. She outfitted herself in the best mourning clothes that she could afford.

Her jacket buttoned, her blouse neatly pressed, her laced corset pulled tight, her undergarments neat and white. Her belt and buckle shining, and her shoes polished and laced, double-knotted to be sure.

She was a soldier, readying herself for battle.

Then, the mêlée that ambushed her sprang from the very quarter where she thought she was safe. It came from her friends and neighbours, the very people at Canoe Lake she thought her equal.

She fought for the freedom to make her own choices, then those closest to her betrayed her trust, and she lost everything. She became undone.

What Winnie knew with complete certainty was that she must not wear a mourning widow's black. That would be unseemly. She could not be so bold as to declare that she and Tom had an understanding. That they were about to get married. That they had secured a cabin for their honeymoon. Not now. Not with him dead and gone before his time.

Theirs was a secret love that had not yet been bruited out from the shores of Canoe Lake. The very breath of those words would have fanned the fires of disapproval. Theirs was a love to last a lifetime, and it did.

His to her and hers to him.

They were familiar and exchanged tenders, in secret of course. The community at Canoe Lake was complicit. It turned its eyes away.

"Let the two alone," it said. "They have so little. Him with his paintings, her with her accounts payable. Let them find love in this north country, where life is tenuous. Southern city folk assume man's domination over the earth.

Northerners know the truth. Life is as fragile as summer love, open and free. It must be carried on in winter under heavy blankets. With the return of spring and the journey into fall, the covers may be thrown off, but are always within reach. A summer's love in the heat is the briefest of couplings. A pleasure that swiftly passes, it is a baring of all and an ecstasy.

May their love's consummation be long and pleasurable, the people of Canoe Lake prayed in their heart of hearts. Without it, life is not worth the living. We will not intrude."

Winnie walked from the train station, past the Lodge and her family's cottage, to the bridge over Potter Creek. There, she and Tom, hand in hand, had enjoyed many a sunset.

"These radiant moments are my favourite," he said. "The way the sunlight filters through the sky and clouds, low on the horizon, dropping into the bay. It comes to life, ever-changing and multi-hued, refracted and pied. A beauty that cannot ever be captured. It is held trembling in the hand and then, let go."

Alone on the bridge, she looked across the lake and said goodbye to the man she loved.

"You are dead and gone, Tom Thomson, and I am completely undone. What good can come out of the days ahead? Even though I watch and pray, I hope this cup will pass from me. Yet I fear, it will not. I know it will not.

I must see my loved one last time before they bury him low in a grave high upon the hill. On earth, I freely gave him my soul, and he took my body with joy. Now, I give him my heart. Please take this offering. I can do no other."

She rowed her solitary boat to the hellish site where Tom's body lay, decayed beyond recognition. Roy Dixon and R.H. Flavelle were preparing it for burial. Winnie needed no Charon to ferry her over to her love and die. She would take this journey herself. Like Jacob, who wrestled with the angel, she would never recover.

Canoe Lake is her Peniel, east of the Jordan River. There can be no return, she knew.

"I have lost my heart, and now I will lose my soul, but it will be on my terms," she said. "I will look on the horror that once was my love and will not turn away. The idea of his decomposing flesh will remain forever in my memory. I will be branded like Cain and left to wander this earth, bereft and broken, and marked forever. From here on is my destiny. I will become an idiot, and I will not care."

Except, when she landed on the shore, that was not to be. The men had put up a tarp to hide the grisly scene from on-lookers. A canvas stretched from tree to tree to obscure, rather than illumine the visible. To make unknown the forever unforgettable.

The smell of rotting flesh filled the air. She breathed it in and retched dry heaves. She had eaten nothing since she had heard. Hardly drank any water. Now her stomach was as empty as her heart.

Mark Robinson grabbed her as soon as she stepped from the boat. "As a favour," he pleaded, his chivalry misplaced.

"No, Winnie, for God's sake, you cannot come here. This isn't for you. Tom is dead and gone. His corpse is bloated and distended. It has burst from the inside out. He does not look the way you want to remember him."

"I will decide for myself," she said as she stormed forward. "No power on earth will hold me back from what I know I must do. I need to see him, or I will be undone forever."

Good, kind, loving Mark Robinson stood up to her. He would not let her proceed. He hugged her and stopped her in her tracks.

Winnie pounded his chest with her fists, and fought like a wildcat, trapped, and enraged. She screamed in grief and thundered forth.

"Let me go," she demanded, but he held her tighter and tighter. "I need to see him one last time to quieten my soul. The demons are already loose. The only way I can exorcise them is to look upon Tom myself. Reality cannot be any worse than what I am already imagining."

She pleaded, she begged, and then she fought, but to no avail.

Mark was too gallant and strong to let her pass.

"No, Winnie, this is not for you. I will not. I cannot let you see Tom in this condition. The memory will haunt you to your death. You will be undone," he said.

"I am already undone, you bastard. This is my right. You cannot decide for me."

She pummelled him with her fists, and she spat in his face. They fell to the ground, he rolled on top of her, putting his full weight upon her body, pressing her down until she could no longer move.

Unable to breathe, she quietened down. He rolled off her. They gasped for air. Their hearts were pounding. She had been beaten and knew it, but she would not give up. She would not forgive, and she would not forget.

"Mark Robinson, you have rolled a stone across the tomb of my grief. You have blocked its escape, and I am imprisoned forever. For God's sake, let me grieve the only way I know. Let me see him, so that I may live."

But while Robinson restrained Winnie, Flavelle and Dixon put the corpse in the coffin and quickly hammered down the lid.

"You will not look upon this man to whom you have plighted your troth," Mark said, lovingly, kindly. "He is gone Winnie, and you must get on with your life."

"Shut up, you bastard," she whispered. "You presume that you can decide for me? You think that you can determine what I can and cannot see? What can I handle? You? For my own good? For God's sake, Mark, you're a pig. I am a grown woman and fully capable. I bear life and death in my body. And you dare suggest that I cannot carry the full force of Tom's decay? Because I am frail?

I am not a child to be trifled with.

There will be hell to pay, Mark Robinson, and you will bear the brunt of it."

Flavelle and Dixon carried the coffin down to the shore and loaded it into their canoe. Robinson wanted to accompany Winnie back to shore, but she refused to have anything more to do with him. He pushed the corpse-laden canoe off and jumped in. The men hurried across the lake to where the funeral procession waited at the dock.

Winnie Trainor followed behind, sobbing, wailing her woe, keening her immeasurable sadness.

The forgotten woman of the lake.

58
The Funeral

Tears streamed down Winnie's face as she stood with the other Canoe Lake residents around the open grave. It was a miserable day with the sky swollen, bloated, and rain gushing out.

As lay minister, Martin Blecher, Sr., read the Service for the Dead from the Anglican prayer book that Mark Robinson always carried with him.

"After Vimy," he said, "I can do no other. I need these comfortable words as near and as close to my heart as possible. Without them, I would die."

The sonorous words flowed over the small congregation. They were too stunned by the blast wave from Tom's death to speak words of consolation to one another. Mute, they grieved as they stared at the casket.

"You bastard, Mark Robinson," Winnie Trainor thought as Mr. Blecher read the service. "How can you look so saintly, you Christ follower. Sound so kindly, and be so mournful here at the grave when a mere hour ago, you were a brute? You ravished my body and my soul.

How dare you deny me the one solace that would have silenced my torment? Yet you had the gall to allow your curious 11-year-old boy to view Tom's corpse. Is he stronger than I? More capable of bearing the woe of the world than I, a grown woman? Mother of God!

I hate you, Mark Robinson. I am so mad that I could spit in your face. Again. And again. You unmanned yourself when you unwomaned me. You ought to be ashamed."

Winnie's clothing was loosened from the fight. Her hair fell from its coiled braids and covered her face. She couldn't care less. She would soon dye it cerulean blue. A grief-stricken memorial to the skies that presided over her lovemaking with Tom.

Her jacket was wrinkled and soiled, her dress awry, her boots scuffed. Her blouse was torn and buttons missing. Mark Robinson violated her when he refused her pleading. Call it what you will. This rape of a sobbing woman.

Mark Robinson cursed Winnie with an everlasting sorrow. Perpetrator and protector, the gentlest of men, violator of her womanhood, well-meaning and sincere, he was completely at fault.

Her brown eyes glistened black and blue from grief. Her hands were raw and bleeding, her heels broken in the sand and gravel. She no longer heard the words that were meant to relieve her sorrow.

Winnie kept a silent vigil for as long as she could.

When the pallbearers lowered the coffin into the grave, she could not hold back any longer.

"Have you consulted the family, Mr. Robinson? Do you know what their wishes are? Did you send them a telegram informing them of the burial, Mr. Fraser? Why are none of the Thomsons here? Why such haste? Surely one more day wouldn't matter. Another 24 hours wouldn't have mattered in the least."

"For God's sake," Robinson pleaded. "Tom's been dead for over a week. He's unrecognizable. That's why I didn't allow you to see him. It was wrong for me to allow Jack a look. I admit that. I didn't want to make the same mistake twice."

"And who appointed you judge and arbiter over Tom's final moments above ground?" Winnie asked.

She could hardly stand to look at the man, he disgusted her so.

"On behalf of George Bartlett, the Park Superintendent. I'm carrying out his orders."

"All I'm asking is that you consult the family before you bury Tom. It is their right to decide, not yours."

"Be quiet, woman," Shannon Fraser swore. "We have a job to do and that's that. As God is my witness, Tom will be buried today, whether you like it or not. I have a business to run and a lodge that I'd like to keep filled with guests."

With that, Fraser grabbed a shovel and filled in the grave. Robinson seized his. The two worked like madmen.

Winnie Trainor bid Tom adieu and hobbled off to the station — her thighs in pain, her shoes broken, and her eyes blinded with tears. With any luck, she could call the Thomsons at Scotia Junction while waiting for her connection to Huntsville.

59
Firmly Afoot

When her train arrived at Scotia Junction, she went to the station call box.

"Mr. Thomson," she said. "They've buried Tom."

"What?" he cried. "But we sent instructions to Mowatt Lodge. Didn't that bastard Fraser say anything?"

"He wanted to bury the body as quickly as possible, so that he could get back to his paying guests."

"Well, I'll be damned. Of course, we want Tom placed in the family plot in Leith, not left by himself at Canoe Lake. He needs to be exhumed and brought home."

He faltered. "I don't know where to begin."

Winnie took charge.

"Of course, I can help, Mr. Thomson. I'll call Flavelle in Kearney. Since he did the embalming and readied the body for burial, he might do the exhumation at your request."

"And if he doesn't?"

"I know Mr. Churchill, the undertaker from Huntsville. He'll do it. No questions asked."

But when she called Flavelle, he flat out refused.

"You've got to be kidding. Embalming that rotting corpse was too grisly for words. And this? It's beyond reason. Let the poor man rest in peace. I will not take part in any further indignity."

He hung up on her.

She phoned the family.

Then, she called Churchill and he agreed immediately.

"Of course," he said. "Business is business. I'll need someone at Canoe Lake to transport the sealed metal casket in a wagon back to the station. Digging up a freshly filled grave is not a problem. The soil won't have compacted yet.

253

Pulling the coffin out of the grave isn't an issue. After all the years I've had in the business? I have the ways and means.

This request, though unusual, is not my first. I've done it before. I'll catch the night train and be done before morning.

Tell George Thomson to meet me at Scotia Junction on the 19th. He can accompany the body to Owen Sound, and I'll return to Huntsville. My fee will come from the estate? I'll give him my bill when I see him."

The train to Huntsville pulled into the station, and Winnie stepped aboard. She settled into her seat for the ride home.

Mr. Churchill trudged upstairs back to his bed.

Dr. Ranney didn't arrive at Canoe Lake until the funeral service was over. He called for an inquest to be held at the Blecher cabin. The chief piece of information that he used in his judgement was the statement Dr. Howland signed about the condition of the body when it was found.

There was a bruise on the right temple that was four inches long, some air was issuing from the mouth, some bleeding from the right ear, but there were no other visible marks on the body.

Dr. Ranney determined that accidental drowning was the cause of death, not murder, not suicide. Just a man, a fish, a wave, and a paddle stroke of bad luck.

He had a quick bite to eat after he concluded the inquest and slept for a couple hours before returning to the station. Then, he was on the 06:00 train back to North Bay, his business at Canoe Lake nicely concluded and the mystery of Tom Thomson's death now firmly afoot.

Later that morning, Shannon Fraser received a telegram, stating that a metal casket would soon arrive, and that Thomson's body would be exhumed for reburial at the Thomson Family plot in Leith. At that point, Fraser couldn't care less.

"That bloody Thomson was a pain in life and is even worse in death."

All Fraser wanted was to be done with the damned funeral. It was bad for business. He had empty rooms to fill.

When Churchill arrived, Fraser hitched up the horses to the Lodge's Democrat to haul him, his heavy bag of tools, and the casket to the cemetery. They unloaded the gear.

"Do you want some help?" Fraser asked.

"No," Churchill replied. "I'll have this done in a couple hours. Come and collect me in time to catch the next train."

With that, Fraser giddy-upped the horses the hell out of there, and Churchill began to dig. When he got down to the coffin, he looped a rope around it and winched it up, one end first, then the other.

"This is not a hard job," he thought. "As long as there aren't any squeamish bystanders on-hand to get upset."

He pried open the coffin and tipped the body into the metal casket. He lit a blow torch and sealed the lid shut.

"Your stink will stay where it belongs, no offensive body fluids will leak out. Your death will be held at bay and your mourners will keep their dignity, dressed in black and covering your grave with flowers."

Then, he threw the empty coffin back into the grave and filled the gaping hole.

At Churchill's gunshot signal into the air, Fraser arrived back in time to load the gear and the casket onto the wagon and get to the station on time.

"I can't believe that you did all this by yourself."

"The labour is easy when you don't have to worry about people's feelings. Covering up someone's death is nothing a few hours' work can't quickly accomplish."

Cold, business-like Churchill warmed sympathetically when he met George Thomson at Scotia Station. He expressed his sincerest condolences and slipped him the bill before returning to Huntsville.

Stiff-lipped and stern and dressed in black, George Thomson accompanied his younger brother's corpse to Owen Sound. He had a funeral to arrange and a mess of bills to sort.

The sun rose on these overnight deeds. Its cruel light brought no solace to the family's grief or the sorrow of Thomson's friends.

When Mark Robinson heard about the exhumation the next day, he was livid. He stormed over to the park office and complained.

"Take it easy, Mark," Mr. Bartlett said. "Let's not make this nightmare any worse. The Thomsons' wishes are clear. They are an influential family, and we don't want to upset them. But check the grave, will you? Make sure that the place is tidy."

With that, Robinson left Bartlett's office and made his way to the cemetery. It was all in good order. "That Churchill certainly knew what he was doing," he had to grant him that. "The cold, unfeeling bastard. He was as efficient as a war machine, dealing with the dead."

Robinson hobbled down the path back to Joe Lake Dam. "I'll never forget you, Tom. We came into our own in this bush and upon these lakes and rivers. Together, we walked these paths before the new day's dawn opened her eyes upon this dark world and wide. We paddled out beyond the horizon and portaged when the water could not carry us further. We set up camp and cooked our suppers over open fires."

The sound of keening filled the air.

"We are grief-stricken and want answers," the community at Canoe Lake demanded. "Tom could not have drowned. He was too good a man for all that. Something untoward must have happened.

Clarity is what we want. In black and white, not muddied and stirred up lake bottom sediment. We want satisfying answers from on high. Our lives have been changed utterly. We are not the same."

60
A Strict Accounting

Winnie Trainor fought every step of the way from her home in Huntsville, to the Arts and Letters Club in Toronto, to attend the autumn exhibition that Dr. MacCallum mounted in memory of her poor, lost Tom.

Half-blind from grief, rage, and utter disappointment, she hadn't forgotten the memories that haunted her since Mark Robinson pinned her to the ground a few brutal months ago. Her thighs ached with phantom pain, reminding her of his weight forced upon her.

She thought that she had recovered, that she'd been away long enough but Tom's death still lingered. The un-memory of his corpse loitered in the shadows of her subconscious. It was always there, a constant unwelcome companion. It troubled her when she was most vulnerable, catching her unawares. She needed to be ever-vigilant and ever-angry. That was when she was safest.

While alive, Tom drove her crazy with his long absences from Canoe Lake. Now his un-composition, his un-painting from six feet under hawked dudgeon gouts against the spit-heavy yellow sky.

Ever-present, his memory tore her flesh and soul apart.

She'd always been shy and insecure, but now she was a firebrand, thin as a match and ready to flare. No man would ever force her again. Robinson's refusal to let her see her dead lover's decaying corpse threw her down the path of unforgiveness.

"I will hold myself together," she vowed. "I will not give that bastard the satisfaction. I will not lose my dignity in this place of all places, where my Tom is finally being honoured. His work is no longer hidden away and buried from view.

It is brought out of dark corners in private collections and basements for all to see. It is finally in the open. I mourn the man I loved.

I am here for him.

I am here for me.

I am here to make sure his paintings are accounted for.

Where are the missing ones? Especially those George spirited away. Where did he take them? Why did he come to Canoe Lake and leave before Tom was found?

What can I do now? How can I count them? They are worth an auditing. There needs to be a tallying of the missing ones. I will not be reconciled until the sums have been tallied and the totals balanced.

There are the paintings that he gave away because he was broke, because he was generous, because he didn't care. There needs to be a telling, for memory's sake. I will not rest until a proper inventory has been taken.

Otherwise, his work will be lost and no good will come of his short life. No good will come of me.

I would like to abide in a Kingdom of Goodness instead of this hell. I am not the same. His death has changed me. I am utterly undone."

She scanned the crowd at the Memorial exhibition for familiar faces before she entered the gallery. Mostly men, she observed, smoking pipes and distinguished. Some young with sun-burned faces, others with greying temples. All subdued. All standoffish, their unsung leader dead and gone.

Tom's memory brought this motley crew together. They were as diverse a group of Canadian men as could be. All white with a touch of wild that gave colour to their palette. Variegated in their beliefs and multihued in their convictions.

With but a few women among them, Winnie ascertained. "The Canadian art world is a man's domain," she concluded. "The world is his dominion."

"We are the playthings to these peckered two-leggéd gods," she rued.

First, he was buried at Canoe Lake where he died, painting his life's work, a soldier on the front. His comrades mourning his loss. His family insisted that his body be exhumed and reburied at Leith. They marshalled together and found solace in one another.

A private mourning for a public figure, not quite famous, not quite known. So many people laid claim to Tom Thomson that the family had to assert their rights. They had no choice. He was theirs. His body was theirs. To do with as they saw fit.

"You cannot intrude," they said. "We have our boundaries. Tom is ours and ours alone. No outsiders were allowed to witness our private grief."

Not quite married, Winnie's betrothal to Tom was a wordless promise to a private act done under the covers of a very short summer's night. Tom's last act of creation. Their banns were unpublished, nothing formalized, nothing written down, except the bill that Tom paid when he booked the cabin for their honeymoon.

That was her only proof of their mutual intent.

After the reburial at Leith, Winnie took the train to Toronto to stay with her old chum Irene whom Winnie regarded as her one true friend. She had to get away from Huntsville and she couldn't return to the Trainor family cabin on Canoe Lake. Not yet anyways.

She had to regain her bearings after all that happened. A trip away would do her a world of good. Help her regain her composure and find purchase in this hard-wild world that no longer held any spring-like hope for her. There would be no return of life.

An unrelenting woe intruded upon the un-summer of her despair, and she was disoriented. Swirling leaves fell on the path ahead of her and she shuffled forward.

"I cannot look back to the places that I held so dear, and I cannot look ahead. The light has completely blinded me. What am I to do now that my Tom is dead and will never return?"

"But they were never a couple?" Irene thought.

For one thing, Winnie hadn't confided anything to her. She was too reserved and shy. She didn't have the vocabulary of love to speak of the affair in her heart.

Not that Irene shared the same regard for Winnie that Winnie held for her. Theirs was an unequal friendship, and both knew it. After all, who could not know when affection is not returned? Yet Winnie accepted Irene's half-hearted gestures. A part friendship is better than none.

"I'll take whatever I can get," Winnie said. "I cannot make it on my own. Perhaps Irene can point me in the right direction. I need her more than she needs me."

For her part, Irene bore the burden that came with being Winnie's only friend. She looked beyond the battered woman in front of her and remembered the young girl she once knew as a child.

"I accept you for what you are, Winnie Trainor," Irene said." You can be yourself," she said without guile.

"But I cannot lower my defenses," Winnie thought to herself. "I cannot allow the hellhounds in.

Could my life get any worse? I am already alone. Am I to be put out of sight and forgotten? Tom's family may have consigned me to the suburbs of their memory, but I will not forget. I cannot forget Tom and I will not forgive his family for their treatment of me."

Winnie confided in Irene, "I have a friend who's found herself in a spot of trouble."

Irene glanced down and knew. Nothing more needed to be said.

"I know of a place in Philadelphia," Irene replied. "They find homes for unwanted babies."

"You won't say a thing?" Winnie begged.

"As God is my witness," Irene replied. "I would never betray your friend."

Irene had long felt that Winnie couldn't recognize the beauty in a thing. She didn't have an artistic soul, just a head for beautiful numbers. How could Tom be satisfied with a lifelong companion like that? One who could put two and two together but could not think beyond the obvious.

"There is beauty in numbers and harmony in balanced columns," Winnie insisted. "Satisfaction in knowing where things are and accounting for them. My art is in figures and audits. Tom's is in paint on canvas. We two are not incompatible."

"Not quite enough," George Thomson insisted when Winnie told him that she was pregnant. "Who's to say it is his? You have no proof."

And he thrust Winnie from the family circle.

They thought her odd; they said so themselves. She with her ringed finger, holding a fly rod in her left hand, her right holding the day's catch, eyes downcast in the bright sun. Clearly uncomfortable in front of a camera, those new-fangled things.

She wasn't quite the woman the family expected Tom to love, woo, and wed. She wasn't quite good enough. Now that he was dead, she was out of the question. They thanked her, reimbursed her for her expenses, and bid her good day.

Irene tried to comfort her friend. "There is so much life to be lived. You must look to the future, not drag yourself into the past. Do not live in a delusion of your own making. You are a worthy woman. Tom photographed you on the shore. He saw you full of life. Do not allow his death to pull you into the grave."

"Then I'll go it alone," Winnie said. "I am already walking in the valley of the shadow of death. I'll revisit his familiar brush strokes and uncomfortable palette. His unmaking of the familiar. Perhaps I'll see the world anew if I can look through his paintings again. Peer into the unknown and find my own way home. I might even unearth his missing paintings," Winnie said, counting her fingers one more time. "Where are they now? The ones that he hung to dry in my cabin? Not that I have any claim on them," she admitted.

It'd be nice to know how they disappeared. Scattered in the wind and gone. Who has them now? The family, she hoped. An outsider? She wasn't privy to that information. She'd have to find out on her own. "A little investigative accounting," she thought.

A tallying of Tom's art. I'm good at that. If they'd let me be.

61
The Memorial
1917

As she passed through the doors of the Men Only Arts and Letters club, Winnie saw a round-faced, elfish man holding court with a group of men encircled around him. Two women were stranded alone on the outer reaches. On opposite sides of the room. They weren't together.

No matter how hard they tried, they couldn't push their way further into the group.

"We all loved Tom and his work," the elfin man said. "If anyone knew the bush, he did. And his use of the brush? I have never been so moved by such an artistic explosion."

The men all laughed at the private joke they shared but did not say out loud. An ejaculation of colour. It split their guts, they laughed so hard.

Tom Thomson's art was manly if it was anything.

"I knew from the moment I first met him that he would take Canadian art to places no one had ever dreamt possible. It's a nasty business, the manner of his death," he continued, lowering his voice.

"The last thing Tom would want is for it to detract from his work and keep you from yours. He laid the foundation, and we need to build upon what he left behind. We need to look forward."

"Couldn't it serve a purpose, though?" a young white-haired woman asked out of nowhere. Obscured by a stand of tall men in black jackets, she stood on tiptoes interrupting their proceedings.

"A scandal has the potential of turning a nearly unknown artist like Tom Thomson into a national icon."

"Who exactly are you?" Dr. MacCallum asked.

"Blodwen Davies," she replied. "Journalist, historian, and travel writer."

"He may be an unknown to you, young lady," Dr. MacCallum replied. "But not to us."

Winnie strained to see the speaker, but the wall of men blocked her from view. She had lain siege to their bulwarks, and they repelled her from their high point, unwilling to surrender their privilege. Their uproar drowned her out.

The plain Miss Davies was not welcome in their club, her credentials notwithstanding.

Winnie fought her way forward, but the men also rebuffed her every step. They would not let her in. She was too old, she was too odd, she did not suit their desire. She was not striking enough to warrant a second look.

Unlike that older, magnificently dressed attractive woman on the other side. She was worth another glance and quick consideration. Winnie didn't know her name, but the men did, and they kept their distance. They excluded her from their coterie. She was too good for them.

"It would be unseemly and undignified to indulge this hearsay," one of the men replied. "Tom's work can stand on its own merit. It doesn't need the scintilla of murder to make it great or the scandal of suicide to prove its worth."

"But you must admit," the little man said, "there is nothing like rumourmongering to draw attention to oneself. A lonely death on a northern lake is easy to ignore. Envelope it in mystery and suddenly, the headlines are reaching for a story.

Thomson's last breath may have been a futile gasp for air, but imply that there was something underhanded going on, and it suddenly takes on a life of its own. Given the right slant, the circumstances of his drowning would suddenly echo and re-echo across the land. Rumour has the power to transform the mundane into spectacle.

His death will put your art on the national stage. His death will bring new life to your work. His death will bring new customers into art galleries."

"His art is all that matters now," the crowd thundered. "Our Tom is dead and buried. We need to focus on his legacy. Give him the honour he is due. But we cannot use him dead and buried for our own ends. That would be tasteless."

"Tasteless?" Winnie asked, the uproar of the men drowning her out. "Tasteless is men talking business at Tom's wake. Tasteless is using the size of their larynx to exclude women from voicing their own opinions. Tasteless is preventing women from making their own choices, participating in society, and sharing in the conversation. Tasteless is respecting women for nothing more than their biological function."

She shouted voicelessly into the storm of sturdy male voices, and no one heard her. No one cared to listen.

"But how did he die?" the young Miss Davies insisted. "He couldn't have drowned, could he? After all, he was an experienced bushman. Did someone hit him with a paddle? Why was the heavy line so neatly tied around his ankle? Who watched him topple out of the canoe and slip without a struggle below the surface? And then it took eight days for his body to rise again from the bottom of that shallow lake. How could this be? Something surely must have happened that no one wants to talk about. Isn't anyone else curious about that?"

"But his death isn't what makes Tom Thomson memorable, my dear," the older, well-dressed woman replied. "There is more to Tom's story than the manner of his dying. It is his use of colour for colour's sake that makes his art so provoking. It expresses his emotional response to the world around him. When you look at these small boards, you can't help but feel the cosmic struggle of the universe. In them, you sense the unity of man with the world around him."

Take his painting of Shannon Fraser, for example," MacCallum said. "That reprehensible man is nearly indistinguishable from the bush in the background and the undergrowth in the foreground. Sitting cross-legged on a log that runs horizontally across the front, he is as vertical as the trees. His face angular and long, the pipe jutting into the shadows.

And the colours. His red hair, red jacket, blue shirt, and pink tie. The white on his neck and the grey on his boots. All daubed together, blues, browns, greys, pinks, whites, and splashes of green at his feet.

A commonplace man made one with a familiar landscape. There is nothing out of the ordinary here, yet Tom Thomson saw beauty in the thing."

"But that man?" Winnie asked. "Of all the men in the world. How could Tom paint him? There is nothing beautiful in him worth noting. Let alone painting."

"With his dark and earthy colours," the woman continued, "Tom used his palette to make the familiar unfamiliar. I'm Mrs. Florence McGillivray (1864-1938) , by the way," she said as she shook hands with Miss Davies. "He is forcing us to look at the world askance.

Is there more to reality than the surface of his painting? Is he calling us to consider deeper truths that lie hidden somewhere underneath? Surely, his work calls us to fall prostrate before the wild world, confess we are unworthy, and realize our oneness and sameness with the universe around us."

"That may be all well and good," Davies replied, "but the manner of his death is the kind of controversy that sells paintings."

MacCallum stepped in, and when she paused for a breath, he took over. "I want his works to increase in value. I applaud the effort to make them a rarity. Not for my sake, don't get me wrong. I have more than enough money for myself."

"But for art's sake?" McGillivray asked. "For Canada's sake? Portraying its ordinary untamed self. Making everyday life a fit subject for art. That is what we're about and what we all want. No longer satisfied with European masters, we need to find our own way as artists. To make our home in this place we call Canada."

Winnie did not know either of the women who spoke so intelligently but recognized a few of the men who had come to Canoe Lake to paint, drink, and fish with Tom. They may have been artists, but she soon learned that they were as raucous as a murder of crows.

All became louts when they were drunk. The more they drank, the stupider they became. Pistols, they fired blanks into the air. Short-lived sparks from a bonfire rising into the night sky and soon snuffed out.

She was familiar with many of the paintings on the A&L walls. Most were small, sketched quickly in the bush among black flies. She'd never seen the larger, formal, and finished ones before. They were completed over long, lonely winters when Tom worked in the Studio Building or lived in the shack that she had heard so much about but had never seen.

They were sold before she could count them.

His last work, painted in the weeks before his death, exploded with colour. *Summer on Canoe Lake.* It hardly represented a recognizable thing, but its effect was heart-stopping.

Winnie had read reviews of Tom's work in newspapers. He caused quite the uproar among the establishment. She walked into the room and nudged her way through the men with their pipes towards the tiny paintings.

Gashing the landscape with razor sharp slashes of colour, most had dried in her cabin and were tokens of much happier times. She peered through brush strokes into the depths beyond the colour and the pigment to the artist himself.

Tom had been hers and now, he belonged to the men who kept stepping in front of her and crowding her out of the way. She was invisible. She no longer had a place in Tom's world.

Then, Winnie saw Mrs. McGillivray shake hands with one of the men. She stepped closer, curious about the woman who seemed so familiar with Tom.

"Tom would have been so pleased to know that you were here" he said. "He was a great admirer of your work."

"And I of his," she replied. "We spent many a long evening in his shack, the woodstove blazing hot. I got to know him and was well-acquainted with his work. We talked of art. Of the galleries I had seen when I was in Europe. I barely escaped, you know, when the hostilities started. It was a trial to get home. I hope the friends I made over there survived."

Her words stung Winnie to the quick. "This woman spent time in Tom's shack, and I didn't? Who the hell is she?"

Winnie couldn't move forward to confront the bitch and didn't know what to say or how to respond. Bile rose to her throat, and she was ready to scream.

This betrayal hurt. She gathered her things about her. All men are bastards and have no room in their hearts for love.

"But my Tom? He loved me, didn't he? I am a woman most forlorn."

62
Unwed

It became clear to Winnie that there was no room for her in this place that Tom vacated. She was on her own and would have to make her own way, the best she could.

With that, Winnie turned on her worn heels and left Toronto behind. It was no place for her to nurse her sorrow or raise Tom's child. She could not return home. She had to unmother her unfathered child.

Winnie arrived in Philadelphia, at the home for unwed mothers that Irene told her about. She sojourned in a cell, awaiting another great undoing of her life. They were days of gruel, thin soup, and harsh judgements. She was a sinner, unworthy of God's grace, and could expect nothing better. Then, no sooner had she given birth, she was on her own again. The sisters forced her out and told her in no uncertain terms to sin no more.

"Damn you, God, for giving me a man who did not live long enough to become my husband. For giving me a baby that I could not raise in his father's image. I hate you to pieces."

Completely shattered, Winnie travelled north towards another un-epiphany, where suffering is without purpose and is without enlightenment. First, Tom's death, then the loss of her living child. Her life unraveled into a long strand of misery, snagging upon one unbearable sadness after another.

Mark Robinson had stolen her dignity and now, this convent gave her new-born child to someone else. Winnie had nothing more to lose.

She packed up her things and returned to Huntsville for Easter 1918. "Perhaps the hope of the Resurrection will return to me," she thought.

Soon, she found work as a bookkeeper, in the windowless back room of a business office. In it, she was out of sight and out of mind. This suited her perfectly. She rose from her sepulchre at the close of every workday and dragged herself home in grave clothes. Her fawn-coloured hair was now dyed blue; her eyes were wild with sorrow.

Winnie the Unfortunate lived out the rest of her days in unbearable woe.

# Part Six

63
Love is Blind

"Hmm, that was delightful," Sadie said, as she and Banting settled into their feather bed. They had registered as Mr. and Mrs. Grant in a hotel well away from the brick four-storey General Hospital, north of the Bow River in Calgary, where the conference was being held.

The last thing Sadie wanted was for pesky Gordon Sinclair of the *Toronto Star* to find out that she seduced her boss, the eminent doctor Sir Frederick Grant Banting. They'd known each other for decades. Getting him to sleep with her was the only way he would listen to what she had to say. She hooked him and he couldn't escape. There'd be no release until she said so.

She needed to speak her mind and he needed to pay attention. Their lives and careers depended on it. They had too much to lose by any further messing around.

The afternoon she spent with him was a thoroughly plotted, pre-meditated strategical act. A controlled-burn on the prairie. To prevent a grass fire from destroying an entire county. Sadie knew the repercussions of desire and took all the necessary precautions. Banting was a most willing and compliant partner.

Say what you will about Fred, he could act the gentleman while compromising the morals he learned from Sunday School. He believed that it was better to commit a minor sin than a graver, more serious one. For him, sex between two consenting adults was an intimate act of no lasting import.

He had a well-developed theology of justification, and Sadie had a planned subterfuge of last resort. He wanted sex and she wanted to talk some sense into him before he got himself killed.

That, however, necessitated the baring of some unfortunate truths. Any post-coital depression wouldn't be about their afternoon's performance. Covering Fred with the sheet on their heat-filled bed, Sadie felt like Abraham on Mount Moriah. A sacrifice offered, a death averted, and a life saved.

Sadie was on a mission.

Fred was scheduled to deliver the keynote address that evening and didn't want to waste any of his precious time attending lectures on the latest research in diabetes. They left the conference proceedings early, walked through what used to be known as Germantown and Little Italy. They strolled through the recently opened Calgary Zoo before heading to their room. He'd lost all interest in his insulin work years ago, but continued on the lecture circuit because the invitations kept pouring in.

Sadie accepted this conference for him because she knew it would enable them to escape the oppression of Toronto's humid summer. They had the motive, the means, and the opportunity to take advantage of a private hotel room in a far-off city.

He was thrilled when she first told him of the booking.

"Finally," he thought to himself. "I can enjoy what's under her covers."

She made a list of topics she wanted to go over with him.

"Why hadn't we thought of this years ago?" Fred asked.

"I had my career to safeguard. Besides, your interest lay elsewhere. I was too over-awed by your stature to consider any sort of liaison with you. Not to mention, you were a brute of a man back then, too full of yourself and all those imagined hurts and slights to be much of a lover. I was never the centre of your attention. You were and remain your sole concern.

In the years since, though? You've mellowed. You're still a beast, but you are a much kinder and gentler man than you used to be. To be honest? Since you've been knocked off your pedestal, I happen to like you more than ever."

"How the mighty are fallen!" Banting replied.

"Failing at something often brings out the best in a person," Sadie continued. "You are an exceptional loser, one who always gets to his feet, no matter how heavy the body blow. I admire your dogged determination. You never quit."

Banting exhaled.

"Your honesty takes my breath away. I've always had the utmost regard for you, Miss Gairns. The reason I respected the boundaries you set for our relationship? I didn't want to lose you. You've always had my back. You are the one sure foundation in my tumultuous life. I can always count on you no matter how poorly I have chosen.

Losing you because of an indiscretion on my part would have been worse than losing a wife. You are patient, long-suffering, and wise beyond measure. Until today, you have been like a sister to me. You are irreplaceable."

"Except I am not your sister, and I am certainly not your mother. I've had it up to here with the other women in your life."

Sadie was so furious with Banting that she sprang from the bed and covered her nakedness with a shawl. "I've put up with far more than either your mother Maggie or sister Essie ever endured back in Alliston."

Banting sat up and watched her closely.

"But those other women who have fallen into your bed? I can only speculate what they saw in you. One moment, you are grumpy, taciturn, or dour, and the next, the most charming man in the world. Why on earth did the elegant and capable Edith wait all those long years while you shilly-shallied around? The war first, your studies second, and finally, your work. You always had a convenient excuse.

Edith had more patience than Job. She persevered through the trials and tribulations you forced upon her. All the while, she wore your ring and waited for you to make good on your promise. Then, I came on the scene. I was there every step of the way. An eyewitness to your foolishness."

Banting tried to say something, but Sadie shushed him. "I must say, I was glad for her when Edith finally gave you the boot. I hope she was eventually rewarded with a quiet, loving marriage out of the limelight. She didn't deserve half the hell you put her through."

She took a breath and Banting took over.

"Edith and I knew each other from childhood. I couldn't keep a secret from her if I tried. The worst mistake I ever made was letting her go. I would have been a far happier man had I settled in London and married her instead of chasing after this fool's dream.

The pain that discovering insulin caused me is worse than making a pact with the devil. That Halloween in 1921? I came to the crossroads and chose the way that led straight to Perdition. As for Marion? I should never have fallen for..."

Sadie stood up before he could continue on his mournful, self-centred lament.

"It was the Nobel Laureate that compelled her to draw her sights on you, and the reason she attended every party with you at her side or not. She married you for the glamour you brought to her life. Baubles and bracelets, sequins and dancing shoes, her closet is full of them. But her heart is as empty as a barrel pitching over Niagara Falls."

"By the time I realized she laid a snare for me, I was hopelessly trapped and couldn't escape," Banting said. "Our failed marriage is entirely her fault. I gave her everything a woman could ever want. She turned her back on me."

Sadie scowled.

"Don't blame her for your wilfulness. You wanted everything she had to offer and more."

Banting sat on the edge of the bed.

"That's a little harsh, Sadie, don't you think?"

"You deserve much worse, especially for your treatment of Miss Davies. You took an unconscionable advantage of that poor young thing. Your potential seduced her. She fell in love with the man you could have become.

MacLeod was a piece of work, but he was not worth the energy you spent despising him. You would have been better served if you had forgotten him."

Banting reached for his cigarettes, hoping that Sadie would soon finish her tirade. She snapped, but he still needed her in the lab. If he opened his mouth, she'd disappear from his life forever.

"The man I now look upon? Blodwen Davies would have loved you forever. Instead, you made promises and broke them. You cast her off and haven't given her a second thought. You are the most callous man that I know."

"Blodwen was a means to an end. I admit it. I regret how the *Toronto Star* blackened her reputation, but I do not apologize for the time we spent together. Did I string her along? Certainly, but she made me feel young again. She worshipped and idolized me, and I loved every minute.

Besides, she's still marriageable. However, if I can be honest, I doubt she'll get over me."

Sadie snorted at that one.

"And the lovely Dr. White? I know what you saw in her, but what did she see in you? Your work on insulin? Your rumpled suit and wrinkled shirt? You look so helpless and endearing. You are a needy man without a woman. Priscilla adored you with all the naïveté of a young girl who has kept her nose in books all her growing up years. You were her Prince Charming."

"If only Joslin hadn't warned her off," Banting said. "I was looking for a woman who could bear me a houseful of children. I'm not interested in someone my age."

"You're saying I'm not a contender for your lasting affection? That I'm an elderly primip? Don't laugh! I have lots of fertile years ahead of me. Modern women can give birth in their fifties. We know each other completely. We've worked together for 14 years. I know your every strength and weakness. I know your failures and successes. I know your flaws, Fred Banting, each and every one."

True love is 20/20.

64
A Lamb to the Slaughter

"The truth is that love requires a clarity of vision and a heart full of grace. It takes open-eyed commitment to make a relationship work. I love you, not because you deserve it, but because I know you. And here I am, happy to be with you, in spite of everything that has happened.

If any couple has ever deserved a weekend of elicit love, we do. I, for one, have no regrets, even if it is for this time only."

"I have none either," Banting said as he lit a cigarette, "except this pillow talk is cutting a little too close to the bone."

"You're out of shape and you smoke four packs a day," Sadie said. "You have to stop, or you'll kill yourself."

"That's not quite right," Banting said, suddenly wheezing and hacking. "Three at the most."

"If you're not careful," Sadie said, "you'll cough up a lung trying to clear your chest. You've got to take better care of yourself."

"I'm in good enough shape to do my duty."

"Are you kidding me?" Sadie asked. She scrambled around the room picking up the clothes they had thrown on the floor. She tossed him his shorts and socks.

"I had to find a hotel with an elevator because you don't have the stamina to climb a flight of stairs. Sure is a good thing you didn't have a heart attack in our bed. What a nightmare that would have been with Sinclair in town, scribbling notes and firing headlines off to Toronto."

"Give me some credit, why don't you?" Banting asked. "I can carry a pack and portage a canoe as well as any man."

"And when was the last time you did that?"

"With Alex, when we tramped around Yellowknife."

"Do you remember how many years ago that was?"

"Not really."

"Then I rest my case," Sadie said.

"It was a tough slog, but I'm sure I'm up for it again."

"You better settle for a genteel painting expedition to civilized Quebec," Sadie said. She took his cigarette, gave it a quick puff, and stubbed it out in the ashtray on the side table.

"Your best course of action? Drive by car, stay in country inns, and paint collapsing barns that aren't too far from the road. That's about all the exertion you're good for these days. And a periodic tumble in the sack with me. To keep your stamina up."

"I don't think that physical exercise is all that it's made up to be," Banting said. "It's a fad that will soon disappear from the public's consciousness. Besides, I am too busy at the lab to waste any time. I have my duty to fulfill."

Sadie laughed at that one.

"Too busy in the lab to exercise? Too busy on the lecture circuit, more like, rehashing the discovery of insulin. You need new material if you want to stay current with diabetes research. There's only so much derring-do you can give before audiences tire of you.

If war comes, you'll be relegated to desk duty because you aren't fit for anything more strenuous. If you want to be a medical officer in the King's Army, then you better quit smoking."

"If war comes?" Fred asked, trying to change the subject. "It's not a question of if, but when."

Sadie fell for his ruse.

"Those Germans are in fighting trim, and the rest of Europe is in shambles. I couldn't believe the poverty and ignorance I saw in Spain," Banting continued. "The Italians, though, under Mussolini? They're waking up. The church is no longer in complete control of their lives. The people are bursting with energy. The country is alive and well and as ready as Germany to flex its muscle.

Don't get me going on the French, though. They are woefully unprepared for an encounter with Hitler's mechanized war machinery. How I loathe them. They capitulated in the last war and will do the same in the next. They whine one minute and parade in silk the next.

As short as it was, the last time I was in Europe made me long for Canada. But then to come home after witnessing all that. And listen to those politicians in Ottawa yelping in favour of Chamberlain's appeasement? They're damned fools.

They may be able to run a country during peacetime, but they haven't a clue about what's coming. The same as the British. You think they'd know better. They need a prime minister who will stand toe-to-toe against Hitler. One who refuses to sit at a table and negotiate. Polite conversations lead only to defeat.

Hitler needs to be beaten into the ground or Swastikas will fly over the Peace Tower."

"If war comes, Freddie," Sadie said, "I don't want you going overseas."

"I'm no hero, Sadie. I'm as afraid as any man. Explosions and airplanes strafing roadways. Civilians trapped with nowhere to hide. Rockets bombing houses and hospitals. I am afraid of snipers trying to blow off my head.

I am no hero. Yet if my country goes to war, I'll do my duty. I'll go where I am commanded. No questions asked."

"As long as you don't look for opportunities to put yourself in harm's way. You have a habit of going to the extreme. I think that you're addicted to danger and the rush of adrenalin. You are most fully alive when your life is threatened. It's almost a death wish.

You know, Fred, sometimes doing your duty means calling it quits on lost causes. You don't have to complete every project you start or drive off every person who loves you."

"What do you mean?"

"The Rous sarcoma[17] experiments."

"But we've had some positive results. A few chickens have resisted the virus after we injected them."

"Maybe five or six of the 1700 we've killed since we started. Three to five birds a week. Enough is enough.

Besides, let me remind you who has been doing the heavy lifting while you've been touring Europe. Drinking yourself under the table with the likes of Norman Bethune (1890-1939)."

"He's a good man with some interesting ideas about rural medicine. He shouldn't be discounted because he's a Communist."

"Don't make a fool of yourself. You know how the *Toronto Star* would have a field day if they heard your mumblings. Listen to me, Fred. Put that Rous sarcoma cancer research to bed. It's a lost cause.

But your silicosis project is making headway. Use your good name and reputation to bring in the funding, so that your researchers can complete the lab work and get their findings published.

I'll keep the program running without a hitch. Leave the administration to me. You're an ideas man. Let others work out the details."

"It'll be the end of my publishing career if I stay out of the lab."

"You don't need a stellar scholarly record to do the work you are good at."

"I refuse to add my name to any publication if I haven't done any of the work. I may be the head of the department, but my staff will get the credit they deserve. I will not do to them what MacLeod did to me."

---

17. A cancer-causing virus

"Your reputation will be established in the success you enable others to achieve. You are not a patrician and never will be. You support others."

"True leaders serve their people," Banting said. "They do not dictate from on high what they want done. They speak the truth in such a way that their followers discover it for themselves.

During the insulin breakthrough, I learned that scientific research is a collaborative process among team members. Under my watch, no single person is in charge. People work together for a common goal."

"So, you agree with me about the chickens?" Sadie asked. "Am I right?"

"You are. We aren't likely to find anything worth publishing. My only consolation is that we're in good company with all the other cancer researchers who are as frustrated as we are. Not one of us is making any headway.

Cancer is a black hole. We may eventually treat its symptoms, but find a cure? Not in my lifetime."

With that, Sadie helped Banting put on his tuxedo. She handed him the leather portfolio with his well-thumbed speech. He had delivered it so many times that he hardly looked down at the text anymore. While she settled down to a quiet evening with a good book, he took the stairs down to the lobby and hailed a cab to the conference.

Breathing heavily, he felt like a lamb being led to the slaughter.

65
Terms

After another long and difficult day at the lab, when nothing ever seemed to go right, Banting dragged himself home to the apartment he bought after Marion sold his house and moved to Oakville. He would never forgive her for the shame she had brought upon him. He certainly didn't deserve the mess he was in.

Not having young Bill close at hand was difficult for Banting to accept. He liked having his son around. He was a welcome reprieve from all his worries at work. They could eat ice cream on hot days. Throw stones in the water on cool ones. Catch frogs in the bog. Do things that boys loved to do.

Saturdays and Sundays with young Bill reminded Banting of his childhood in Alliston. He was a kid again and happy to be alive. At least for the weekend.

Weekdays at the lab were another thing altogether. Frustrated by the minutiae of running a department as large as the Banting Institute, he left its administration to Sadie Gairns. She kept the place shipshape. He worried about where the money would come from for the salaries, lights, and equipment. His staff focused on their research projects, publications, and careers.

He wondered how MacLeod kept his wits about him, publishing all those books and keeping the department of Physiology in good order. That man had more going for him than he liked to admit.

If only Sadie would get off his case about that young graduate, Miss Henrietta Ball — Henrie to her friends.

"I know you, Fred Banting," Sadie said. "She's too young for you. In two years, it'll be Marion Robertson all over again. I don't think I could put up with another one of your failed love affairs. She's too good a student to let you have your way with her and jeopardize her studies."

"She's piqued my interest, Sadie. I can't help it."

"She's aroused more than your interest, Fred. Be honest. Every male in the department thinks she's a cute young girl that they can enjoy. Did you hear them laugh when she dropped that vial of TB at your feet?"

"Good thing it didn't break," Banting laughed. "The sweet kid."

"Exactly! No one respects her as a researcher. She's the only female in a room full of males. They shunt her aside. As Department Head, you should be defending her right to study unmolested, not trying to seduce her."

"But she has a splendid pair of hips," Banting thought to himself as he unlocked his apartment door and turned on the lights. "I'd give anything to mount her and sire a houseful of babies."

He hung his coat in the hall closet and placed his fedora on the shelf. He sat on the bench, unlaced his shoes, and wriggled his feet into a pair of slippers.

"What a relief," he thought. "No Marion to criticize me for my choice of footwear."

The apartment was chilly, so he turned on the fireplace. "I can't believe how early winter has come to Toronto. It'll be a long one. Of course, any day after Hallowe'en without snow is a gift."

He poured himself a tall glass of Gooderham.

"In my younger days, I'd drink it neat to prove my manhood, I suppose. Now for a splash of water."

He ran the tap in the kitchen for a few seconds before adding some to his glass. The whiskey turned opaque. He swirled the glass and breathed in a hint of bitter orange before taking a sip.

He turned on his top of the line Zenith Z-1000 Stratosphere. The salesman said it was a rich man's radio. He heard Louis Armstrong singing.

"Henrie's refused me for 11 months now. What more does she want?" Fred asked.

"Terms," she had been telling him again and again. "I will become intimate with you, but not before you and I come to an understanding. You want to engage in pre-marital sex but that'll put my studies at risk.

As soon as you've had me, you'll look for someone else. I know you, Fred Banting. I've been side-stepping your parries and thrusts for over a year now.

You're no better than the other men in the department. They'd like nothing better than to slip off my panties and then go home satisfied to their wives. At least you're single, but you have baggage. That gives me pause. I am not a schoolgirl you can seduce with false promises.

I'll give you what you want, but on my terms only."

"A wedding?" Fred asked. "Is that what you expect?"

"For a start, if I may be so bold. And a guarantee that I'll get into medical school. It need not be a grand affair."

"But children. I want a houseful of children."

"I'll give you as many babies as you want, but you'll have to be home for them. I won't raise them alone."

Banting couldn't believe what he was hearing. It drove him mad. This woman and her ultimatums. She expected him to compromise his career so she could have hers. He wanted to retire when he turned 50 and spend his days painting. But change shitty diapers and listen to squalling babies? That was another matter. He needed time to think.

"I'm going to England to study obstetrics and gynecology," Henrie said. "You can reach me there when you've made up your mind." Then, she walked out of his life.

Banting took another sip of whiskey and changed radio stations. He tuned in to the BBC. The Night of Broken Glass — *Kristallnacht.* Apparently, some Jew attempted to assassinate the German ambassador in Paris. Then, spontaneous demonstrations broke out across Germany. The police couldn't intervene. The public outrage was unstoppable.

Banting reflected on a conversation he had when he was last touring Europe.

"It's all their fault," a young Berliner said to him. "They have too much power. They take their profits out of Germany and invest them in numbered Swiss bank accounts. They're crippling our economy."

Since his Nobel Prize, Banting realized that anti-Semitism wouldn't exist if anyone considered the achievements of Jewish scientists.

He took another sip of his whiskey and felt the oily resin burn at the back of his throat. "But that doesn't mean Canada should become a safe haven for Jewish refugees. So what if they are being singled-out in Germany.

After Hans Kist (d. 1932?)? That Communist rabble rouser? Good thing Canada deported him. He was a threat to the state. Could you imagine if a boatload arrived on our shore begging for asylum?

How could we separate Nazi infiltrators from German Jews? Adults can get circumcised. Females can be spies. There's no telling. Accepting Jews into Canada is not worth the risk when our security is at stake.

I've always maintained that we should only accept refugees if they have something to offer that is in our national interest. Certainly, if they have a set of skills Canada needs. But Freudian psychologists? Jewish surgeons? Only if they have the required qualifications.

If I had known so many Jews were diabetics, I wouldn't have bothered with insulin."

66

Truth in the Roistering

"Of course, you can't send him overseas to serve on the front lines," Velyien Henderson said.

"Major Banting won the Military Cross for his bravery during the Cambrai Offensive of September 1918," General Andrew McNaughton (1887-1966) replied. "He enlisted and will follow whatever orders we give him."

"He's too valuable to be sent to the front to treat wounded soldiers," Sadie Gairns insisted.

"He wants to relive the solidarity that men under enemy fire have experienced," McNaughton said. "Civilians will never understand the bonding between soldiers who have fought together. If we intend to beat the Hun, we need battle-hardened men who faced death and survived. In spite of his injuries, he refused to leave his post until his men were safe."

"He was the luckiest boy in France," Gairns said. "By the time his arm healed, the war was over. Can't you see? He wants to do his duty in the simplest, least-complicated terms he can, treating the wounded. Not bothering about fragile egos and petty turf wars."

"But he's a gold-mine of a fundraiser," Henderson insisted. "His name alone brings in more money than the rest of us combined."

"That won't prevent him from trying to get overseas," Gairns replied. "Put Dr. Banting on a speaking tour across the country. Start at Halifax and work his way to Vancouver, stopping at every university and town hall along the way.

Let him be an ambassador for medical science. Put him on a fact-finding mission to find out what science departments can do to contribute to the war effort.

But whatever you do, do not send him overseas."

"He's a humble sort of fool who disarms his detractors with his candour," McNaughton said. "He'll drink a beer with any of the boys, no matter how junior their rank. He has the common touch and is deeply interested in what everyone he meets has to say."

"He'll talk to anyone about their work, Dr. G. Edward Hall (1907-1972) said, "and freely admit he doesn't have a clue what they're going on about."

"I once saw him get soaked when he was teaching us the proper way to tap open a keg of beer," Henderson said. "And the bawdy songs he led us in.

I'm glad his new wife wasn't there to hear us. She would have flushed red with embarrassment and anger."

"There is truth in the roistering when men get drunk together," McNaughton said.

"He's an ideas man who refuses to report for the first time the findings of others," Hall said. "He has a sketchy understanding of the basics and very little to contribute to the research. However, his strength is in the people he gathers around him."

"But what about insulin?" McNaughton asked. "A serendipitous fluke?"

"Absolutely. That's why he has the reputation he has. People hear what they want to hear and ignore what they don't. However, he was smart enough to win a Nobel Prize. That says something."

"He's learned to let people follow their noses," Henderson said. "The Banting Institute would most certainly fail if we didn't have him as its head and Miss Gairns here steering its course."

"Then send him on a junket," McNaughton said. "Have him raise money."

"We do need funding for a decompression chamber," Hall said. "If we could introduce recruits to the physiological effects of high-altitude flying, we'd have a better idea if they could handle the sudden changes in pressure and G-forces of a fighter plane."

"Cheaper and safer too," McNaughton said. "Maybe deploy him as a gunner".

"The expansion of air force training in Canada means our new research equipment is being used exclusively for RCAF training flights," Hall said.

Banting wants to test the effects of gravity on the flying suit that Wilbur Franks (1901-1986) designed. It has compartments filled with water. The suit doesn't need to cover the whole body; just the groin area to keep blood from pooling in the legs.

The heart has to pump blood into the brain to keep the pilot from becoming lightheaded and passing out. It's tricky, though, finding the right fit. Using real airplanes in flight is too dangerous and time-consuming because of the weather. Not to mention a security risk. The testing needs to be done inside a top-secret facility, not in the open air.

Air force Training Command cannot have complete use of the centrifuge. We need it to study the response of the human body to high altitude flying. These new airplanes are capable of far more than the human body can endure."

"Just don't send him overseas," Gairns insisted. "If you let him go, he'll find a way to stay there and not return. He is a national treasure. His worth exceeds anything he could ever accomplish in a lab or field hospital."

"Canadians need heroes like him to inspire them during these dark days," McNaughton said. "He is our Winston. Did you hear Churchill's recent speech?

We are in action in Norway and Holland, and we have to be prepared in the Mediterranean. The air battle is continuous. We have nothing to offer but blood, toil, and tears."

"For the sake of Canada's involvement in the war, Banting needs to be protected from his own heroics," Gairns said. "He will stop at nothing to defeat the Germans."

"We can hardly keep him out of the lab, experimenting on himself," Henderson said. "I thought the mustard gas wound on his leg would never heal. He walked with a cane for months."

"Then there was the time that he was in the decompression chamber," Hall said. "They had to pull him out because his oxygen mask froze up and he was delirious. He almost died."

"While Dr. Banting's away, Miss Gairns could run the lab," McNaughton said.

"She already is," Henderson replied, turning to her. "You have an attention to detail and a knack for administration that few others can match. Without you, the department would be in shambles."

"If you send him overseas, you bastards," Gairns said. "I'll quit this department, and you'll never hear from me again. His life is too precious for you to waste in your schemes. Do not let him die alone on a cold and lonely shore beside a frozen lake in a foreign country."

"If it weren't for Banting's advocacy, Canada wouldn't be a leader in aviation medicine," Hall said. "That alone is worth a Nobel Prize."

"Too bad he turned the British off with his alarmist views of biological warfare," McNaughton said. "He spent so much time at their Porton Downs facility, they drove him off."

"Once he gets an idea in his head, he won't let it go," Henderson said.

"The Brits must have figured out it's more effective to bomb the hell out of the Germans, than to infect them with microbes and viruses. How they'd drop germs to the ground without them being dissipated by the wind, I haven't a clue."

"If needs dictate, we have that newly acquired 1,000 square mile tract of land north of Suffield out in Alberta," McNaughton said. "It'll do nicely for live arms training and chemical research."

"For chemical warfare?" Gairns asked.

"For surviving whatever the enemy throws at us," McNaughton replied.

"First, we have to convince the good people of Bemister, Bingville, Brutus, Kalbeck, Learmouth, and Tripole to vacate the premises," Hall said.

"They'll do it willingly or be accused of collaborating with the enemy," McNaughton said. "Once this war is over, there is no telling where medical research will end up. The only way we'll defeat the bastards is through science and technology."

67
My Two-Bits

Twelve-year old William Robertson Banting trained the sights of his Hawker Hurricane on the Messerschmitt Bf 109F-4 Number 7285 that Franz Xaver Baron von Werra (1914-1941) was flying.

"Got you, you bastard," Bill said. He pulled the trigger on his guns. Werra was the only German prisoner of war to escape custody on Canadian soil. One thousand Axis POWs landed in Halifax on January 21st, 1941. They were being transported by train to a newly constructed prison camp on the north shore of Lake Superior.

On the night of the 23rd, while the train was picking up speed from the yard at Smiths Falls, Ontario, Werra jumped headfirst out of the window and rolled into a snowbank. He lay still until the lights on the caboose faded in the distance. Standing, he brushed the snow off the long civilian overcoat his friend Erhard Köstler had given him.

"At least, you won't look like an escapee if someone sees you from a distance," Erhard said. "But don't open your mouth."

"I'll tell them I'm a Dutch pilot and got kicked out of my girlfriend's home when her parents caught me in her bed."

They laughed and then he dove out the window.

Under the cover of darkness, Werra made his way down to the road. He crept past farmhouses and was ready to leap into the ditch at the first sight of a vehicle coming toward him. Dogs barked in the distance, but not at him. He was too good at nighttime reconnoitering ever to be caught. The moon in Sagittarius was a waning crescent. It gave him enough light to see a few metres ahead. The guards on the train didn't discover that he was missing until the following morning.

By then, it was too late.

He travelled southeast toward the frozen St. Lawrence River that he'd have to cross if he were to reach the neutral United States. "Maybe sixty kilometres," he thought. He marched double time, scrambled for cover at the first sign of danger, and half ran when the coast was clear, not once pausing to rest.

He was perfectly fit. After his tour of duty in Russia, he could survive anything. He couldn't stop. Out in the middle of the frozen river, he was an easy target. The dawning of the new day would be the death of him if he were caught.

When he came to a patch of open water in the middle of the river, he turned back to shore and found a rowboat under a tarp. He dragged it down the bank and over the ice to the flowing water. He rowed across the current to the American side and handed himself in to the police at Ogdensburg.

He asked for asylum and contacted the German consulate in New York City.

It was bad luck for the bastard Werra when young Bill descended from the clouds wearing the new Frank's Flying Suit that his father helped design.

"This is all hush-hush," Major Banting whispered to his wide-eyed son before he boarded the Lockheed Hudson bomber on his ill-fated flight to England.

"Not even your mother can know the work I am doing. That's the reason I'm flying overseas. To complete a top-secret mission. We've got to get the Hun before they invade Canada.

When I get home, son, let's go fishing in Algonquin Park. I hear there's a lake there with the largest trout in the world. What do you say about a camping trip? We could sleep in a tent and cook our meals over an open fire. Maybe rent a canoe and go out on the water? We'll paddle out into the middle and while the canoe is drifting in the gentle wind, we'll cast our lines, and try our luck. Can you imagine the sound of the waves, the cry of the loon, and the stars shining in the night sky? I can hardly wait.

Look after your mother while I'm gone. She and I have had our differences, but she's a good woman. With me gone, she'll need you more than ever."

Those were the last words young Bill heard his father say and he took them to heart.

The flying suit with its compartments of water kept young Bill from experiencing the full G-force and blacking out during the rapid descents, sudden turns, and ascents of the high-altitude dog fight he was in.

With it, he had the advantage he needed to blast Werra to smithereens.

"I've trained my entire life for this one moment in time," Bill said as he watched the Messerschmidt burst into flames and fall into the sea north of Vlissingen, near the port of Antwerp.

Had Werra's body floated to the surface, Bill would have strafed it with all his guns blazing. There's no way he'd allow that bastard to survive.

"Kids can be heroes, too," he said to himself, proud that he had contributed his small part to the war effort.

He gave a thumbs up to the memory of the other members of the RCAF No. 1 Squadron who had flown with him. He remembered their service in the air and on the ground. Duncan Hewitt (1920-1940), Robert Beley (1919-1940), Bob Edwards (1912-1940), and George McAvity (1911-1940). They did their duty and paid the price.

They had been called out again and again. They flew sortie after sortie, several times a day, bombing run after bombing run.

Then, they were shot down.

Bill and his pals were instrumental in saving the entire world from the Nazis. They had a small part to play, and it made all the difference.

Bill's mission had come straight from Fighter Command. "Seek out and destroy the German ace Werra."

Bill knew from the Intelligence reports that Werra made it back to Germany in April 1941. That rankled him to the core.

Bill's grandfather, Dr. Robertson, had a heart attack in Elora and died March 1941. His mother and Aunty Vera were suddenly alone and bereft.

Bill was now the man of the family. It fell upon him to care for his mother. She'd been sorely treated since the divorce. He had to be strong so that she could regain her health. She depended on him, but he was up to the challenge.

His father told him that a man does not shirk from his duty. He does what needs to be done and then he does it again. Just to be sure.

"I'll make you pay, Werra, for the pain you caused my family and my country. If you hadn't escaped last January, my father'd still be alive. His plane wouldn't have crashed, and he wouldn't have frozen to death alone.

I'd still be spending weekends with him and Henrie. She and I don't really get along. She has more important things on her mind. Besides, I'm too much for her to handle.

But Father was needed overseas, and he went. Simple as that. Now, he's gone and I'm here to take his place.

You Germans lost the Blitz because the RCAF is better trained and equipped than yours. No question. We beat you because of my Dad's work. He may have been part of the team that discovered insulin, but he is the undisputed Father of Aviation Medicine.

You don't have a chance. With men like him and boys like me.

This is my two-bits worth. It's not much, but it's what I have to offer."

The End

Bibliography

Bator, Paul with Andrew J. Rhodes. *Within Reach of Everyone: A History of the University of Toronto School of Hygiene and the Connaught Laboratories.* Volume 1, 1927-1955. Ottawa: Canadian Public Health Association, 1990.

Bliss, Michael. *The Discovery of Insulin.* Toronto: McClelland & Stewart, 1982.

Clowes, Alexander W. *The Doc and the Duchess: The Life and Legacy of George H.A. Clowes.* Indianapolis: Indiana University Press, 2016.

Davies, Blodwen. *Tom Thomson: The Story of a Man Who Looked for Beauty and For Truth in the Wilderness.* Toronto: Discus Press. 1935. Rpt. Vancouver: Mitchell Press, 1967.

Defries, Robert D. *The First Forty Years, 1914-1955: Connaught Medical Research Laboratories, University of Toronto.* University of Toronto Press, 1968.

Dejardin, Ian A.C. and Sarah Milroy. *North Star.* Fredericton: Goose Lane Editions, 2023.

Dickin, Janice. "'By Title and by Virtue': Lady Frederick and Dr Henrietta Ball Banting." *Great Dames,* 245. University of Toronto Press, 1997.

FitzGerald, James. *What Disturbs Our Blood: A Son's Quest to Redeem the Past* Toronto: Random House, 2010.

Feasby, W.R. *The Story of Insulin: Forty Years of Success Against Diabetes* London: The Bodley Head, 1962.

Grace, Sherrill. *Inventing Tom Thomson: From Biographical Fictions to Fictional Autobiographies and Reproductions.* Montreal: McGill-Queen's Press, 2004.

Klages, Gregory. *The Many Deaths of Tom Thomson: Separating Fact From Fiction,* Dundurn Press, 2016.

"Lady Henrietta Banting: a Life of Service." *Canadian Medical Association Journal. 8,* 1977.

Little, William T. *The Tom Thomson* Mystery. Toronto: McGraw-Hill, 1970.

MacGregor, Roy. *Northern Light: The enduring mystery of Tom Thomson and the woman who loved him.* Toronto: Random House Canada, 2010.

Milroy, Sarah. Ed. *Uninvited: Canadian Women Artists in the Modern Movement.* McMichael Canadian Art Collection: 2021.

Moloney, Mary V. *Behind Insulin: The Life and Legacy of Peter Moloney; A Man's Catholic Faith and Bold Science.* Toronto: Lulu, 2016.

Murray, Joan. *Trees.* Toronto: McArthur & Company. 1999.

Palme, Rachel Delle. "Dr. Henrietta Banting." *Banting House.* March 8, 2019.

Popa, Denisa. "Henrietta, the Other Dr. Banting: Early Mammography Research at Toronto's Women's College Hospital (1967)." *CSTHA,* August 17, 2020.

Reid, Dennis. Ed. *Thomson.* Art Gallery of Ontario and National Gallery of Canada. 2002.

Rutty, Christopher J. "'Couldn't Live Without It': Diabetes, the Costs of Innovation and the Price of Insulin in Canada, 1922-1984," *Canadian Bulletin of Medical* History 25 (2008): 407-31.

Blodwen Davies

The Storied Streets Of Quebec (1929)

Old Father Forest (1930)

The Story Of Agriculture (1930)

Daniel Du Lhut (1930)

Paddle And Palette: The Story Of Tom Thomson (1930)

Saguenay, "Saginawa", The River Of Deep Waters (1930)

Ruffles And Rapiers: Being The Half-Forgotten Romances Of The Gallant Women And The Doughty Men In The Days Of Colonial Adventure (1930)

Mother Marie Of The Incarnation (1930)

Storied York: Toronto Old And New (1931)

The Story Of Hydro: White Thunder (1931)

The Charm Of Ottawa (1932)

Romantic Quebec (1932)

Margaret Hall Discovers Upper Canada (1934)

A Study Of Tom Thomson: The Story Of A Man Who Looked For Beauty And For Truth In The Wilderness (1935)

Planetary Democracy: An Introduction To Scientific Humanism And Applied Semantics (1944)

Couchiching Views World Problems with Oliver L. Reiser (1946)

Youth Speaks Its Mind (1948)

Gaspe, Land Of History And Romance (1949)

The Reesor Family In Canada: Genealogical And Historical Records (1950)

Quebec: Portrait Of A Province (1951)

Nestles The Seed Perfection (1951)

Ottawa: Portrait Of A Capital (1954)

Payepot And His People (1959)

Tom Thomson: The Story Of A Man Who Looked For Beauty And Truth In The Wilderness (rpt. 1967)

A String Of Amber: The Heritage Of The Mennonites (1973)

Acknowledgements

There are a number of people who took time from their busy lives to respond to my queries about Fred Banting, Blodwen Davies, Tom Thomson, and Métis language and culture. Thanks to Jodi Ashkoi, Jerome and Lionel Berthelette, Sherrill Grace, Gregory Klages, Joan Murray, Matthew Oliver, and Danielle Siemens. This book could not have been written without your expertise.

It is a truth rarely acknowledged that writers sequestered in cold windowless basements for hours at a time must have tried the patience of their longsuffering English instructors.

The unsung heroes who graded the last minute scribbles that I tried to pass off as final drafts include my junior high school teachers from Stonewall Collegiate in Manitoba: Mrs. Campbell, Mr. Hendricks, Mr. Lavery, and Mr. Prime; my high school teachers Mr. Currie-Johnson, Mr. Wittenberg, and Mr. Wiebe from Abby Senior in Abbotsford, BC; and my college English instructors Graham Dowden from Fraser Valley College and Rod Harvey from Medicine Hat College.

When I first tried writing fiction, Ronenne Anderson, Caterina Edwards, Glen Huser, John Keeble, Keith Liggett, and Maria Scala guided me down this long and lonely road.

For the friends who read my work in progress, I am grateful. PJ Groeneveldt, Karen Howell, Karen Mills, and Ilona Ryder come immediately to mind. There are many others whose names escape me right now. I cherish your support.

For each one of you, I sing your praises.

My writing cadre includes Fred Clark, Teresa Dobson, Eldon Evans, Stuart McKay, and Tom Pedersen. They read my work, act as a sounding board for my ideas, catch my errors, call out my nonsense, and encourage me to continue. You have made all the difference.

The last word of thanks goes to my wife Sandy. Without her, none of this would be possible.

I am a fortunate man.

Also by James Gregory Randall

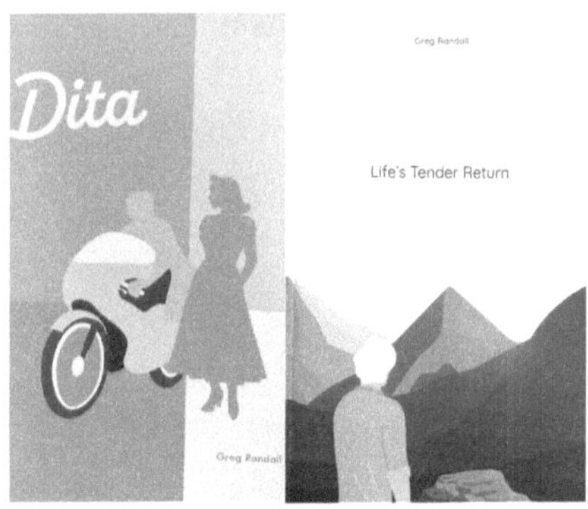

By special order from your favourite bookstore, including

https://www.aospublishing.com

https://www.audreys.ca
https://benmcnallybooks.com
http://www.bookmanpei.com
https://bookmarkinc.ca
https://bookstoreonperron.com
https://mtl.drawnandquarterly.com
https://www.indigo.ca/en-ca
https://www.mcnallyrobinson.com
https://www.munrobooks.com
https://www.nextpageyyc.ca
https://pageskensington.com
http://pulpfictionbooksvancouver.com
https://www.russellbooks.com
https://pennyu.ca
https://shelflifebooks.ca

https://turning.ca
https://upstartandcrow.com
https://westminster.bookmarkreads.ca
Amazon.ca

If possible, please leave positive reviews. Independent authors need help getting the word out about their work. Ask your library to order copies.